Don't miss any of these exciting thrillers by
#1 *New York Times* bestselling author

IRIS JOHANSEN

ON THE RUN

"Johansen gives her readers what they have come to
expect from the queen of suspense." —*Booklist*

COUNTDOWN

"[A] thrill ride . . . Action, romance, castles, bomb
plots and a booby-trapped hideaway in snowbound
Idaho—what more could Johansen fans want?"
—*Publishers Weekly*

BLIND ALLEY

"Johansen has become adept at mixing supernatural
elements with intriguing suspense, and her new tale
will please both fans and new converts with its
unpredictable journey from Atlanta to the
archaeological digs of Herculaneum in Italy."
—*Booklist*

P9-CNB-384

DEAD AIM

"Smoothly written, tightly plotted, turbocharged thriller . . . Megaselling Johansen doesn't miss."
—*Kirkus Reviews*

"Readers will stay up all night reading this cat-and-mouse chase." —*Booklist*

"The nonstop action and slick plotting won't disappoint." —*Publishers Weekly*

NO ONE TO TRUST

"With its taut plot and complex characters, [*No One to Trust*] is vintage, fan-pleasing Johansen."
—*Booklist*

"Fast-moving plot . . . another zippy read from megaselling Johansen." —*Kirkus Reviews*

"Gritty, powerful and fast-paced, *No One to Trust* starts off with a bang and never lets up. . . . This is one thriller that will keep you on the edge of your seat."
—*Romantic Times*

BODY OF LIES

"Filled with explosions, trained killers, intrigues within intrigues . . . It all adds up to one exciting thriller." —*Booklist*

"A romantic thriller whose humanity keeps the reader rooting for its heroine every step of the way."
—*Publishers Weekly*

"[Johansen] doesn't let her readers down."
—*Newark Star-Ledger*

FINAL TARGET

"A winning page-turner that will please old and new fans alike." —*Booklist*

"A compelling tale." —*Atlanta Journal-Constitution*

"Thrilling . . . will have fans of the author ecstatic and bring Ms. Johansen new readers."
—BookBrowser.com

THE SEARCH

"Thoroughly gripping and with a number of shocking plot twists . . . [Johansen] has packed all the right elements into this latest work: intriguing characters; a creepy, crazy villain; a variety of exotic locations." —*New York Post*

"Johansen's thrillers ooze enough testosterone to suggest she also descends from the house of Robert Ludlum. Johansen pushes the gender boundary in popular fiction, offering up that rarity: a woman's novel for men." —*Publishers Weekly*

"Fans of Iris Johansen will pounce on *The Search*. And they'll be rewarded." —*USA Today*

THE KILLING GAME

"Johansen is at the top of her game. . . . An enthralling cat-and-mouse game . . . perfect pacing . . . The suspense holds until the very end."
—*Publishers Weekly*

"Most satisfying." —*New York Daily News*

"An intense whodunit that will have you gasping for breath." —*Tennessean*

THE FACE OF DECEPTION

"One of her best . . . a fast-paced, nonstop, clever plot in which Johansen mixes political intrigue, murder, and suspense." —*USA Today*

"The book's twists and turns manage to hold the reader hostage until the denouement, a sure crowd pleaser." —*Publishers Weekly*

"Johansen keeps her story moving at breakneck speed." —*Chicago Daily Sun*

BOOKS BY IRIS JOHANSEN

IRIS JOHANSEN

STALEMATE

BANTAM BOOKS

STALEMATE
A Bantam Book

PUBLISHING HISTORY
Bantam hardcover edition published January 2007
Bantam mass market edition / January 2008

Published by
Bantam Dell
A Division of Random House, Inc.
New York, New York

This is a work of fiction. Names, characters, places, and incidents either
are the product of the author's imagination or are used fictitiously.
Any resemblance to actual persons, living or dead, events,
or locales is entirely coincidental.

Library of Congress Catalog Card Number: 2006023433

Bantam Books and the rooster colophon are registered trademarks of
Random House, Inc.

ISBN 978-0-553-58654-1

Printed in the United States of America
Published simultaneously in Canada

www.bantamdell.com

OPM   10   9   8   7   6   5   4   3   2   1

STALEMATE

1

The phone was ringing.

Ignore it, Eve told herself, her fingers moving swiftly on the skull reconstruction she'd given the name of Marty. She could call whoever it was back when she was through working. The phone was set for speaker and she could pick up if it was Joe or Jane. She was getting too close to that important last step in the sculpting.

On the sixth ring the answering machine picked up.

"I need to speak to you. Answer the phone, Ms. Duncan."

She froze, her fingers stopped in midstroke. Luis Montalvo. Though she had spoken to him only twice that faint accent was unmistakable.

"I know you're there. You haven't left that cottage in the last week." His voice became faintly mocking. "Your dedication is admirable and I understand you're brilliant at your job. I look forward to having both focused soon on my behalf." He paused. "Do pick up the phone. I'm not accustomed to being ignored. It upsets me. You don't want to upset me."

And she didn't want to pick up the phone. He might jar her out of the zone of feverish intensity she needed when she was working this close to completion. Dammit, she had hoped he wouldn't call her again after she'd turned him down when he'd phoned her the last time, over a week ago.

"I won't give up, you know."

No, he probably wouldn't. Montalvo had been polite during the first call and even after she'd refused his offer, the second time he'd phoned he'd displayed no anger. His voice had been smooth and soft, almost regretful, yet there had been a note beneath that velvet courtesy that had puzzled her. It had made her uneasy then but tonight it filled her with impatience. She had no *time* for this now. Marty was waiting.

She strode across the room and picked up the phone. "Montalvo, I'm very busy. You've had your answer. Don't call me again."

"Ah, how delightful to hear your voice. I knew you wouldn't be so rude as to leave me hanging on that dreadful answering device. I hate impersonal machines. I'm a man of emotion and passion and they offend me."

"I really don't want to hear what you love or hate. I

don't care. I want to get off this phone and forget you exist."

"I realize that sad fact. You're absorbed in your latest reconstruction, of that boy found buried in Macon. Have you named him yet? I understand you name all the skulls you work on."

She stiffened. "How did you know that?"

"I know everything about you. I know you live with a Detective Joe Quinn of the Atlanta Police Department. I know you have an adopted daughter, Jane MacGuire. I know you're possibly the best forensic sculptor in the world. Shall I go on?"

"That could all be public record. And how did you know about the boy murdered in Macon?"

"I have many, many contacts around the world. Do you want to know who killed him? I could find out for you."

"I don't believe you."

"Why not?"

"Because you're not even in this country. You're a scumbag of an arms peddler and you live in Colombia where you can hide out and deal your poison to the highest bidder."

He chuckled. "I do like frankness. Very few women I know are willing to tell me the truth as they see it."

"Then I'm grateful to not be one of the women you 'know,' you sexist bastard. If I were, I'd probably be tempted to cut your nuts off."

"Such violence, such passion. I believe we're very much alike, Ms. Duncan."

"No way." She drew a deep breath. "The answer is still no. I've no intention of coming down there and doing your reconstruction."

"You were very polite and businesslike, almost sympathetic, when I first made you the offer. The second time you were much more curt. I suppose you had Joe Quinn check me out?"

"Yes, of course. I don't deal with crooks and murderers."

"Everyone deals with whoever can make them the best bargain."

"I told you the last time that I wasn't interested in any of your fat fees."

"And I was duly impressed. I don't believe I've ever had anyone turn down a million dollars for a few days' work."

"Dirty money."

"Not true. All my cash is very well laundered."

"I thought you'd accepted that I wouldn't work for you."

"Because I didn't argue with you? I don't believe in spinning my wheels. I just go away and find another lure. It took almost a week for me to decide what that would be."

"And?"

"I'm convinced you'll be my guest in a very short time."

"Why?"

"That would spoil the surprise. I like to see a plan unfold like a beautiful night flower."

"You mentioned Joe and my adopted daughter. You touch them and I'll kill you."

"That violence again." His tone was amused. "I'd never be that stupid. That would be the trigger that would send you into the fray to take me down. I want your cooperation."

"I'm hanging up."

"Very well. I just wanted to offer you the opportunity to change your mind. It would make me happy if you would come to me for mercenary reasons. Much less stressful for all of us."

"Are you threatening me?"

"Heavens, no. You'd know it if I were doing that. There would be no question. Won't you come and make me happy and become rich in the process?"

"No."

"Too bad." He sighed. "Good night." He hung up.

Eve slowly pressed the disconnect button. He had said he wasn't threatening her, but what else could she call it? It was subtle, but the threat was all the more chilling for the casual, understated way it was delivered. He'd been so calm when she'd turned down his offer that she'd honestly thought he'd accepted her refusal and was out of her life. It was clear she'd been wrong.

Should she call Joe and tell him Montalvo was still on the scene?

And have him think she was worried and rush home from the precinct?

She wasn't worried. She was uneasy. Montalvo

had said her family was safe and she believed him. As he had perceived, any danger to them would have made her angry and rebellious. He'd made no direct threat at all and he might just be trying to intimidate her into doing his job.

Maybe.

Yet he'd seemed to know entirely too much about her movements. Was she being watched?

Yes, she'd definitely tell Joe. But there was no use in alarming him right now. She'd tell him tonight when he came home for dinner. Okay, so she wanted to get back to Marty and she was afraid talking to Joe about Montalvo would keep her from doing it. She wasn't about to let Montalvo disturb her concentration on her work. That slimeball would probably enjoy the thought that he could control her to that extent. He might even call her again and try to reinforce that control. She'd be damned if she'd let him. She turned off the house phone and then her cell phone before moving back toward the reconstruction on the easel across the room.

Block Montalvo out of her thoughts. Think of Marty and the chance to bring him home. Think of the boy who'd been murdered and buried and left alone with no name or place.

That was better. Montalvo's words were blurring, fading away as she began to work.

Talk to me, Marty. Help me to bring you home....

·   ·   ·

"Pity." Montalvo looked down at the phone. "I was hoping she'd give in to greed like a normal person. It's easy to be noble for an hour, a day, but then they start to think and perhaps dream a little. A week should have whetted her appetite and made her start making excuses why she should take the job."

"Not everyone thinks that money is the be-all and end-all of everything, Montalvo," Soldono said.

Montalvo smiled. "Almost everyone. It's unfortunate that Eve Duncan is in the minority." He rose from the carved chair at the head of the dining table. "Oh, well. One must make adjustments."

Soldono tensed. "Don't do it, Montalvo."

"She's giving me little choice. You're giving me little choice. You didn't talk to her, did you?" He shook his head. "I told you what you had to do but you were looking for an out. I can see you scrambling frantically to avoid bringing her into the picture until time got away from you. Well, that time has come."

"Why her?" Soldono asked. "There's a fine forensic sculptor in Rio de Janeiro. Use him."

"Sanchez?" Montalvo shook his head. "Technically brilliant but he's not what I want."

"Eve Duncan is an American citizen and she's known and respected by every police department on the planet. She turned down your money and you'll be stirring up a hornet's nest if you try to force her."

"And you wouldn't like that. The CIA tries to be very low-key these days."

"Let me try to get Sanchez for you."

"You don't understand."

"Then tell me."

He gazed musingly down at the depths of the wine in his glass. "It's a matter of passion."

"What?"

"I told Eve Duncan that I was a man of passion. It's true."

Soldono hadn't noticed any emotion in Montalvo, much less a passion. The man was brilliant, innovative, and he kept any feelings or thoughts hidden behind that faintly mocking smile. "Why Eve Duncan?" he repeated.

"She has passion too. I've studied her file and nothing could be clearer. It's like a whirlwind spinning around her. She grew up on the streets with a drug addict for a mother and gave birth to an illegitimate child as a teenager. She turned her life around and went back to school and became a model mother. Then her daughter was kidnapped and presumably killed, but the body was never found. Instead of being crushed, the lady became a forensic sculptor and tried to bring closure to other parents by identifying the remains of their missing children."

"I know all that," Soldono said impatiently.

"You know the facts but you've never studied Eve Duncan the way I have. I believe I may know her better than she knows herself. I know what drives her. I know what makes her tick."

"Yeah, sure." He couldn't keep the sarcasm from his tone. "Passion?"

"Don't underestimate it. Da Vinci had it. Michelangelo had it. It's the difference between art and creation. Eve Duncan has it." His tone was smooth but hard. "And that's why I have to have her. Don't try to pawn anyone else off on me."

"Find another way. You promised me that you'd—"

"And I'd keep my promise if you'd kept yours." His tone was threaded with mockery as he continued, "But since the lady is not being accommodating, I must have cooperation from someone. You can see that, can't you?"

"No."

Montalvo's smile faded. "Then your vision had better improve quickly. I told you yesterday that if I didn't get the answer I wanted, then I'd move. You obviously chose to think I wasn't serious. I'll give you another four hours to persuade her, Soldono. No more, no less." He looked at his watch. "Ten tonight."

"I can't strike a bargain like that."

"Of course you can. Don't bullshit me. You do it all the time. A life for a life." He turned away. "Finish your dinner. The tiramisu is magnificent. The chef will be upset if you don't try it."

Soldono was seething with frustration as he watched him walk away. Sleek, graceful, and as dangerous as a stick of dynamite too near the flames. Bastard.

Would he do it?

Why was he even questioning it? Montalvo didn't

bluff and he would carry out any threat he made in exactly the method he'd outlined.

He had four hours.

He'd hoped to find a way to stop Montalvo without involving Eve Duncan but time had run out. But was it to his advantage to make a trade for the woman? Why not let it go? He had to be sure it was worth it.

Four hours.

He reached for his phone and quickly dialed.

"Montalvo's given me four hours. Dammit, he'll do it. How the hell am I supposed to stop him?"

Venable was silent for a moment. "It's time you offered Eve Duncan a choice."

"Some choice. Okay, I'm on it. I'll call you back when I get through." He hung up and looked in his book for Eve Duncan's phone number.

"Jane called me," Joe said as he came into the cottage two hours later. "She tried to reach you but she couldn't do it. She said she'd made reservations for us at the Doubletree in Phoenix and that I was to remind you that the show was this Saturday." He smiled. "I told her that there was a fairly good chance that you'd remember."

"What?" She tried to shift her attention away from the skull. It was like fighting her way through a thick fog. "Of course I remembered." Eve managed to tear her gaze away from Marty. "It's a very important show for Jane. I wouldn't miss it. She should know that."

"Yeah." He went over to the phone and turned it back on. "She also knows that you've been working day and night to finish that reconstruction."

"Marty is difficult." She looked back at the reconstruction of the eight-year-old boy. At least, the forensic team's estimate was eight years. "I had to practically put his splintered facial bones back together before I could begin work."

"Do we have a clue who he is yet?"

She shrugged. "You know I never look at police files before I finish the reconstruction. The Macon police have photos of children who disappeared around the time that they estimate the boy was killed. We'll see if we have a resemblance."

"DNA?"

She grimaced. "Come on. The DNA labs are so backed up with current murders that they're not going to be in any hurry to process a five-year-old cold case." She pushed the hair back from her forehead. "But if I do a good enough job I have a chance to bring him home."

"You'll do a good job," Joe said. "But not if you get so tired you lose judgment." He headed for the kitchen. "Did you eat dinner?"

"I think so . . . I don't remember."

"Then we'll assume that you didn't. I'll warm up the beef stew in the refrigerator and put some garlic bread in the oven. That means you have fifteen minutes to clean up your studio and wash up."

"I can catch something later."

"Now." He opened the refrigerator. "Scoot."

She hesitated. Montalvo. She'd meant to tell him about the call from Montalvo as soon as he came in but it didn't seem important now. As she'd worked on the skull, everything had faded but the reality of the work itself. Marty was important. The other lost children were important. She'd tell Joe about Montalvo later. "I should finish tonight. I want to do the computer three-D image before we leave for Phoenix."

"According to forensics, the boy's been dead for five years. He can wait a little while longer." He glanced at her over his shoulder. "No arguments, Eve. I let you wear yourself into the ground because you give me no choice, but not this time. You'll have a fight on your hands. I'd bet you've lost five pounds this week."

"I don't think—" She wearily shook her head. Maybe he was right. She was exhausted and she probably had lost weight. This case had been particularly painful. She should be used to dealing with the cruelty of the monsters who killed innocent children after all these years of forensic sculpting. Yet the mindless brutality of the violence visited on this small boy had ripped aside the scar tissue. "I want to bring him home, Joe." Her lips tightened. "And I want to kill the son of a bitch who did that to him."

"I know," he said. "Give me a chance and I'll do the job for you. For that poor kid and for what his killer is doing to you." He slammed the refrigerator door. "I was hoping this damn obsession was lessening but along comes a nasty case and you're right back where you were."

She stiffened. "This is what I do. This is what I am. Why are you so angry about it now?"

He didn't speak for a moment. "Because I'm tired. Because sometimes I can't stand to see you in pain. Because the years pass and I think the miracle will happen and it never does."

He was talking about Bonnie. She felt a ripple of shock. She couldn't remember the last time he'd spoken about her daughter. Yet Bonnie was always there, a silent presence. "I'll find her someday."

"A miracle," he repeated. "After all these years that's what it would take." He turned his back on her and moved to the stove. "Go get cleaned up. If I upset you any more, you won't eat and I'll be defeating my purpose."

She studied him. Something was definitely wrong. His motions were jerky and that remark about Bonnie was an instant tip-off. She would have noticed earlier if she hadn't been distracted by both her work and the aftereffects of that call from Montalvo. "I'm not the only one who's upset. What the devil is wrong with you?" She crossed her arms over her chest to keep them from shaking. "And don't tell me that you're just fed up with living here with me.

If you don't want to stay with me, no one is forcing you."

"Particularly not you."

"Shut up." She tried to steady her voice. "I don't have any right to ask you to stay. I'm an emotional cripple. As you said, I'm obsessed and I'll probably remain that way for the rest of my life. Sometimes I wonder why you haven't left me before this."

He didn't look at her. "You know why."

"Joe."

"I have my own obsession. Now get your ass in gear. We need to get some food down you." He shot her a glance. "It's okay. I'm over it. It just had to come out."

"Why now?"

"Why not?"

She hesitated, gazing at him. It wasn't over. She could sense the turbulence, the reckless energy whirling below the surface.

"You're down to ten minutes."

She tried to smile. "You used up five telling me what an obsessive wacko I am."

"Takes one to know one." He turned on the oven. "And you're my wacko."

She felt a sudden surge of warmth. He was the only man she'd ever known who could make her flit from emotion to emotion in the space of a heartbeat. She'd been angry, upset, defensive, and yet now she was feeling this powerful surge of affection. She turned away and headed down the hall. "Wackos of the world, unite."

"I only want to unite with one wacko and I fully intend to do it later tonight. After I feed you and stoke up your energy level."

"Promises, promises."

She was still smiling as she stepped into the shower a few minutes later. She could feel a tingle of sexual anticipation and excitement start within her. Jesus, you'd think after all these years with Joe that sex wouldn't be this urgent. Wasn't it supposed to become merely comfortable after a while? Their coming together was just as wild and passionate as that first time. Her body was tensing, readying at the thought.

She took a deep breath and closed her eyes as the water flowed over her. She'd tell Joe about Montalvo's call over dinner but right now she wanted to relax and forget about everything but Joe. . . .

Joe was taking the garlic bread out of the oven when his cell phone rang.

Soldono.

He was tempted to let his voice mail pick up.

Shit.

He punched the button. "Quinn. Go away, Soldono. I'm not talking to you. We're done."

"If we were done, you wouldn't have answered the

phone. Have you talked to her? It's almost nine-thirty, dammit. Time's running out."

"No, and I'm not going to."

"You will. You have a conscience."

"My conscience concerns Eve, Eve's physical safety, and Eve's mental well-being. Period. Bottom line."

"And what does her conscience dictate, Quinn? I've heard Eve Duncan's conscience is a little more encompassing. What would she say?"

"I'll never know. Neither will you, Soldono." He hung up the phone. Keep cool. He'd already let Soldono get under his skin or he wouldn't have answered the phone.

"Who's Soldono?"

He turned to see Eve, wrapped in a terry robe, standing in the doorway. "No one important."

She frowned. "If he weren't important to you, he wouldn't be able to make you this angry."

"I'm not angry."

"Who's Soldono? An officer at the precinct?"

"No." He placed the garlic bread on a plate. "We've got to both eat this to cancel the odor out. Maybe garlic wasn't such a good idea. Of course, it's supposed to keep away vampires."

"Is Soldono a vampire?"

"Drop it, Eve."

"Why?" She sat down at the table. "I've an idea he may be one of the reasons you were on the attack tonight. Who is he?"

He put her bowl of stew in front of her. "CIA. Satisfied?"

"No. Is that all I'm going to get?"

His lips lifted in a sardonic smile. "Soldono says that it's not. But it's all you're going to get now."

Her forehead wrinkled in thought as she remembered something. "When you came into the house, you turned the phone back on. No comment. You just turned it on."

"Jane couldn't get in touch with you."

"But you didn't ask me why I turned it off."

"You were working."

"Joe."

He didn't answer.

"Talk to me. You knew about my call from Montalvo, didn't you?"

"Yes." He poured some coffee. "Why didn't you phone me and tell me about it?"

"I thought it would wait until you got home." She grimaced. "Okay, I didn't want to think about him. It was interfering with Marty. It was just a kind of follow-up call to see if I'd changed my mind. And he didn't exactly issue any firm threats."

"You should have called me. I don't like being shut out."

"Neither do I. What does Soldono want with us?"

He didn't answer for a moment. "He doesn't want us. He wants you."

"What?"

"He wants you to go down to Colombia and do

the reconstruction Montalvo is asking." His hand tightened on his cup. "He doesn't give a damn that once you're down there, your chances of getting out alive stink. If knowing the identity of that skull is important to Montalvo, he's not going to want anyone else alive and walking around to share that knowledge."

"You're preaching to the choir. I've no intention of going down there."

"Good. Then we'll forget both Montalvo and Soldono. Eat your stew."

"We won't forget it. Why is the CIA involved with Montalvo? You said he was a crook."

"The CIA sometimes has strange bedfellows."

"I want to know, Joe."

"Okay." His lips tightened. "Soldono called me because he couldn't reach you and he was on the hot seat. Montalvo called you because he expected Soldono or one of his superiors to have already put the screws to you."

"Why would they do that?"

"Soldono had an informant, Pedro Gonzales, in Montalvo's camp. Montalvo found out about him and has been holding him locked up in his stockade. He offered to release Gonzales if Soldono could get you to come."

"And if he couldn't?"

"What do you think happens to traitors?"

"He'd kill him," she whispered.

"He's a dirtball," Joe said harshly. "Even Soldono

admitted that Gonzales was every bit as much a criminal as Montalvo. He just wasn't as smart. That's why he was trying to find a way to get him out that wouldn't involve an innocent U.S. citizen."

"He was helping the CIA."

"For money, Eve. For money."

"Yes, but he..." She moistened her lips. "Life is precious. I could save him."

"And get killed yourself."

She rubbed her temple. "I know. I'm just trying to think of a way.... How much time do we have?"

"Not enough."

"How much?"

He glanced at his watch. "Twenty-five minutes."

Shock jolted through her. "My God, and you weren't going to tell me?"

His lips twisted. "Evidently I was or I wouldn't have done it. Maybe I was just trying to save my ass when you found out later."

"Call Soldono."

"No, you're not going."

"I didn't say I was. Tell Soldono I'll talk to Montalvo. Maybe I can stall him until the CIA can free Gonzales."

Joe stared at her without speaking.

"Dammit, Joe. I don't care if he's a crook. Maybe he was trying to change if he was working with the CIA. What do we know? What will it hurt me to make the attempt to stop him from being killed?"

"I don't know and I don't want to know."

"Don't do this." Her hand clenched into a fist on the table. "There's too much pain in the world. I don't want anyone hurt or killed if I can prevent it. It's only a phone call, Joe."

He hesitated and then took out his phone and dialed. "It had better be only a call." When Soldono answered the phone, he said curtly, "Tell Montalvo she'll talk business to him if he wants to call her back."

"Jesus, you cut it close enough. I've only got fifteen minutes."

"Then get off the line and talk to him." Joe hung up. "This is a mistake, Eve. He'll take it as a sign of weakness."

"I don't care." She picked up her coffee cup and cradled it in her hands. The warmth felt good to her. "I don't want to enter into a battle of wills with the bastard. I just want to buy a little time to save a life." She looked at the telephone. "I suppose I should expect a call from him tonight."

"Yes." Joe stood up and pushed his chair back. "And I want to hear every word. Put him on speaker."

She nodded. "I'd record it but I don't imagine he'll say anything incriminating. You said he was smart."

He nodded curtly. "I wish you'd have been as smart."

"Would you really have let Gonzales die if I hadn't pushed you to tell me about Soldono?"

"What do you think?" He took the plates to the sink. "You know the answer. I don't give a damn about a son of a bitch like Gonzales. Hell, I probably wouldn't have cared if he was a priest instead of a crook. Not if it meant trouble for you." He put the plates into the dishwasher. "Now go in and make yourself comfortable on the couch and wait for the slimeball to call."

"It's the right thing to do, Joe."

Montalvo didn't call.

One hour passed.

Two hours.

Three.

Joe called Soldono's number and got only the voice mail.

Four.

Five.

"Come to bed." Joe pulled her to her feet. "He's playing games with you."

"Why would he do that?"

"How do I know?" He put his arm around her waist and led her toward their room. "But we didn't hear from Soldono either, and he would have called if he hadn't been able to reach Montalvo with the message."

"Why don't you call Soldono again?"

"As soon as I get you tucked into bed."

"You're treating me like a child."

"Not a child." He pushed her down on the bed. "There's nothing childlike about you. Sometimes I wish there were." He lay down beside her and pulled up the covers. "I'd celebrate the child in you. I'd give a party every day with red balloons and firecrackers." He pulled her close. "Now relax and try to sleep. You did what you could and now it's up to Montalvo."

"Call Soldono again."

"Nag." He took his cell phone out and dialed the number. "Still voice mail." He put the phone on the nightstand. "It could be that Montalvo gave Soldono orders not to talk to us before he did."

"Maybe." She didn't know what to think. Her nerves and expectations had been screwed up to face Montalvo and then there had been nothing. She felt flat and anxious at the same time.

And tired. Very, very tired.

She nestled closer to Joe. "This isn't what I was anticipating for tonight." She had a sudden thought. "Or were you trying to distract me?"

"You think I was trying to lure you with my manly body."

"You would have succeeded."

"Past tense."

"If you—"

"Hush." He pressed his lips to her temple. "Neither one of us is going anywhere. It can wait. I can wait. Love isn't only sex." He chuckled. "Though it's a damn entertaining part of it, isn't it?"

"Yes." She cuddled her cheek into the hollow of his shoulder. "I can't be a child for you. That part of me isn't alive any longer if it ever existed, but I still like the red balloons and the firecrackers. There are celebrations and then there are celebrations. Sex is a celebration. So is lying here close to you."

His arm tightened around her. "God, you're easy to please. Go to sleep, Eve. The celebration will still be going on when you wake up...."

2

*D*on't go, Mama."

Eve opened her eyes to see Bonnie sitting in the rocking chair across the room. She was dressed in jeans and the Bugs Bunny shirt Eve had last seen her wearing that day she was taken. "I'm not going anywhere, baby. I just have to see if I can help that man."

Bonnie shook her curly red head. "Joe's worried. He's afraid you may go."

She looked at the indented pillow next to her. "Where is Joe?"

"He's on the porch trying to call Soldono again. He waited until you were asleep. He doesn't want you to know. He doesn't like it when things scare you."

"I'm not scared."

"You should be. You will be."

"Okay, Miss Know-It-All. You'll forgive me if I take your predictions with a grain of salt. Your crystal ball doesn't always work."

"I don't know it all. Sometimes I just get a feeling. Usually when it concerns you." She leaned back in the chair and tucked her leg beneath her. "Joe's not the only one who worries about you, Mama."

Eve cleared her throat to ease it of the tightness. "No, Jane does too."

Bonnie chuckled. "You never give up. Me, Mama."

"Which probably means that I'm worrying about myself, since you're undoubtedly a figment of my imagination."

"Not 'undoubtedly.' You have plenty of doubts and we both know it. You're just afraid to admit it."

"That you're a ghost? You're damn right I'm afraid to admit it. I told Joe that I was a wacko, but that would put me beyond the pale." She stopped, frowning. "Why are you laughing?"

"Because you're worried because you said 'damn' in front of a kid."

"I am not." But she'd had a fleeting moment when that thought had crossed her mind. "It's all part of the fantasy. They could probably write a textbook on me."

"It shouldn't bother you," Bonnie said gently. "I'm not a kid anymore, Mama. Not really. I couldn't stay seven forever. It doesn't happen like that."

She had told Eve that before but to Eve she looked exactly the same: curly red hair, bright eyes, luminous smile.

Her Bonnie . . .

"I am your Bonnie. I'll always be with you."

Bonnie hadn't been with her during that year after that monster had taken her away and killed her. Eve had gone almost insane herself and was spiraling ever closer to the step *that would have given her peace. Then she had begun to have the dreams of Bonnie. They had saved her and helped her to start living again.* "You haven't come in a long time."

"I have to give you a chance to go on without me. It's a rule. You've been happy with Joe."

"I think you make up the rules as you go along." *She quickly corrected,* "Or I do."

"You slipped." *Bonnie's freckled nose wrinkled as she grinned in delight. Then her smile faded.* "I don't make the rules. But I'm glad we have something to go by. Otherwise I'd stay with you all the time."

"I'd love that."

"But it's not good for you."

"Bull." *She paused.* "Then why are you here now? Montalvo?"

"Partly. I was going to come anyway. I don't like it that you're so unhappy about Marty."

"I'm unhappy about all the lost ones."

"Yes, but this one is hurting you more than usual. I can feel your pain. Why?"

"I don't know." *She thought about it.* "Maybe it's not Marty." *She wearily shook her head.* "It could be that I've done this too long. These days every one of those skulls they bring me makes me flinch. Maybe it's all the lost ones, all the terrible brutality in the world. Children should be safe and loved. We should find a way to keep the monsters away from them. But we haven't and it goes on and on."

"And you go on and on. That's pretty wonderful, Mama."

"It doesn't bring you back to me. I want to bring you home, Bonnie."

"I'm home whenever I'm with you. It will come."

Love flowed through Eve in a warm tide. Jesus, she mustn't cry. Change the subject. *"You said the reason you came was partly Montalvo. What part?"*

"The fear. It's all around you."

"I told you I wasn't afraid of him."

"Because you don't know him. He's not what you think. He's not what anyone thinks. The fear will come." She sat up straight in the chair. *"I have to go. Joe's finished with his call. He couldn't reach Soldono. He's going to come back to bed."*

"Why leave?" she asked with sly mockery. *"Why not stick around to say hello?"*

"You're kidding me. You don't want me to do that. You've never shared me with Joe. I don't know why."

Neither did Eve. Trust? That couldn't be the reason. She'd trust Joe with her life. They were closer than any couple she knew. Yet she'd never told him about the dreams of Bonnie.

"Not dreams," Bonnie said softly. *"Not dreams, Mama. Close your eyes. I'm going now."*

"And you don't want me to see you vanish like something in a Star Trek *transporter?"* She closed her eyes. *"You used to like those* Star Trek *reruns. Do you remember how you—"*

Aching emptiness. Sadness.

She opened her eyes. No Bonnie. The rocking chair was vacant. Tears stung her eyes. Stupid. Weeping because Bonnie had drifted away from her again.

Beloved dream. Beloved spirit. Beloved Bonnie.

She could hear Joe's quiet steps coming down the hall.

She instinctively shut her eyes again. She didn't want to have Joe know that she was crying. She couldn't bear to make explanations right now. Better to pretend to be asleep.

He slipped into bed and drew close to her. He whispered, "Eve?"

She didn't answer.

He hesitated and then lay back against his pillow.

She felt as if she'd betrayed him. There shouldn't be pretense between them. Why couldn't she lower the barriers and confide in him? He was so good to her. Even if he didn't understand he'd never condemn her.

She couldn't do it. Lately it was as if there was a growing distance between them. Sometimes the closeness was there, sometimes she had to work to keep it firm, keep the substance of their love in focus.

Like Bonnie, drifting back and forth into her life like a puff of smoke.

Like Bonnie...

She was asleep. Eve hadn't been asleep when he'd come to bed but she was sleeping now.

Joe stared into the darkness. He wanted to touch her, wake her, make love to her. He *needed* to do it.

Christ, how insecure could he get? Sex should be pleasure, not a frantic effort to bring her back to him. They were so fantastic together physically that it was always a temptation to use it when he was frustrated in any other aspect of their relationship.

And he'd use it again if he had to do it. He'd use anything he had or could dredge up from heaven or hell. She'd been the center of his universe for years and he didn't know if he could survive without her.

He wouldn't have to do that. All he had to do was get past this remoteness he'd sensed in her during the last months. He'd blamed it on weariness. She always worked herself into exhaustion if he didn't watch out for her. Then he'd blamed it on the fact that Jane was grown and on her own. It might have been a period of adjustment. It might be that—

He was losing her.

No! He instantly rejected the thought. He would not lose her.

And he wouldn't let her be killed by Montalvo or be drawn into the machinations of Soldono.

Why the devil hadn't Soldono answered his voice mail?

In the morning he'd try again and then get on the phone and contact a few people he knew in the CIA in Washington.

He turned over and looked at Eve.

Lord, she was beautiful. She always told him he was crazy and that she wasn't even pretty. Her features were more interesting than attractive. Her red-brown hair was clean and shiny but she always kept it short and simply coiffed. When she worked, she wore horn-rimmed glasses.

But there was a world of intelligence and strength in those brown eyes and her lips were beautifully formed and sensitive. He loved to watch her expressions and try to bring a smile to those lips. Hell, he loved to watch her, period.

He started to reach out to touch her.

He stopped. No, this wasn't the time to be impulsive. She was very delicately balanced right now.

And their relationship was even more fragilely balanced. She'd probably deny it, but he sometimes believed he knew her better than she knew herself. He'd studied her, agonized with her, watched her with pride as she slowly healed and grew to be the woman she was.

No, he'd be patient, he'd watch and wait.

They had to get past this business with that bastard Montalvo before he could concentrate on clearing away any obstacles between them.

Sleep. Don't touch her. Don't reach out and grab because you're beginning to feel desperate....

Joe was on the phone when Eve walked out on the porch after nine the next morning. He looked at her as he hung up. "No answer from Soldono."

"What the devil is going on? Do you suppose something's happened to him?"

"Do you mean do I think Montalvo got pissed off

at him and killed him?" Joe shrugged. "We'll find out. I'm going to make some calls. I'll see if Venable in the CIA can track him down."

Venable. She vaguely remembered the name. "Will he talk to us about CIA business?"

Joe's lips tightened. "Oh, yes, he'll talk to me. Go get yourself some breakfast. I'll get back to you as soon as I can."

"I just want some orange juice." She turned toward the door. "I have to get back to work on Marty. I should have worked last night instead of fretting over something I couldn't help."

"You're allowed to be distracted occasionally."

"No, I'm not. Not when I have a job to do." She moved toward the easel where Marty waited.

Concentrate. Think about the boy who was lost. Forget everything else. Her fingers moved searchingly, delicately, molding the clay over the cheekbones. It was the last stage of the reconstruction and the most definitive one.

Let her hands work without thought.

Smooth.

Mold.

Smooth.

Help me, Marty. . . .

It took Joe almost an hour to get hold of Venable, and when the agent came on the line, his tone was reserved and unencouraging.

"I can't talk about Soldono, Quinn. He's an agent on assignment. You were FBI at one time and you know that it puts our man at risk to discuss that assignment."

"We didn't go to Soldono. He came to us. Now tell me what's happening."

"Same answer."

"Venable." Joe's words spat out hard and fast with bullet velocity. "I don't know what this is all about, but your man screwed up handling Montalvo. I don't like having Eve put on the spot to correct that screwup. I don't like it so much that if Soldono is still alive and kicking, I'm tempted to go down there and strangle the bastard. But Eve isn't like me. She's going to worry until she knows that Soldono is okay and that he reached Montalvo in time to stop him from executing a man. So you tell me what's happening, dammit."

Venable was silent a moment. "I don't know what's happening. I haven't heard from Soldono since he called me and told me that Eve had consented to deal with Montalvo. He was going to contact him immediately after he hung up and check back with me."

"He didn't call?"

"He didn't call. I've been trying to reach him all night."

"Shit."

"I've sent a man to Montalvo's compound to try to

check on Soldono, but I won't chance losing another man unless I'm sure Soldono is in danger."

"You ran a risk for that mole in Montalvo's camp."

"Gonzales was valuable. Most of Montalvo's men are loyal to him and the chances of getting another informant in his camp are practically nil. We have to know what he's doing."

"Why? A two-bit weapons dealer?"

"There's nothing two-bit about Montalvo. You didn't check deep enough. He's the big man to go to for weapons in South America. He supplies drug dealers, rebels, militias, anyone with the money to pay. If we can't stop him, we need to know where those weapons are going."

"And Gonzales was telling you."

"Until Montalvo caught him last week. He contacted Soldono and invited him to the compound for a discussion. You know the rest."

"A screwup."

"If it was, I have to bear the brunt of the blame. I told Soldono to stall, to find a way that wouldn't involve pushing an American citizen into jeopardy." He paused. "Actually, I was surprised that Montalvo thought Gonzales's life or death would even matter to her."

"It would matter. When you work with death as much as Eve does, life takes on a very special value. But it worries the hell out of me that Montalvo would realize that about her. You wouldn't think he'd—I want to know more about Montalvo."

"He's smart, he's deadly, and not always predictable. I don't have time to fill you in on anything
else about him right now. As you can see, I have a
problem. I'll phone you when I find out anything
about Soldono." He hung up.

Joe slowly pressed the disconnect. His uneasiness
was growing. Montalvo's insight into Eve's character
was chilling. No threats to her family, she had said.
Nothing that would trigger instant antagonism. But
he'd still played on the sensitivity that was Eve's core.

He rose to his feet and went into the house. Eve
was totally absorbed, her fingers flying over the features of her reconstruction. She didn't look up as he
came into the room. She had forgotten everything
but her Marty and the task of bringing him home.

For once he was grateful for that single-minded
dedication that was a key quality of Eve's. She
wouldn't even realize that time was passing if Venable
didn't get back to him right away.

Eve carefully set the brown glass eyes into the sockets
of the reconstruction and took a step back. It was the
best she could do. She only hoped it would be good
enough. "What about it, Marty?" she whispered.
"You were a very handsome little boy, you know.
Lord, I hope you have a safe haven somewhere now.
I'll do the computer work and then we'll see if we can
bring you home."

"Finished?"

She turned to see Joe sitting on the couch. She nodded and reached for the towel to wipe her hands. "Finished. It took a long time. It wasn't coming." She arched her back to ease the ache. "It's almost dark."

"It was dark an hour ago."

"Oh." She shook her head to clear it. It was always like this after she'd finished a reconstruction. Exhaustion, disorientation, and sadness. "Longer than I thought."

But the world was coming back to her now. "Did you get through to Soldono? No, that's right, you were calling Venable."

"Venable hasn't called me back yet. He doesn't know anything about why Soldono isn't answering his phone. Why don't you take a shower? I'll put a pizza in the oven and we'll—" Joe's cell phone rang. "Quinn." He listened for a moment. "Okay, call you back."

"Something wrong?" Eve asked.

"I don't know. Venable got an anonymous message on his voice mail."

"What's that to do with us?"

"It was only two words. 'Duncan. Porch.'"

Her gaze flew to the screen door. "Porch." She was across the room in a heartbeat.

Joe beat her to the door. "Get the hell away from there." His shove was not gentle. He opened the window to the right of the door, jerked the slender flashlight out of his pocket, and shone the beam out onto the shadowy porch. "Nothing. No one." He swung over the windowsill onto the porch and crouched low. The beam played over every inch of the porch. A moment later he straightened. "No one's here."

"False alarm?"

"I didn't say that." The beam of his flashlight was focused over a rectangular Styrofoam box before the front door. "But at least the delivery boy is gone."

Eve jerked open the door and looked down at the box. Jesus, she was shaking. "What is it?"

"No wires. That doesn't mean that it's not explosive."

She bent down and touched the top of the box. "It's . . . cold."

"Keep your hands off it. Evidence."

"I don't care. Dammit, Montalvo wouldn't want to blow me up. Open it. If you have to preserve your damn evidence, do it. But open the box."

"The two actions don't coincide. Oh, shit." He took his penknife and carefully cut the tape binding and slowly opened the lid. "Step back while I—"

Blood.

"Oh, my God," Eve whispered.

Joe slammed the lid of the box shut.

"No." Her voice was shaking. "I'm okay. Open it again."

"You've seen it. It's a man's head."

"Open it."

He hesitated and then opened the box again. Brown eyes stared blindly up at her from the man's head lying in the box.

"Gonzales?" she whispered.

"I don't know. We have no idea what he looks like. It could be Soldono."

She felt sick. "Why? I told him we'd talk."

"He might be nuts. He might have recognized it as a stall. Who the hell knows?" He took out his phone. "But I do know I'm going to get a forensic team out here to examine this box."

She nodded. "You're right. I probably shouldn't have asked you to—" She stopped, gazing down at the head. "Wait. There's something wrong."

"Tell me about it. Very wrong. The bastard beheaded him."

"No. The eyes..." She extended her hand toward the head.

"Don't touch him."

"I don't think..." She moistened her lips. "At least, the eyes..." Her fingertips touched the left eye. She drew a deep breath. "Bring the box inside."

"I'm not moving it."

"I want more light." She picked up the box herself. "If you won't help, get out of my way." She could hear Joe cursing as she set the box down on the floor inside the door. "It's not what we thought."

He's not what you think. He's not what anyone thinks.

Bonnie had said that about Montalvo, she thought absently. Or maybe Eve had sensed it from her conversations with Montalvo.

"What do you mean?" Joe asked.

"The eyes. They're glass."

"You're sure?"

"I wasn't until I touched it. It just struck an off note when I was looking at him. I've put thousands of glass eyes in reconstructions over the years. And if he has phony eyes, he could—" She turned on the top light and looked at the bloody head. "That son of a bitch."

Joe muttered a curse. "It's a fake."

"Not even a good fake. If it hadn't been so dim on the porch, we would have been able to tell. And the blood didn't help. It was immediate shock value." She was shifting the model from side to side in the box, examining it. "Dry ice to make us believe it had to be refrigerated. Everything done very elaborately just to scare the hell out of me. It's like a bratty kid's practical joke. I want to—" She stopped as she caught sight of something lying in the pool of blood in the bottom of the box. An envelope. She picked it up and tore it open.

"A letter?" Joe asked.

"No letter. A photograph." It was a photograph of a young, good-looking, dark-haired man with his arm around a smiling woman. Two children, a boy of about four and a girl who looked to be eight or nine, were standing before them. The little girl wore a stiff white dress and the boy was wearing a white shirt and tie. They looked like they were dressed up to go to church, Eve thought. "What the devil is this?" She turned the photo over and brushed a smear of blood that had leaked through the envelope to obscure the writing on the back. The ink had also smeared but she could read it. "Pedro and Maria Gonzales. Manuel and Rosa on her First Communion." Her hands were bloody from handling the photo, she noticed dully as she dropped it. "The head definitely resembles the man in the photo. I suppose Montalvo wanted us to know who he was. It's absolutely bizarre." She whispered, "I hope that's what he wanted to do."

"We've got to call Venable."

"Wait."

"Why?"

"Montalvo's going to phone me." She sat back on her heels. "Any time now. He must have known we'd find out fairly quickly that his surprise package was a fake. He's going to do a follow-up."

"Maybe."

"No maybe." Her gaze was fastened on the head. "He's going to do it. I couldn't be more certain."

The house phone rang.

She jumped to her feet and ran toward the phone.

"Did you get it?" Montalvo asked.

"What kind of sadistic bastard are you? What did you think to accomplish by that macabre joke?"

"You did get it. Then my timing is impeccable. I couldn't have my courier stick around to make sure. There was always the chance Quinn might set out on his trail, and the man is valuable to me."

"I got it. And it didn't fool me for more than a minute. Whoever did it was no expert."

"I didn't have a lot of time to have it done properly." He paused. "I had to examine my options. I was going to send you Gonzales's head, but I liked this alternate better. I figured it would get your attention."

"Is Gonzales still alive?"

"Perhaps. Perhaps not."

"Tell me."

He didn't speak.

"I told you I'd talk to you about the reconstruction."

"You were stalling me. I knew that would be your first reaction. Since I couldn't get a commitment from you, I thought I'd take our negotiations a step further."

"Did you kill Gonzales? Soldono thought you would."

"And Soldono believes he knows me very well."

"What about Soldono? We couldn't reach him."

He didn't answer her. "Did you like the photo? I took it from Gonzales's wallet. It's a good likeness of him. Much better than that exhibit I sent you."

"Is he still alive?"

"And his wife and children? A handsome family, aren't they? His wife and the boy and girl live in a village near the compound. He got a note from them yesterday. They don't understand why he didn't come to see them this weekend."

"Then let him go."

"I can't do that."

"Because he's dead?"

"Why don't you come here and see for yourself?"

"Tell me."

He didn't answer for a moment. "I don't like playing these games with you. He's not dead...yet. Neither are his wife and children."

"His family? You were going to kill his family?"

"Ask Soldono what the punishment is for traitors among we savages here in the hills. One must have a deterrent to keep men from stepping over the line. Examples must be set."

"Children?"

"No one knows better than you that children are far from sacred."

"You son of a bitch."

"I'll make you a bargain. You come and do my reconstruction and I'll forget about setting examples. I'll send Gonzales and his family away and forget they exist."

"I couldn't trust you."

"You can, you know. I keep my word."

"Bullshit."

"You're quite right. You don't know me. I'll have to give you something you want enough to take the risk. Let me see...Ah, I have it." He was silent a moment. "I hear a faint echo. Am I on speakerphone?"

"Yes."

"Because you wanted Quinn to hear every word. Turn it off. This is just between you and me."

"I'd only tell him what you said after you hang up."

"It's possible. Why don't we see? Turn it off."

Joe motioned for her to turn it off.

She picked up the phone and pressed the switch button. "Talk. What are you going to offer me that I can't refuse?"

"What do you want most in the world? What drives you and haunts you?"

She found herself stiffening. "I want answers, not questions."

"You want one answer." He paused and then said softly, "Bonnie. It's all about Bonnie, isn't it?"

"I'm going to hang up."

"No, you won't. Because there's no road you won't go down to find your Bonnie. Even one as murky as the one where I live. I'll be very brief. You want to find the remains of your daughter. You want to find her killer. The pervert they executed didn't kill her. You thought you'd found the true killer years ago but you're not sure. You couldn't prove it. I'll find your Bonnie for you. I'll find her killer. And if you want me to do it, I'll dispose of him for you so that you don't have to rely on the courts to do it."

"You can't promise me that."

"I can do it. I have a lot of strings I can pull and I know that criminal underbelly very well. I've been dealing with them ad nauseam of late. We strike a bargain and you get what you want. I get what I want."

"I get lies. You get your reconstruction. I probably end up in a grave in the jungle."

"That won't happen. I give you my word. But I can see how you might doubt my capability to do what I'm claiming. I can understand your skepticism."

"I'd be crazy not to be skeptical."

"When you refused the money, I thought it might come down to this so I started making plans. I thought I'd set up a test for myself to show you that I can do what I say."

"A test?"

"The reconstruction you're working on. Have you finished it?"

"Yes."

"Fax me a photo."

"Why?"

"You want to know who he is and who killed him. I'll find out for you. I told you I had many contacts."

"The police can find that out once they have the photo."

"Will they try as hard as I will? Even after they know who it is, will they go after the killer with every means possible? I don't think so."

She didn't think so either. The ratio of murderers found and convicted even after the bodies were identified was not that impressive. "How would you do it?"

"Oh, I wouldn't murder anyone unless that's what you wanted. Intimidation. Bribery. Whatever it takes." He paused. "Send me the photo. What do you have to lose? You haven't committed. It's only a test to see if I can give you what you want. This is a freebie. The big pot of gold is at the end of the rainbow. I don't give you Bonnie until you do the reconstruction. I'll expect the photo within the next twenty-four hours."

"You won't get it."

"I think I will."

"What if I don't send it? Is it going to affect what you do to Gonzales or Soldono?"

"Every action has a reaction. A lack of action can also cause events to change. Have you ever seen a time-travel movie where the hero changed the future simply by what he did or didn't do?"

"This isn't science fiction, this is real life."

"The principle is the same."

"You're not going to answer me."

"Figure it out for yourself. It's a good idea for you to think about me, guess at my reactions. We need to get to know each other very well. We're going to become very close. You'll be given my fax number in the next few hours." He hung up.

"What's the story?" Joe asked as she hung up the phone.

"He wants to make a trade."

"The lives of Gonzales and his family for you to go down there? No way." His gaze narrowed on her face. "There's something more."

Bonnie.

"Yes." She moistened her lips. "He offered to prove he'd keep his word. A kind of test."

"What kind of test?"

"Marty. He said he'd have someone find out who he was and who killed him if I'd send him a photo."

"That could take years."

She nodded. "He said that he already had people in place to do the work but there's no way that he could—It's crazy."

"Right. Then you won't be doing it. Call and tell him he's wasting his time."

She was silent.

"Eve."

"What could it hurt? I didn't promise anything and it might bring Marty home sooner."

"Because he's drawing you closer and closer with every action he's taking. First that damn bloody head to shock and throw you off balance and then he offers you the promise of bringing that little boy home. The threat and then the stroking."

We're going to become very close.

"He didn't kill Gonzales yet. If I stall long enough, the CIA might get him and his family away."

"You're not stalling, you're dealing with Montalvo."

"I'm doing both." She slammed the lid of the box down. "If I decide to do it. I'm not sure I will."

I'll find your Bonnie.

"You're pretty damn close to committing," Joe said roughly. "I'm not blind, Eve."

"He's not asking me to do anything yet."

" 'Yet.' That's the key word and it means—" Joe's cell phone rang. He looked at the ID. "Soldono." He answered. "Quinn. Why the hell didn't you answer my calls?" He listened for a moment and then held out his phone to Eve. "Montalvo wouldn't let him use his phone until he'd had time to spring his little surprise package. He wants to talk to you."

She took the phone. "Is Gonzales still alive, Soldono?"

"He was a half hour ago. Montalvo took me down to the stockade to see him. He wanted me to be able to tell you that." He paused. "I don't know for how long. I don't know what the devil Montalvo is doing. He's obviously handling you with kid gloves but he could change in a heartbeat."

"Can you arrange to get Gonzales and his family away and out of the country if I can stall him for a few days?"

He was silent, obviously thinking about it. "Maybe. I could try. The wife and kids should be fairly easy, but Gonzales...Can you do that?"

"It's possible."

"He told me to call you and give you a fax number. It's not here at the compound. He doesn't want to chance his machine being monitored. It's at a house in the village." He rattled off a number and she took it down. "What does he want you to send him?"

"He's testing himself." She lifted her gaze to look Joe in the eye. "And I'm going to let him do it."

"As long as you don't expect him not to cheat to get the results he wants. He's a wily bastard."

"I don't expect anything of him. I didn't promise him that I'd give him what he wanted in exchange. For me, it's a win-win situation providing you can get the Gonzales family out of Colombia."

Soldono didn't speak for a moment. "Montalvo usually doesn't make one-sided bargains. If he did, then watch your back."

"Does he keep his word?"

"As far as I know."

"That's not clear enough. Do you believe he would have kept his word about releasing Gonzales if you'd prodded me as he asked?"

He hesitated. "Yes."

"Okay, then tell Montalvo I'll send the photo in the next six hours. I'll consider five days an adequate time for him to find out what I need to know. Is that enough time for you?"

"I hope it is."

"So do I. One other thing. I want Venable to send me a complete dossier on Montalvo."

"Why?"

"He seems to know entirely too much about me; I need to know everything about him."

"I'll tell Venable. He'll get it to you right away." He paused. "I'm sorry we had to involve you in this, Ms. Duncan. We did our best to avoid it."

"I'm sorry too. Just get me the dossier." She hung up the phone and said to Joe, "Well?"

"What do you want me to say?" he said curtly. "It's a mistake. He's going to suck you down and swallow you alive if you let him."

"I won't let him." She stood up and went toward Marty's easel. "A photo isn't a commitment. He's going to do something I want very much and he's not asking anything in return." She bent over and opened the cabinet and started pulling out the photographic equipment. "And the delay could save lives."

"Why five days?"

"I didn't want to have to deal with him when we're going to Phoenix this weekend. And he wanted a test; I gave him a humdinger of a test. It gives Soldono enough time to get the Gonzales family out but it also limits the time I have to deal with Montalvo."

"It would be a miracle if he pulled it off."

Miracle. Joe had said only last night that to find Bonnie would be a miracle. It was almost as if he sensed that Montalvo had offered more than to bring Marty home. Perhaps he did have a premonition. Joe knew her so well....

And why hadn't she told Joe what Montalvo had promised about Bonnie? She hadn't lied but she hadn't told him. Omission was also a lie.

She could still tell him.

She wouldn't lie to herself as well as Joe. She wasn't going to tell him because she knew what his reaction would be. She knew that he would worry, that he would try to stop her from even considering what Montalvo had said. It made no sense to involve Joe when she knew as well as he did that Montalvo's lure was a siren call that was totally false.

Men like Montalvo dealt in death, not miracles.

3

The castle in the painting was wreathed in mists that seemed to be otherworldly.

"MacDuff's Run?" Eve asked Jane. "You made it look like Camelot."

Jane grinned. "That's how MacDuff sees it." She lifted her glass of wine to her lips. "It's like the song in the musical. Magic."

"I'm surprised he doesn't want to buy the painting."

"I didn't tell him I painted it." She tilted her head, appraising it. "I don't usually do landscapes, but I couldn't stop thinking about the place. Maybe it is a little magic. Do you like it?"

"Very much." Eve looked around the crowded gallery. There wasn't any question the show was a success. Sold signs had been popping up on Jane's paintings all afternoon. "But I like all your paintings. I love the one of Toby sleeping on the hearth rug."

"That's one of Toby's favorite sports these days. He'd rather count sheep than chase squirrels."

"That's a dog's privilege. Toby isn't a puppy any longer. When are the two of you coming home for a while?"

"Soon. Maybe next week. As soon as I get through here. I'm ready for a rest."

"Good." Eve took a sip of her wine. "We miss you. How's Trevor?"

"Fine." She smiled and waved at the man talking to Joe across the gallery. "He's just returned from Johannesburg. He promised he'd make the show."

"He looks well."

"He looks like a bloody movie star and every woman in the room is salivating," Jane said with a grin. "I always need Trevor present to give my shows star quality."

"You've got star quality yourself. Ask any of those people who bought your paintings."

Jane shrugged. "I can't see myself as a Rembrandt. I love the work, not the praise." Her glance shifted back to Eve. "And it seems pretty trivial compared to your work."

"Not to me. Art is both a joy and a healer. My reconstructions may offer closure but there's no joy."

"You look tired. You've been working too hard again."

"Maybe." She changed the subject. "What about you and Trevor?"

Jane's smile faded. "What about us?"

"Jane."

She wrinkled her nose. "Okay. He's sexy. He's smart. We're great together." She paused. "And I'm scared to death of commitment. There's no hurry. There are a million things I want to do with my life before I settle down. Satisfied?"

"Temporarily. Sorry if I seemed prying. I worry sometimes."

"God knows I don't want you worrying about me. You have enough problems in your life." She glanced at Joe again. "Why is he on edge? He's trying to be offhand but he's..." She searched for a description. "Ready to spring."

Eve should have known that Jane would sense the turbulence in both of them. Jane had grown up on the streets and she was both savvy and intuitive. Besides the fact that she was close to both of them. "He's being protective. There's a job I'm considering that he doesn't want me to take."

"Then don't take it."

"I probably won't." She changed the subject. "We're going back to Atlanta in the morning. Can you have dinner with us or are you going to be tied up with all these highfalutin art patrons?"

"Screw them." Jane grinned. "I know who's important in my life. I'll meet you at the hotel at seven. Okay?"

"Great." She put her glass down on a table. "Now I'd better let you mingle and influence people if I'm going to monopolize you this evening." She started to weave her way through the crowd toward Joe and Trevor.

She was only a few steps into the throng when her cell phone rang.

"Are you having a good time?" Montalvo asked.

She stopped short, her hand tightening on the phone. "I was until I answered your call. What do you want?"

"Your Jane is a wonderful artist and a beautiful girl. You must be very proud of her."

"More than you could dream. What do you want?"

"It's been three days since you gave me my deadline. I thought you deserved a report."

"Are you going to tell me that you want more time?"

"I said 'report.' Your little boy is Peter Dandlow. Nine years old. He's not from Macon. His parents lived in Valdosta, Georgia. He was reported missing five years ago. He was a latchkey kid and was supposed to call his mom at work when he got home from school. One day she didn't get the call. She never saw him again."

She was so stunned she couldn't speak for a moment. "How did you find that out?"

"Computer files of all the police-department records in the area. It's not easy to break in to them but not impossible for a computer geek. I gave my men enough money to give them incentive to work hard and fast. Some of the cities' records were scanty so I sent a man into the precincts of a few of the towns to check through the back files in their morgues." He paused. "You did a great job on the reconstruction of the boy. You should be quite proud. I've sent a fax to your hotel with the boy's picture and your reconstruction. It should be there by now."

She tried to keep her voice even. "How do I know that any of this is true? You could have doctored the photograph."

He chuckled. "How suspicious you are. I approve. By all means, have Quinn check with the Valdosta police. For my part, I'm sure that Peter Dandlow is your victim. I've moved on to step two."

"And what is that?"

"I told you that I'd try to find the boy's killer. Now, two days isn't much time, but I've made certain strides already. I don't believe the boy was killed by his parents, although I understand it's not uncommon in these cases. His father left the boy's mother before he was born and the extent of the boy's injuries would indicate a certain strength and brutality. I could see the mother hitting the child and killing him but not a continuous pounding that—"

"You actually believe you're going to be able to find his killer? No way."

"I'm not saying I'll catch him. The time's too short. But I'll find out enough to point the way."

"It's a cold case, Montalvo."

"Then I'll warm it up. I'm good at making things happen. But I'm disappointed you gave me such a short time. I like to finish what I start. Wouldn't you like me to drag the boy's killer to lie at your feet?"

"No."

He said softly, "What about your Bonnie's killer?"

She went rigid.

"I'll call you in two days, Eve." He hung up.

Her heart was beating hard. She couldn't breathe. She had to get out of here. The crowd around her seemed to be pressing closer and closer...

She made it to the side exit and ran into the alley. The air was cool and crisp. She took a deep breath and then another.

What about your Bonnie's killer?

Damn him. Liar. Liar.

But he'd found out who Marty was in three days.

That didn't mean he could find Bonnie or Bonnie's killer. It didn't mean he was even telling the truth about Marty.

"I saw you run out. What's wrong?"

She turned to see Joe standing behind her in the doorway. "I needed some air." She moistened her lips. "I got a call from Montalvo. He says that Marty is a missing boy from Valdosta. Peter Dandlow. He's sent a fax with the boy's photo to our hotel."

"He's a crook. It could be doctored."

"That's what I said. He said you could check with the Valdosta police."

"You're damn right I will."

She said slowly, "I don't think it's a fake."

"Why not? That head he left on the porch was a fake."

"That's different. He knew I'd find out almost immediately about that. He had a purpose."

"He has a purpose now."

Yes, he did, but not the one Joe thought. "You should have heard his voice. He was...exhilarated. He likes the idea of doing something this difficult. I can see him sitting there, thinking, pushing, demanding, putting the pieces together."

"Then stop thinking about him," Joe said roughly. "You're talking about Montalvo as if you know him. He's trying to con you."

She was beginning to feel as if she did know him. There was no question that he knew which of her buttons to push. Bonnie. Always Bonnie.

She tried to smile. "It's never a bad thing to know the enemy." She moved toward the door. "We'd better go back inside. Jane might be concerned."

"She was surrounded by a crowd of adoring fans when I came out here. What are you going to do? Run back to the hotel to get the fax?"

"No, this is Jane's night. I'm not even going to look at the fax until we get home from dinner tonight."

"Hallelujah." He took her arm. "And tomorrow I'll check with Valdosta. I hope the bastard is lying through his teeth."

"I don't. If it's true, it means Marty will be brought home to his mother."

"And that makes Montalvo a hero?"

"No, it means that what I worked for will come to pass. I don't care how it happens, just so it happens."

He was silent a moment as he opened the door for her. "Sorry. I'll be glad if you're able to bring your Marty home. I just wish it had happened some other way."

"I do too." She didn't want to think Montalvo was some kind of wonder worker.

She didn't want to feel this dark stirring of hope.

She picked up the fax at the front desk when she and Joe arrived back at the hotel before midnight. She waited until they had reached their suite to look at it.

The photo of Peter Dandlow looked amazingly like the reconstruction she had done. The two photos side by side on the fax were very similar. There were differences, of course. There were always differences when you weren't copying but relying on tissue depth and instinct. But she had done a good job, she realized thankfully.

She handed the fax to Joe. "Close."

"Very close. May I have it?"

"Of course." She went to the bathroom and closed the door as pain poured through her. That smiling, sweet boy, full of life and joy. It was always the same. Satisfaction at a job well done and then the poignant regret.

"Eve."

"I'll only be a minute."

"Let me in." He opened the door. "For God's sake, don't close me out." He pulled her into his arms. "I know what you're feeling. I've always helped you through it. What's different now?"

"Nothing." He had a right to be bewildered. She had acted instinctively when she had run away from him. There was no rhyme or reason why she would do that. "I guess I didn't think."

"That's what worries me." He pulled her closer. "We disagree about what you did. That doesn't mean I won't be here for you."

"I know." She buried her face in his shoulder. Dear heaven, she loved him. Why did she feel this desperate sense of loss and regret lately when she was with him? "I know, Joe…"

They were close to the dirty bastard.

Montalvo plunged into the water and waded downstream. He could hear the dogs up ahead yelping as they caught the scent.

Soldono caught up with him. "I'm not going any farther. I don't hunt men like prey."

"Yes, you do." Montalvo's hand tightened on his rifle. "You do anything you have to do, what your orders tell you to do. This kind of hunt isn't usually necessary for you." His lips thinned. "It's very necessary in my world."

"But you're enjoying it."

"Am I?" He plunged ahead. "Think what you like.

Just follow me and keep your mouth shut or I'll leave you in this jungle to rot."

He could see Miguel up ahead with the dogs. "Across the clearing," Miguel shouted. "Shall I turn the dogs loose on him?"

"No, call them off. Both of you stay here. Leave him to me." He moved forward, darting from tree to tree, taking shelter where he could. It brought back memories of the years he'd spent with the rebels. The same instincts tuned to excruciating acuteness, the adrenaline racing.

A bullet whistled by his ear and buried itself in the tree next to him.

He dodged to the left.

A palmetto bush moved up ahead.

Meant to draw him out and into a line of fire.

Circle around and approach the area.

Move softly, quietly.

Aquila was waiting ahead with his rifle aimed on anything that moved.

Another slight shiver of movement to the left of the tree.

The light was flickering, changing. Montalvo waited for his eyes to become accustomed to the gray pearl of dawn.

The last movement was not a ploy. He could see Aquila's faint outline against the bushes.

He dropped to one knee and aimed his rifle. It was not an easy shot. Poor light, long distance, and Aquila could move at any second.

Concentrate.

His finger pulled the—

Aquila moved to the left!

Take the shot anyway. Make the shot two feet to the left to allow for—

He pulled the trigger.

Aquila fell to the ground.

Playing dead? Wounded? Or really dead?

He circled and cautiously moved toward him. Aquila was a snake and he had no desire to be bitten by him in his death throes.

No danger.

As he drew closer, he could see Aquila lying crumpled on the ground, the top of his head blown off. It had been a true shot.

"Is this what I'm supposed to see?" Soldono asked.

He turned around to watch Soldono and Miguel coming toward him. "Yes." He told Miguel, "Bury him here, where he fell."

Miguel nodded. "I'll get a shovel from the truck." He disappeared into the shrubbery.

Soldono was looking down at Aquila. "Who was he?"

"Someone who made me very angry."

"Why?"

"That's not important to anyone but me."

"It's important for me to know why you dragged me through the jungle to watch you blow a man's head off."

"I saw an opportunity and I took it." He turned

and strode in the direction of the truck. "I thought it was a good idea."

He could feel Soldono's bewildered and faintly repulsed gaze on his back as he moved through the trees. Ordinarily he wouldn't have chosen to have him along when he went after Aquila, but as he'd said, the opportunity was there.

Dawn was beginning to break. By the time he got back to the compound it would be full daylight. He'd grab a nap and then he'd call Norton in Macon and see what information he had for him.

Eve Duncan was waiting.

The dossier on Montalvo was waiting for Eve when they got back to the lake cottage the next day.

"I suppose you want to look at it before dinner," Joe said.

She nodded absently as she opened the envelope. "I'm not really hungry."

"I'll make a pot of coffee." Joe went into the kitchen. "But you've got to eat later. Jane made me promise to make you put on the weight you've lost."

"Okay." There wasn't much in the envelope. A few photos and two sheets of paper. "From what Venable told us I expected a rap sheet the size of a telephone book."

Joe came back and picked up one of the sheets. "No jail time. Ten years ago he was picked up for suspicion of weapons trafficking a few times. After that, nothing."

"How can that be? Venable said he was a big-time dealer."

"He's either very smart, has contacts in high places, or has enough money to bribe his way out of trouble. Maybe all three."

"I believe you're right." She glanced through the photos. Montalvo wasn't a conventionally handsome man. His nose had been broken at some time, his lips were well-shaped but large. His dark hair was threaded with silver at the temples and his eyes were dark and stared out of the photo with direct boldness. "How old is he?"

Joe scanned the report. "It doesn't say. Presumed early forties."

"Presumed? Venable couldn't even get his birth date?"

Joe shook his head. "Not according to this dossier. He was supposed to have fought with the rebels when he was younger."

"Presumed? Supposed? Personal information? Where was he born? Family members? For God's sake, if he was picked up by the police they must have had some record."

"The CIA's first contact with him was when he was selling weapons to the rebels ten years ago. He'd set up a compound in the jungle and ran it like a feudal castle. They probed; they asked questions and came up with zilch."

"A mystery man?"

"There's no mystery that can't be solved. Perhaps they know more than what's on this sheet."

"That's more logical than them not being able to trace his background. Soldono and he seemed to be in each other's pockets." Her hand clenched. "I want to know more, dammit."

"You know enough. He's a crook, he has no compunction about killing a man and his entire family, and he'll use you if you let him. I'd say that about covers it."

"I guess you're right." She looked down at the photos again. "It's just . . . he's very . . . it's hard to dismiss him without knowing what makes him tick. What reconstruction does he want me to do? Why doesn't he try for DNA? He must have the money. He's going to a hell of a lot of trouble to get me down there."

"Including making you think about him nonstop." Joe threw the sheet down on the coffee table. "You've turned down criminals before when they've come to you. What's different about Montalvo?"

The others hadn't offered her Bonnie.

She tried to smile. "I guess I won't find out what's different about him from this rap sheet."

"You've got what you want from the bastard. You've found out who Marty is. Walk away from him."

"When Gonzales and his family are free and clear.

Soldono hasn't called yet to say he's gotten them out. I'll call him tonight to see if there's any progress."

"And I'll check with Valdosta to see if the kid is who Montalvo said he was." He went back to the kitchen. "The coffee should be finished. Want a cup?"

"A little later. I think I'll go for a walk by the lake. Do you want to come along?"

He shook his head. "I want to call Valdosta. I hope they tell me that fax is a fake."

"I don't think that—I don't know. He was just so pumped when he was talking to me. I don't believe he was lying." She opened the screen door. "I'll be back in half an hour."

"Okay." He was already dialing his phone, his expression intent on the task at hand.

Joe was always intent, she thought as she went down the steps. Intent, focused, totally involved with whatever he was working on. That's what made him a brilliant cop.

The lake was smooth as glass.

Peace.

She loved the peace of this cottage and she loved the solid security of her life with Joe. He'd formed cushioned walls around her to protect her from all harm.

She didn't want to leave this haven. She wanted to stay here forever surrounded by Joe's love and care.

Why was she even thinking of leaving? That thought had come out of nowhere. She had no intention of altering her life or taking a chance on...

On what? Going down to Colombia on the chance that Montalvo could do what he'd promised. Risking her life on a criminal who cared nothing for the peace she loved.

Her telephone rang.

Soldono. A rush of hope surged through her. Give me an out, Soldono. Tell me you've gotten Gonzales away and I've no excuse to go to Montalvo.

No excuse but Bonnie.

"What's happening?" she asked as soon as she picked up the phone. "Gonzales?"

"Not yet." Soldono paused. "It's difficult. Montalvo must expect me to make that move. They're very well-guarded."

"That's not what I wanted to hear." She paused. "How serious is he about killing the family?"

"Too serious to discount the possibility."

"The dossier Venable sent us didn't mention any penchant for violence." She added with frustration, "But then it mentioned damn little about anything. Doesn't anyone at the CIA know more about him?"

"Not that I'm aware."

"Are you telling me the truth?"

"I don't have any reason to lie to you. But I wouldn't count on Montalvo not being violent just because it's not on his rap sheet."

"He could have sent me Gonzales's head in that box and he sent a fake instead."

"That could only mean he's smart enough to realize that would turn you off. He got your attention and now he still has Gonzales to bargain with. Believe me, he doesn't hesitate to kill."

"How do you know?"

"Because he wanted me to know." He paused. "I was invited on a hunting expedition last night. No, not invited, commanded to come along."

"Hunting?"

"A man named Aquila. I don't know what he'd done to Montalvo but it was enough to make him so scared he took off into the jungle. Montalvo and his first lieutenant, Miguel, went after him. There wasn't any question of bringing him back alive. He was a dead man from the moment Montalvo started after him."

"He caught up with him?"

"After five hours of tracking. Then Montalvo went on alone to get him. He blew half his head off."

"Jesus."

"And then he told Miguel to bury him in the jungle and went off about his business." He paused. "And I'm sure that business was you."

"Why?"

"Because Montalvo is no exhibitionist. He had a reason for making me go along. He wanted me to see him put down Aquila. He wanted me to tell you about it."

"Because he knew I'd ask the same questions of you that I did. He wanted to let me know that he'd follow through." Lord, Montalvo was intelligent. He seemed to know what she was thinking, what she would do before she did it. "Did he do it just to make a point?"

"No, he said it was an opportunity that presented itself."

She shivered. "Some opportunity."

"Well, you have your answer."

Yes, she had her answer to everything but the question she'd first asked. "Can you get that family away without Montalvo blowing their heads off?"

"I'm doing my best. Venable's sending help."

"That's not good enough."

"I know," Soldono said wearily. "Half the time the work I do isn't good enough. It's all compromises. I'm doing what I can. I'll call you when I know more." He hung up.

She hoped when he called her it would be to give her better news, she thought with frustration. She'd been impatient with Soldono, but he'd probably been doing his job in the most efficient way possible under the circumstances. He was sitting in Montalvo's house and being constantly watched.

It was strange but she felt as if Montalvo were also watching her. She could imagine him sitting like a panther, waiting, watching, blocking every exit before she reached it.

She stared out at the lake. The sun had started to go down and red flames streaked the water. So much beauty. At times it took her breath away. She would remember moments like this forever.

Remember? She experienced moments like this every day of her life. There was no need for memory.

She had to get back to Joe and tell him about the call from Soldono. Maybe not tell him quite everything. He was already on edge and disturbed. He didn't need to know about the man Montalvo had killed. It wouldn't have surprised him, but it would give him more ammunition to hurl at her for dealing with Montalvo at all.

She turned and headed back toward the cottage. She wasn't going to be dissuaded from continuing her contact with Montalvo but she, too, needed ammunition. That dossier was ridiculously sparse and it made her feel helpless. She couldn't tolerate feeling helpless. There had been too much of that agony after Bonnie's death. It was the primary reason she had gone back to school to be a forensic sculptor. It had been a way to strike back, to have a purpose.

Knowledge was power. Knowledge was strength. To deal with Montalvo she'd need quantities of both.

"Soldono called while I was down by the lake," she told Joe when she went into the cottage. "He's striking out. He hasn't got Gonzales and his family out of the country yet. Venable's sending him help." She went to the coffeepot on the counter and poured a cup. "And he doesn't know any more information than what's in that report. Or so he says." She lifted the cup to her lips. "I tend to believe him. If the CIA is keeping his background under wraps, they haven't told Soldono."

"It's not bright not telling an agent information he might be able to use in the field."

"I agree. We need all the information we can get about Montalvo." She paused. "That's why I'm going to call Galen."

"I'm not surprised. I could see it coming. He may not be able to help, you know."

"And he may. Galen deals in buying and selling information, among other things. The CIA may not be able to find out anything about Montalvo but I'd bet on Galen."

"You have in the past." He looked down at the coffee in his cup. "But you haven't even spoken to him for months. Elena and he have a little girl now. You're his friend but relationships have a tendency to break down when new bonds are formed."

"Not with Galen." She and Galen had become too close in the time they had spent together. "He'll have time for me. I'm not asking him to fly off to Colombia and scout out Montalvo. All I want is information. I'll call him right after supper." She opened the freezer. "How about me putting a frozen lasagna into the oven?"

"Fine." He paused. "You didn't ask me about my check call to Valdosta."

She took out the lasagna. "Oh, what did you find out?"

"The fax wasn't doctored. But that's what you expected, wasn't it?"

"It's good to have it confirmed." But she'd really

had no doubt that Montalvo had been telling the truth. It would have been too easy to check and he wouldn't have wanted to be discredited in her eyes. He'd gone to extreme lengths to make sure that she didn't think he was either a liar or a charlatan. "Thanks for going to the trouble."

"No trouble." He turned on the oven. "I have a feeling the trouble is yet to come."

"Montalvo?" Galen repeated. "I've heard of him. But nothing that you'd call confidential information."

"Can you find out anything for me?"

"Of course, luv." Galen sighed. "I'd offer to dispose of him for you but my Elena would object. She's making me as tame as a pussycat."

Eve chuckled. "I can't see it. Particularly since Elena was once more lethal than you."

"She was *not*." His English accent became more pronounced in his indignation. "We came together on equal ground. Of course my ground sometimes is a bit more equal than hers. Oh well, we're compatible in almost every other way."

"I imagine you are since you managed to conceive a child between bouts. How is Elspeth?"

"Glowing, beautiful, sweet, clever, amazing, I don't see why they say two is so terrible. She's an absolute—" He broke off. "No, Elspeth, do *not* take a bath in the dog's drinking water. That's not a good thing. You may be clean but the puppy isn't so lucky.

Why aren't you listening to me?" Eve heard the sound of a child's crowing in the background and then a cry of protest. "Okay, I've got her under my arm. What was I saying?"

"Elspeth is clever, amazing, and sweet."

"Also stubborn, single-minded, and utterly dictatorial. And being almost two has nothing to do with it. She's her mother's child."

"And Elena probably says the same about you."

"Undoubtedly. They gang up on me. You have no idea how a daughter can rule your life until you—" He stopped. "God, I'm sorry, Eve. I didn't think."

"Stop it. Do you think I don't wish you every minute of joy with Elspeth? It's one of the greatest experiences you'll ever know. Just hold her close, Galen."

"I do. I will." He paused. "Before Elspeth came to us I thought I felt sorrow for you but it's nothing to what I feel now. I didn't understand. Maybe I still don't understand but, my God, how I empathize."

"Thanks, Galen." She cleared her throat. "I'll let you go so you can get back to Elspeth."

"She's okay. She's playing with her piano now. No, dammit, she's on top of her piano. Oh, hell, I said it again. Every curse word and we have to put a dollar in her college fund. She's got enough for Harvard already. No, Elspeth, we don't jump off—" He hung up.

Eve was still smiling as she pressed the disconnect. Lord, it was wonderful to hear Galen so happy. She had told him the truth. She wouldn't have cheated him of one precious moment just because those moments were no longer hers. Bonnie. Elspeth. All the other children who shared the magic of childhood and made the days golden.

"He's going to help?" Joe asked.

"Yes. He said he'd get right on it but I'm not sure when I'll hear from him. He seemed to be busy with dog water and pianos."

"What?"

"Elspeth."

Joe nodded. "And any delay is forgiven in the name of the baby girl."

"Of course. Galen has his priorities straight." She got to her feet. "I have to go through the mail and send a refusal to the Moscow police department for the job they asked me to take on."

"I thought there was a possibility you'd do their reconstruction."

She shrugged. "I changed my mind. If they're willing to delay, I may still do it. If they want it right away, they'll have to get someone else."

"But you're clearing your calendar."

She didn't answer directly. "Dealing with the Russians can be a headache. They have so many current mafia problems they're not interested in cold cases." She went to the mail basket and got the sheaf of letters. "I don't need any more headaches right now. Marty was difficult enough...."

4

Montalvo didn't call when the five days were up. Nor did he call on the sixth day, nor the seventh.

On the eighth day her cell phone rang at 3:32 P.M.

"Have you been waiting with bated breath?" Montalvo asked. "I assure you it wasn't a strategy on my part. I hate not being able to meet a challenge with utmost efficiency. I was most unhappy with my head operative, Norton, in the U.S."

"Are you going to shoot him as you did that man Aquila?"

"Ah, Soldono discussed it with you. Actually I wasn't that displeased with Norton. There's no similarity in the cases. Aquila was armed and would have killed me given the smallest chance. Inefficiency deserves replacement and withdrawal of favors. That punishment is usually enough in most situations. However, since I'd given you my word and the issue was earning your trust I was particularly irate."

"I'd never trust you."

"But you could trust my ability to do what I promised," he said softly.

"I had no faith in you. There was no way you could find the killer in such a short time."

"But I did."

She went rigid. "What?"

"I've no concrete proof. There wasn't time, but I believe I located him."

"How?"

"I had my men checking the police records of all child molesters in the towns surrounding Valdosta and Macon. None of them seemed a match. There were two attempts at kidnapping in Columbus, Georgia, and Stockbridge at about that time. But those men were apprehended almost immediately. No reports of attempts in Macon. Yet the boy was found in a grave outside Macon."

"So?"

"I studied the situation and decided to focus in on Macon. If I was looking for victims, I wouldn't commit a crime in my own backyard. I'd pick up the victim in another town and dispose of the body in a grave some distance away."

"And you found a suspect in those records?"

"No, we located a few sex perverts who were in Macon at the time. It took a little while to track down and eliminate them. And, no, I don't mean that literally. Though I'm sure they deserved it. Two were in jail at the time. The other offender had an alibi. I thought we'd run into a stone wall. I don't like to be wrong."

"You said you found him," she prompted.

"Impatient? I'm getting to that. Since I didn't want to admit being wrong, I went down another road. If he wasn't a known sex offender and didn't have a record with child molestation, what was the answer? Macon is a big college town. What if one of the students was the killer? It was a long shot but I gave the order to scan police records for any students picked up loitering near schools or day-care facilities. Donald Palker came up in the computer. He had a bottle of whiskey in the car and claimed he'd passed out after a frat party in front of Jolly Time Day Care. The Macon police get a lot of students who can't hold their liquor. Palker was a sophomore, clean-cut, got good grades, and was polite and apologetic. They let him go."

"And Marty died," she whispered. "He wasn't arrested again?"

"Yes, but not in Georgia. Last year he was put on trial in Connecticut for suspicion of murdering a ten-year-old boy. The evidence was compromised and he was released."

"He's still loose?"

"Yes, he's living with his parents in upper New York State. As I said, I didn't have time to get proof. I have a man watching Palker now. If you can have

Quinn get Valdosta to search through their forensic records for DNA other than the boy's, we can get a match." He paused. "Or if you don't want to bother, Palker can disappear. It would save the courts a good deal of money and maybe save a life. It's up to you."

She shuddered. "And land in an unmarked grave? We'll get the DNA."

"I thought that would be your response. You have a horror of unmarked graves."

"Is that why you told your Miguel to bury Aquila in one?"

"No, that was purely for my convenience. Not all of my actions revolve around you." He chuckled. "But certainly a good portion of them do at the moment."

"I've no desire to be the focus of your attention."

"Nevertheless, you are." He paused and when he spoke again all trace of humor was gone from his tone. "I didn't keep to the letter of the test you gave me, but you have to admit I did very well. I showed you I was capable of giving you what you want."

"No, you didn't. Marty's murder was recent history compared to Bonnie. She was killed a long time ago. Joe and I have been searching for years with no result. We've explored every avenue. And you think you could just step into the picture and actually find her?"

"It's not what I think. It's what you think," he said softly. "Or what you hope, Eve. Right now, you're re-membering all the information I gathered in just eight days. You're wondering whether if you pass up the opportunity you'll ever be able to forget that you might have found your Bonnie."

"My God, you're sadistic."

"No, I'm desperate. This is no game to me. I have to have you. You do this for me and I promise I'll find your little girl."

"And if I don't?"

"I've stacked the situation with good and bad cards. It's up to you how I play them."

"I'm responsible? Don't lay your blame on me."

"I'd never do that. I take total responsibility for everything I do. I'm going to hang up now so that you can consider the gift I've offered you."

"A gift has no strings."

"True. Good-bye, Eve. I'll be—"

"How long have you known about Palker?"

"I found out last night."

"And why didn't you call me then?"

"Why don't you tell me, Eve?"

"You didn't want to keep me in suspense. Your ego would have told you to call me as soon as possible so that you would have at least come closer to your deadline."

"Really?"

"Really."

"Then why didn't I do it?"

"Joe. You knew Joe wouldn't be home at this time of day. You didn't want him to hear what you said to me before. You don't want him to know now."

"Very good. You *are* coming to know me."

"Not enough. How many people did you pay off to keep any information about you buried as deep as that man you killed and threw in the ground?"

"A good many. I'm flattered you've been interested enough to try. And, as I told you before, this is between the two of us. I'm sure Joe Quinn has been putting up roadblocks since the moment I called you. He gets in the way. You know that as well as I do. I can't have him doing that. He stands over you like a guardian angel protecting you from my devilish ways."

"He's a good man and I listen to his advice."

"I know. That's one of the things I've had to overcome. But I have overcome it, haven't I? When all is said and done, you don't care if you're being wise. You don't care if there's danger. You're tired and hurting and you want your heart eased of pain." His voice lowered to soft urgency. "I'll give you that ease, Eve. Come to me. Help me and I'll help you."

Christ, she was bending, yielding to his words as if he were indeed Lucifer tempting her with untold riches.

But the riches were not unspecified; she knew exactly what she would get from him.

"Call me when you're ready to come and I'll make arrangements." He hung up.

Dear God.

She rose to her feet and went to the window to look out at the lake.

Help me and I'll help you.

Lord, she did need help. She needed someone to tell her she was crazy to be drawn into the web Montalvo had woven. Yet that was what Joe had been doing all along and she had been ignoring him, fighting him.

Because she didn't want to be saved. From the moment he had mentioned Bonnie she had wanted to risk everything for the chance that Montalvo was not lying to her. Somewhere deep within her she had desperately wanted Montalvo to be successful in finding out Marty's identity and locating his killer. If he could do it once, he might be able to do it twice.

And he had done what he had promised. He had met the test.

Help me and I'll help you.

She closed her eyes as the words repeated over and over in her mind.

Help me and I'll—

Her eyes flicked open and she turned away from the lake. There was no need to dwell on Montalvo's words. They had already done their work. He hadn't even had to be particularly persuasive after the first attempt. It had been overkill. On a subconscious level she had been persuading herself these last days.

And there was no question in her mind or heart that she was going to let Montalvo help her find Bonnie.

·   ·   ·

She phoned Montalvo back thirty minutes later. "I'm coming. But on my terms, not yours."

"What terms?"

"You're not sending any plane for me. I'll arrange with the CIA to bring me to you."

"Agreed."

"And you'll have Gonzales and his family waiting when I get off the plane and they'll board it and the CIA will fly them out of Colombia."

"Agreed."

"And you won't wait until I finish the job to get your people working on finding my daughter. You'll start at once."

"Agreed. Anything else?"

"No." She paused. "I'm good, but I'm not a miracle worker. I may not be able to do what you wish. I'm bargaining for the attempt, not the success."

"I've seen your work. At times you come very close to miracles."

"I mean it, Montalvo."

He didn't speak for a moment. "As long as I feel you're giving it your best effort, I won't quarrel with you."

"I can't do anything else but my best. It's the only way I work. One other thing. Joe Quinn."

"He can't come with you."

"I don't want him to come with me. I may be willing to risk my own neck with you, but I won't risk Joe's. But he's not going to see it my way. I need a promise from you. Under no circumstances will you harm my family, particularly Joe. No matter what he does, what he says, how much trouble you believe he's going to cause, you will not hurt Joe Quinn."

"That may be a most difficult condition. I've checked his background. Police, FBI, ex-SEAL. He could cause a disturbance."

"You're damn right he could. Ask me if I care. Give me your promise."

"Would you trust my word?"

"Probably not. But if I make it a part of the bargain you'd know it was a deal breaker."

"I do keep my word. It's one of my eccentricities."

"We'll see. Give me your promise. I want the words."

He sighed. "Under no circumstances will I harm your admirable Joe Quinn. Satisfied?"

"No, I'm not satisfied about anything connected with this. I'm just trying to minimize the damage."

"And you've done a good job. I'd expect nothing less of you." His voice became crisp. "Now let me go over arrangements. You'll be landing at a strip in a small village, San Cristal. The countryside is rough and it's difficult for even a helicopter to land near the compound. You'll be brought by jeep to within one mile of the compound, where you'll go through the checkpoints."

"Very isolated. How do you do business?"

"By staying alive and not inviting anyone too close. My men know the jungle around the compound and can spot anyone who gets too near."

"Like Aquila?"

"Yes, he got much too near. When may I expect you?"

"I'll let you know. I have to talk to Venable."

"He'll be full of warnings and gloom, but he'll go along with you. He's very concerned about Gonzales. For such an experienced agent, I found he has a conscience where innocent bystanders are concerned."

"You act as if that's rare."

"I appreciate those who have a code and stick by it. Most of us change with the winds."

"Speak for yourself. I don't. Neither does Joe. I'll call you when I firm up the flight with Venable." She hung up.

Committed.

Fear. Uncertainty. Excitement.

And the excitement was growing, she realized. Facing the unknown, a challenge to be met, a chance to find Bonnie. She suddenly felt vibrantly alive. She hadn't expected this reaction. Now that the decision was made it was as if every facet of her mind and body were readying for a battle.

And that's exactly what it might prove to be, she thought ruefully.

Well, time to call in reinforcements. She looked up the number and quickly dialed Venable.

"It's my duty to try to dissuade you," Venable said. "You're putting yourself at risk and we're not in a position to help you if you need it." He added wearily, "I'd think you'd realize that. We haven't even been able to help Gonzales."

"I won't ask for help. This is my choice. If I get in trouble, it's up to me to find a way out."

"What about Quinn? What have you told him?"

"Nothing." She paused. "He's not involved with this."

"Yet."

"He's not going to know anything until I'm halfway to Colombia. He's going to be angry and he's going to try to get you to do something to get me out of Montalvo's compound. You're not to do it. If you come for me, I won't go with you. And you may lose men trying to make me. Do you understand?"

"Understood. But there's no way you'll get Quinn to understand. He may come after all of us."

"I'll try to explain—I have to do this. Try to keep him away from me and safe, Venable. You owe me for Gonzales. Pay me back by protecting Joe." She had to get off the phone. She was getting too emotional. "I'll be waiting for someone to pick me up at nine-thirty in the morning."

"I'll have a man there. You won't change your mind?"

"I won't change my mind."

She stood there a moment, fighting for control, after she'd hung up. Talking about Joe had brought the effect on him of what she was doing to the forefront. He would understand her going, he would not understand her not letting him go with her. He would regard it as a betrayal of their relationship.

So be it. She would worry about damage control later. She had done all she could to keep him safe. She just had to forge forward.

But that was not going to be tonight. She had Joe for one more night. The next days ahead would be for Bonnie. She would take tonight for herself.

"We have to make a trip to the village tomorrow, Soldono," Montalvo said as he turned away from the phone. "I'm going to have a visitor."

"She's actually going to come?"

"With many stipulations." He smiled. "She very wisely hedged her bet as much as she could. But the bottom line is that she's coming."

"God help her."

Montalvo's smile faded. "God helps he who helps himself. Eve Duncan is doing what she can to help herself. We must hope that she continues in that vein." He turned away. "Now go and tell Maria Gonzales and the children to pack up. I won't release her husband until the last minute before we leave for the landing pad. It won't hurt him to sweat a little more."

"You're releasing them?"

"A condition of your Ms. Duncan's. I expected it." He gave Soldono a cool glance. "You were wise not to make the attempt to get them out before this. I was a little worried you might not be as intelligent as I thought you to be. You might have set my plan back severely if you'd made me use violence when I'd tracked you down. I'm being forced to strike a very delicate balance with Eve Duncan."

Soldono met his gaze. "If I'd found a way, I would have done it." He turned away. "And I wouldn't have been as easy as Aquila."

Montalvo laughed. "Good for you. A break at last in your demeanor. I was getting tired of you being so diplomatic with me."

"There was a man's life at stake. I did what I had to do."

"And now the man is going to be freed and you can be yourself. It will be a relief to both of us." Montalvo waved his hand. "Go get the woman and children. Miguel will give you cash to set them all up far away from me."

"Why?"

"It may discourage me from obeying the rule I set up for the compound." He paused. "Or it might not. So don't tell me where you settle them."

"You're a strange man, Montalvo."

"Strange is better than ordinary. I swore when I was a child that I would never be run-of-the-mill. I've kept my word."

"That you have." Soldono was heading for the door. "There's no use me being here if you're releasing Gonzales. I'll be boarding the plane with them."

"No, I want you to stay here."

"Why?"

"Eve Duncan will feel safer here with you on the scene."

He hesitated. "I'll have to check with Venable."

"We both know there won't be a problem. Not only will you be providing security to a U.S. citizen, but you'll continue to be in a position to spy on my operations. After all, that's how all this started in the beginning."

"I have to warn you that I'll provide her with all the security of which I'm capable. I won't be a cardboard figure, Montalvo."

"Good. The safer she feels, the more productive she'll be."

Soldono shook his head and strode out of the room.

Montalvo stood up and moved across the office to the window to stare out at the jungle. Excitement was tingling through him.

She was coming.

It had been a hard fight but he had won. He had been patient and not reached out and grabbed. He had used his mind and not muscle.

Are you as excited as I am, Eve? I believe you are. I could hear it in your voice. I could sense it.

I'm getting closer, you son of a bitch. One step at a time, one person at a time. You can't stop me, Diaz.

She was coming.

.   .   .

Nekmon hesitated outside the bedroom door. Diaz had a new woman with him and he usually didn't like to be disturbed. Screw it. Diaz had told him to report as soon as he knew anything about Aquila. If he didn't do as ordered, he'd be in trouble anyway. Damned if he did, damned if he didn't.

He knocked. "Nekmon."

"Come in. Come in," Diaz said impatiently.

The scent of perfume and marijuana hit his nostrils as soon as he opened the door. "I'm sorry to bother you, but you said—"

"I know what I said." Diaz sat up, leaned back against the padded velvet headboard, and lit a joint. "Talk and get out."

Nekmon carefully avoided looking at the naked woman lying next to Diaz. "Aquila reported in night before last. He didn't have much. Montalvo has been very quiet lately and staying close to home. He did come up with one name several times during surveillance. Something about a job and an Eve Duncan."

"Who the shit is Eve Duncan?"

"I went to the Internet. If it's the same one, she's some kind of big-time forensic sculptor."

Diaz stiffened. "What?"

"My report's on your desk. I could get it for you now."

"No, not now," he said absently. "But I want to know if Aquila calls with any other info."

"We haven't heard from him in twenty-four hours.

He should be calling every eight hours per your orders."

Diaz muttered a curse. "The idiot was probably clumsy."

"That's my guess. Do I send someone else?"

Diaz nodded slowly. "Send Duarte."

Nekmon's brows lifted. "You believe that will be necessary?"

"It can't hurt. I like to be prepared." He murmured, "Eve Duncan. The bastard must be getting close."

"Can I do anything else?"

"Not in here. I don't like sandwiches." He handed the joint to the woman next to him.

Only it wasn't a woman, Nekmon noticed. It was a girl not over eleven or twelve. He vaguely remembered seeing her working on one of the coca farms. Evidently Diaz had seen her, too, and decided he liked what he saw. It didn't surprise him. Diaz usually liked the young ones. He often bought girls even younger from the whorehouses in Bogotá.

"I'll go then. Good night, Mr. Diaz."

Diaz didn't answer. He was already moving over the young girl. "Now let's see how well you've learned your lessons, little *puta*...."

"Again, Joe?" Eve's voice was breathless as she cuddled closer to him. "Don't tell me I've worn you out?"

"Okay, I won't tell you." He rolled over and was on top of her. "Now put up or shut up."

"You mean put out." She smiled up at him. "No problem."

"I hope not." His hand caressed her cheek. "That's what I want for you, Eve. No problems ever."

"There are always problems." She turned her head to kiss his palm. "But moments like this make us forget about them. You're a wonderful man and a hell of a lover." She whispered, "I love you, Joe."

"I gathered that by the way you seduced me tonight. You didn't let me eat my supper before you set out to do your best to get me in the sack."

"You were easy. It didn't take my best. Are you complaining?"

"If I were, you should send me to a shrink." He bent down and kissed her, slow, lingering. "God, I'm glad to be seduced. I was trying to be reserved and not use sex to influence you."

"How stupid can you get? Use it." She chuckled. "It won't get you anywhere, but we'll have a hell of a good time."

"What a healthy attitude." He started to move. "I believe I will...."

Joe was carefully getting out of bed and heading for the bathroom. The door closed silently and she heard the shower.

He didn't want to wake her, Eve knew. It was

six-thirty. He'd get dressed and be on the way to the precinct within thirty minutes.

She'd lie here and pretend to be asleep and hope he didn't turn on the light and see the tears staining her cheeks. This was going to be the most difficult time. She wanted to talk to him, tell him everything. She wanted to draw him back to her and forget about Venable's agent, who'd be here in a few hours. Why was she doing this when she could have Joe and hours like the ones that had spun by like molten gold?

Golden nights and silver mornings.

Who had said that?

Jane. After she had come back from MacDuff's Run.

Last night had been golden. But this morning was anything but silver. It was shoddy metal and was leaving a taste of bitter brass in her mouth.

The decision was made. Good-byes were always hard. If she didn't go today, she would go tomorrow or the next day. She knew herself too well not to know that.

She just had to hope that Joe didn't turn on the light.

5

She got a call from Galen when she was boarding the private jet at the Atlanta airport.

"Do you have a minute, luv?" he asked. "I need to talk to you."

"I have time. You've found out something?"

"Not as much as I'd like. Enough to make me uneasy."

"You? Uneasy? It takes a lot to rattle you."

"I'm not rattled. Don't insult me. I'm merely a bit troubled."

"And what about Montalvo made you troubled? We all knew he was bad news."

"We didn't know that there was a connection with Ramon Diaz."

"Diaz . . . the name's familiar, but I can't—"

"Colombian drug lord. Scum of the earth. Very powerful. He controls half the politicians in the government."

"And Montalvo is his buddy?"

"I don't know. Digging for information about Montalvo is a study in frustration. I need to go down there and do the job myself."

"No," she said sharply. "That's not what I asked. I want you to stay home and do any digging long-distance."

"I may have sounded like a hausfrau yesterday, but I still do my job, Eve. Long distance isn't cutting it."

"What did you find out?"

"I think he's forty-two and was born in a village in the south. I can't trace his parents yet. As far as I know, he could have been hatched. The next info places him with the rebels when he was in his twenties. Very good. Very lethal. That's all until he emerges years later as this weapons guru."

"And Diaz?"

"I don't know. My informant says it's only a whisper, not a fact. But that whisper keeps repeating over and over."

"Maybe it's like the telephone game. It starts out as one thing and ends up completely different."

"Maybe. But if there's any connection at all you want to get as far away as possible from him. Diaz shoots priests because they preach against growing coca. I don't know how nasty Montalvo operates, but if he works with Diaz, he's bound to be an ugly customer."

"A whisper."

Galen was silent a moment. "And you don't want to hear that whisper, do you? Why not?"

"I'm listening."

"I can hardly hear you with all that background noise. Where are you?"

"I need to hang up anyway. Call me if you hear anything concrete." She was climbing the steps of the jet. "But don't you leave Elena and Elspeth. I don't need the information that badly."

"You sounded fairly urgent before. What's different?"

The difference was that bad or good, she was going to find out for herself. "Thanks for trying, Galen."

"I don't try, I do. You know that or you wouldn't have called me in the first place. I'll get back to you when I know more. Good-bye, Eve."

"Good-bye, Galen. Remember what I—"

He was gone. Dammit, she'd unleashed Galen's boundless curiosity, and coupled with his pride in his profession, she'd never be able to call him off until he was satisfied.

The pilot came out of the cockpit. "We need to take off, Ms. Duncan."

"Fine." She settled in a seat and fastened her seat belt. It wasn't fine. In a matter of hours Joe would be home and getting the note she had left. Galen might decide to leave his family and go to Colombia and she was on her way to a man who was not only a criminal in his own right, but hobnobbed with scum like Diaz.

No, nothing was fine at this particular moment.

The note was propped up on the coffee table where Joe couldn't miss it.

He muttered a curse as he tore it open.

> *Joe,*
>
> *I had to do it. I'm on my way to Montalvo. Don't come after me. It will be much riskier for both of us if you're on the scene. Montalvo doesn't want to hurt me. He needs me. I won't answer my phone for a while but I'll keep in touch. Just don't come after me. Please.*
>
> *I can see you now, angry and frustrated as you read this. You're thinking I'm stupid and blind and you're asking yourself why I fell for the line he gave me. I fought it but in the end I couldn't do anything else.*
>
> *He promised me Bonnie.*
>
> *I love you.*
>
> *Eve*

Shit.

Joe's hand slowly crushed the note. He wanted to strike out, to crush more than this damned piece of paper. He should have known that she was on the edge, preparing to move. Eve was always up-front and eager about sex, but last night she had been almost aggressive.

And damn wonderful.

If good-bye could ever be wonderful.

The son of a bitch. He had dangled the one bait Eve could never resist and done it with a cleverness that made it almost acceptable to her.

Yes, she was safe while she was working on the reconstruction. But she knew as well as he did that once the work was done, all bets were off. She didn't care. The chance to find Bonnie was worth the risk to her.

Pain surged through him. Well, it wasn't worth it to him. He wouldn't lose her.

And her plea for him not to follow her was crap. No way.

He pulled out his cell phone. No use to call Eve. If she said she wouldn't answer, she wouldn't do it.

He dialed Galen and said when he picked up, "I need to know everything you can find out about Montalvo's compound, how it's manned, any weakness."

Galen was silent a moment. "How soon?"

"Yesterday."

Galen gave a low whistle. "Not easy. Would you care to give me a reason for the urgency?"

"Sometime tonight Eve will be going through the gates of that compound."

"Shit."

"Exactly. She left me a note to tell me to stay home and tend to my knitting."

"Fat chance. I can't believe she'd take that risk. Particularly after I told her about Diaz."

"Diaz?"

"I called her this morning and told her that there might be a connection between Montalvo and Diaz. It would be a very nasty combo. Drugs and weapons." He paused. "I think she was at the airport this morning when I called. The noise..."

Diaz. Jesus. What Joe had heard about him was ugly and lethal. "Montalvo is nasty enough. He played Eve like a maestro."

"Eve doesn't manipulate easily."

"He promised her Bonnie."

"Christ. That would do it. I'll get on the phone and see what I can find out for you. When are you leaving?"

"Tonight."

"Call Venable before you go and see if you can find out any information from him. It can't hurt. We may need all the help we can get."

"We?"

"I'll meet you in Bogotá and we'll go from there."

"No."

"Screw you. I'm going with or without you. Eve asked me to do a job and I haven't finished it. You try to operate without me and you'll be going in blind. My sources wouldn't trust anyone but me."

And Galen had the best information sources Joe had ever run across. "Then I won't argue with you. Eve probably would. She was looking very mushy and sentimental when she was talking about your Elspeth."

"I've no intention of not coming back. We go in, we get Eve, and we get out." He paused. "If we can persuade her to go. That's up to you."

"Thanks. She'll come back with us if I have to tie and gag her. I'll call you when I have my flight information." He hung up and sat there for a moment. Fight the panic. Galen was right. The big battle would be to persuade Eve to abandon her deal with Montalvo and come with them.

He'd find a way. He had to find a way. Stop sitting here and start moving. He'd call Venable on the way to the airport. He stood up and headed for the door.

San Cristal

It was after midnight when the helicopter Eve had switched to in Bogotá set down on the landing strip of the small village that was only a dot in the middle of the blackness of the jungle.

She drew a deep breath, trying to ease the tenseness of her muscles. Now wasn't the time for nerves. Being here was her choice. So she felt isolated and uncertain. Suck it up and face it.

"Welcome, Ms. Duncan." The door slid open. "Did you have a good journey?"

Montalvo. In the lantern light he looked younger, stronger, more vibrant than his photographs. Also, considerably more dangerous; the photographs had not shown the gun that was holstered at his hip.

"Considering where I was going." She unfastened her seat belt. "And why have I become Ms. Duncan when you were calling me Eve the last few times you phoned?"

He chuckled. "I thought it would put you more at ease if I was more impersonal. No?"

"No. Nothing is going to put me at ease until I get out of here. Call me what you like." She ignored his hand and jumped down from the helicopter. "Where's the Gonzales family?"

"Inside the hut. The children were frightened."

"Of you?"

"Possibly." He grabbed her two bags. "Is this all?"

"Clothes and my equipment."

"I should have told you that you didn't need the equipment. I have all you'll need at the compound."

"I like my own equipment."

"I can understand that. I have weapons that I've used for years and the familiarity is comforting." He threw the bags in the back of the jeep. "There's a certain feel..."

Her gaze went to the gun on his hip. "Death?"

The smile never left his face. "I never thought about it. Don't you think that your tools would reflect death more than mine? You actually work with human skulls."

"Not to destroy them."

"Good point. I do destroy on occasion." He waved his hand at the hut. "We'll get the Gonzales family on board and then get you to the compound. You must be tired."

"I'm perfectly fine."

He turned and met her eyes. "No, you're not fine. You're tense and a little frightened. Oh, not of me. I don't frighten you. But you're wondering somewhere deep inside if you've made a mistake. If it's worth quarreling with your Joe. If I'll do what you want me to do."

Jesus, he must be a mind reader. That was exactly how she felt.

"And the answer to all those questions is no," he said softly. "And yes, and yes. You've done the right thing for both of us. And I won't let you regret it."

She tore her gaze away from his. "We'll see." She shifted her eyes to the woman who was hurrying toward the helicopter with two children in tow. She stiffened. "Where's Gonzales?"

"Ye of little faith. Not that I don't approve of suspicion." He waved his hand again. "Soldono is bringing Gonzales separately. I wanted the bastard to sweat up to the last minute about whether I'd actually let him go."

"Cruel."

"He deserves it. He betrayed me. He's lucky to get out with his skin."

She watched the thin, dark man bolt out of the hut and run toward the aircraft. He cast one panicky glance at Montalvo and then dove into the helicopter. A moment later the door was closed and the rotors whirled. "I'd say he was sweating even enough to please you."

"No. I don't like traitors. Even Soldono didn't object when I decided to punish him a little. He knows Gonzales got off lucky." He turned to the man coming toward him. "Don't you, Soldono?"

Soldono was a tall, lean, sandy-haired man in his thirties who looked rawhide-tough. "I guess you could say that. He's not dead." He held out his hand to Eve. "Mark Soldono, CIA. I'm sorry for my part in involving you with this mess. I hope you'll let me do everything to make your stay easier at the compound."

She felt a surge of relief. "You're coming with us?"

He grimaced. "Montalvo wanted to provide you with a sense of security. I guess that's me." His glance shifted to the helicopter that was lifting off the ground. "Though you've done a better job than I have so far. I don't like the price you paid but thanks anyway."

"It wasn't all about Gonzales," Eve said. "He was just a fringe benefit."

Montalvo chuckled. "I enjoy your turn of phrase. 'Fringe benefit'..." He got into the driver's seat of the jeep. "I'll have to see what other fringe benefits I can find for you."

"You can't beat a human life."

"Yet neither of us is here because of life, but death. What does that say?" He started the jeep. "Never mind. It's not fair to argue philosophy when you're so tired. Sit back and relax. It's ten miles to the compound. The last mile has three checkpoints."

"You're very careful."

"It's how I've stayed alive for all these years. I'm an old man for my business."

"Forty-two?"

"You've been asking questions. Forty-one, actually."

"And running guns is so dangerous?"

He shrugged. "Everyone in this part of the world wants weapons, and if they can get them without paying, then they'll do it. Weapons are like drugs. The more you have, the more you think you need."

"How very profitable for you."

"Yes, it is." He turned to look at her. "Do you want to discuss it? I'll be happy to do it, but it's not a subject that's going to make us get along with any degree of harmony."

She gazed at him for a moment before glancing away. She hadn't expected him to be like this. No anger, no ugliness, every antagonistic remark met with calm control. She had realized he was intelligent and persuasive, but often when people got what they wanted they changed. "I don't believe anything is going to make our relationship harmonious. But there's no use doing anything to make it worse." She leaned against the back of the seat. "All we have to do is survive each other."

"Very sensible." He looked back at Soldono. "Perhaps I didn't need you after all, Soldono. She doesn't seem at all nervous with me."

"She's barely met you," Soldono said dryly. "Give her an hour or two. I'm staying, Montalvo."

Montalvo smiled. "Of course you are. I just thought I'd ruffle you a bit so that you could show Eve how forceful and determined you can be." He turned on the CD player. "Chopin. That's your favorite, isn't it?"

Yes, she loved Chopin. She could feel a chill go through her. How the hell did he know a little detail like that?

"Sorry." Montalvo turned the CD off. "I intended to make you feel comforted, not threatened. Okay, no music. No conversation."

The knowledge that he had read her response so easily wasn't guaranteed to make her feel less threatened. She looked straight ahead. "Do what you like. It doesn't bother me."

He didn't answer and when she shot him a glance it was to see a faint smile on his face.

Let him smile, she thought wearily. Let him feel confident and powerful and all-knowing. She needed a night's sleep to fully recover from the emotional and physical drain that was sapping her of strength. She'd deal with Montalvo tomorrow.

The compound was encircled by high stucco walls and looked like an armed fort. No, it *was* an armed fort, Eve saw as she entered the tall wooden gates into the courtyard. The battlements were manned by guards with rifles. Mounted at two points she noticed something even more threatening.

"Missiles?" she asked as she got out of the jeep. "My God, are you preparing for a war?"

"I'm always prepared for war. That's what keeps it at bay." He took her luggage out of the jeep. "But you'll be relieved to know they aren't nuclear."

"That makes me feel much better," she said sarcastically. "No wonder the CIA is so interested in you."

"One has to be a bit special to earn such interest. It's quite flattering."

"Don't be flattered," Soldono said as he got out of the jeep. "You'd be surprised at the scum we deal with."

"No, I wouldn't." He turned to a tall, good-looking man dressed in khakis who was approaching. "This is Miguel Vicente. He'll show you to your room. There are guards in the hall. If you need anything during the night, just ask one of them to get it for you. I have breakfast at nine. I'll send Miguel to get you tomorrow morning and bring you to the dining room."

As she looked at him, she realized that Miguel was more boy than man. Probably not more than nineteen or twenty. But he also wore a holstered pistol on his hip. Good God, talk about an armed camp.

He smiled. "If you'll come this way, Ms. Duncan."

"Miguel doesn't have to come for you in the morning, I'll do it," Soldono said. "Good night. Sleep well."

She nodded. "Good night, Soldono." She inclined her head in a cool acknowledgment of Montalvo before she followed Miguel.

Jesus, she'd need a guide in this place, she thought as she moved through polished rosewood halls and chandelier-lit staircases. It was a bloody palace. The beauty of hand-carved chests and velvet drapes was in complete contrast to the military encampment outside these front doors.

And the room to which Miguel took her was as luxurious and beautifully furnished as the rest of the house.

"I hope you're comfortable here," Miguel said. "I was told you must be happy. Does it please you?"

He was frowning anxiously and she was once more aware of how young he was. "It's fine."

"Truly?"

She nodded as she gazed around the room. More carving on the headboard, fine Persian rugs on polished wood floors. "It's like something out of a *Zorro* movie."

He smiled. "I saw that movie, but he was in prison

a good deal of the time. I hope that's not what you meant."

"No, strictly Spanish hidalgo." She went to the huge bed where Miguel had placed her bags. "Do you work in the house?"

He shook his head. "Only for you. I'm a soldier for the Colonel."

"Colonel?"

He opened the French doors. "Colonel Montalvo."

"Montalvo?" She stared at him in bewilderment. "If he's an officer, it must be purely self-assumed."

"I'm a soldier for the Colonel," he repeated. "The bath is the door to the left. May you sleep well." He was gone before she could answer.

A colonel? Oh, well, maybe he liked the idea of styling himself as an officer to match his little army here at the compound. She wouldn't have thought he would be that vain. No, that's right, Galen had mentioned something about him being with the rebels but nothing about being an officer.

But what did she know? She'd only scratched the surface of the man. If she was lucky, she'd not have to dig any deeper. She'd finish the job he gave her. She'd demand the payment he'd offered and be off and back to the lake cottage. Dear God, and perhaps if Montalvo kept his word, she'd be at peace at last.

If Joe would allow her to come back to him. He'd be hurt and angry and he wasn't going to be easy or forgiving. In his eyes her greatest sin would be leaving him behind. He'd been through too much with her.

Don't think about Joe. It hurt too much. She felt very much alone in this big, palatial room so different from the small, comfortable cottage to which she was accustomed. She wanted to go home.

Stop whining. She grabbed her nightshirt out of the suitcase and headed for the bathroom. Take a shower. Go to bed. Tomorrow she'd dive into work and close everything else out.

The skull.

Montalvo hadn't given her any details about it. She should have asked him on the way here but she'd deliberately avoided it. She had been going through too much emotional trauma to want to concentrate on anything but taking the first steps to adjusting.

Tomorrow she would ask about the skull.

She hadn't asked about the skull.

Montalvo leaned back in his office chair and opened the well-thumbed Eve Duncan dossier on his desk. He was tired but he knew he couldn't sleep. The adrenaline was still flowing through him like strong wine. Or maybe it was the meeting with Eve that was intoxicating. She was as strong as he'd expected but that hint of vulnerability had struck him by surprise. He supposed it shouldn't; he'd studied her, listened to her lecture tapes, read everything he could find about her. This picture in her dossier didn't do her justice. Her body was slim and strong, but the fineness of her bones gave her a breakable fragility that was highly provocative, almost sexual.

He'd expected Eve to confront him the moment she arrived and it hadn't happened. Not that he wasn't relieved. The longer he could put off her questions the better.

He looked up as Miguel came into the room. "How is she?"

"Well. She appeared tired." He hesitated. "She's ... pleasant. She's not going to be hurt, is she?"

"Not if we can help it. One can never be sure. You know that, Miguel."

"Yes, I know that. It's just ... I think I like her."

"So do I. Same answer."

He nodded. "I'm sorry. I didn't mean—" He rushed on to another subject. "I took a message on the house phone. It was Delk from Atlanta. He said that he'd been trying to reach you on your cell."

"I had it turned off. I didn't want to disturb our guest with listening to my business calls. She's a bit sensitive to my occupation." He chuckled. "No, she thinks I'm Satan. But then she's never met Satan. What was the message?"

"Joe Quinn left today on the six-thirty jet for Bogotá."

Montalvo's smile faded. "Already? He didn't waste time."

"You said he'd be coming."

Montalvo shrugged. "I thought perhaps I might

have a day or two to prepare. Sometimes men have difficulty dealing with the initial emotions of anger and rejection and have to work their way through them. It seems I was wrong. It just means we'll have to move faster."

"Do you want him dead?"

"No, I promised I wouldn't kill him. Which makes it even more difficult."

"I could do it for you. I made no promise."

"It's an implied promise that would include my men."

Miguel smiled. "But I don't understand implications. I'm just an ignorant boy from the country. My father is in trouble so I must help him."

He frowned. "I'm not your father. For God's sake, I *killed* your father."

"And must supply me with another to replace him. I chose you."

"Miguel, you chose wrong. Leave while you—" He broke off. "You're not listening."

"I listened. I won't kill Joe Quinn. You want to wait until you can do it yourself." He turned. "I'll go and tell the men to be on the alert for Quinn. Will he really come after her against such heavy odds?"

"I would."

Miguel stopped at the door to look curiously at him over his shoulder. "Why?"

"She's an extraordinary woman. You don't find one like her every day. You're lucky to find one in a decade."

"Yet you may let her die."

"Yes, I may let her die." He looked down at the dossier in front of him. "Any news from Diaz?"

"No. But they must be missing Aquila. They'll either send someone else or make another move."

"You've become very canny about strategy."

Miguel smiled again. "I'm my father's son." He strolled out of the study.

Montalvo muttered a curse beneath his breath. He had to do something about Miguel. He'd sent him away before but he always came back. No, admit it, he'd let him come back because he was a selfish bastard and he was closer to the boy than to anyone else in the world.

He closed the dossier and stood up. He'd worry about Miguel after all this was over. Hell, he might be on the run himself by that time and that would make the problem of sending the boy away from him a moot point.

Now he'd go to bed and get a good night's sleep and prepare himself for the confrontation with Eve tomorrow morning.

And try to think of a plan to get rid of Joe Quinn without actually doing the job himself.

6

Eve was dressed and ready when Soldono knocked on her door the next morning.

"How did you sleep?" Soldono asked when she opened the door. "You look a little tired."

"I'm fine." She joined him in the hall. "And yes, I had a lousy night. What do you expect?"

"I expected a sleepless night and a few regrets. What I didn't expect was for you to come down here and put yourself under Montalvo's thumb." He grimaced. "Though I'm grateful that you saved my bacon by getting Gonzales out of here. I was going to have to do something myself and that could have been fatal."

"Montalvo's attitude toward you didn't appear to be antagonistic."

"No, but he has rules, and Gonzales broke one of the major laws that govern his men. If I got in the way, he wouldn't think twice about killing me."

"Laws. Rules. A military compound. This man is a criminal running a criminal organization. What's happening here?"

He shrugged. "Search me. It works for him. His men are loyal and thoroughly intimidated by him." He paused. "And they admire him. That keeps them in line more than any other factor. We had a devil of a time locating one of his men who'd turned traitor to him. It took me more than eighteen months to find Gonzales and another three to persuade him."

"How did you do it?"

"Money. A great deal of money and a promise to get him away before Montalvo found out."

"Which you didn't do." Her gaze wandered around the hall they were going down. "This is a palace. I was surprised when I got here. It was weird to see a place like this in the middle of the jungle. Montalvo evidently likes his creature comforts." And he had appeared perfectly at home here last night, she remembered. Civilized, graceful, handsome. "He built a military fort and then set himself up as emperor."

"According to Gonzales, he didn't build either the fort or the palace. About ten years ago he took them from a Hector Caranda who was the local drug lord in the area."

"Took?"

"Caranda and his men aren't around any longer. I imagine if you looked hard around the jungle you might find their graves."

"Wonderful." She looked at him. "You don't appear upset."

"If criminals fight criminals, it leaves less for us to get rid of. They can all kill each other for all I care." He gestured to the curved arch just ahead. "The breakfast room. His Highness awaits."

"I'm flattered, Soldono," Montalvo said from behind them. "I was wondering if you noticed my regal air." He nodded at Eve. "He's been filling your ears with poison about me. Probably most of it is true, but it's still unpleasant." He waved her into the room. "And I don't 'await.' I've been busy working since six."

He held her chair for her at the gleaming oak table. "To keep myself calm and harness my anticipation for our meeting this morning." His gaze raked her face. "I see you've also been anticipating it. Perhaps with not so much eagerness but definitely with curiosity." He waved his hand and a white-coated servant appeared from the door across the room. "I understand you don't eat a large breakfast so I ordered eggs, bacon, and a piece of toast."

"That's too much."

He smiled. "And in case you said that, I ordered orange juice and coffee and a bagel. Sit down, Soldono. You're boringly predictable. He always has French toast and Canadian bacon, Eve. You wouldn't think he had a sweet tooth, would you?"

"I don't know him. I wouldn't speculate on what he'd like."

"What about me?" He sat down across from her. "By all means, speculate."

She met his gaze. "I think you already had your breakfast at six. Probably something light. Juice, coffee...maybe toast."

He chuckled. "Right. Except for the toast. I always have a tortilla. It brings back memories of my childhood. One of the pleasant ones. It's always best to hold on to whatever happy memories we can revisit. Don't you agree?"

She lifted her orange juice to her lips. "Why are you talking about food and childhood memories? I don't give a damn about your blasted tortilla. I'm not here to socialize or to get to know you. I came here to do a job."

"Yes, you did." He leaned back in his chair and gazed at her. "You look exceptionally good in all the light pouring into this room. Not many women can bear daylight truth but it wraps around you as if it loves you. I wondered how you'd look having breakfast here."

"Bullshit."

"But I did."

"And I didn't anticipate sitting here having breakfast with a man who goes around wearing a ridiculous pistol as if he were some Old West gunslinger. It's a little over-the-top, Montalvo."

He laughed as he glanced down at his holster. "But necessary on occasion. I've been a soldier too long. I've learned you can't count on being safe just because you're on home ground."

"My job," she prompted. "The reconstruction."

He nodded and turned to Soldono. "Would you excuse us? I think you'll find the terrace very comfortable this morning. I'll have your breakfast served there."

"Eve?" Soldono asked.

"I'll see you later," she said.

Soldono shrugged, stood up, and strode out the French doors.

Montalvo nodded at a servant, who hurried after Soldono.

"Soldono will be tempted to eavesdrop but he'll get such excellent and hovering service it would prove too awkward." He lifted his coffee to his lips. "It will be frustrating for him."

"Where is the skull? Where am I to work?"

"I have a studio set up for you in the library."

"Let's go."

"Finish your breakfast. You've barely started your bagel."

"I don't want the bagel. I want to see the skull."

"The bagel is your better bet."

She stiffened. "What?"

"The skull isn't here at the compound."

"Where the hell is it?"

"It's not been unearthed yet. It's buried about ninety miles north of here in a small cemetery."

She said through her teeth, "I don't rob graves, Montalvo."

"You won't have to rob this grave. I'll do it. I just couldn't do it until you were here and ready to do the job. You'll have to work faster than you've had to at any time in your career."

"And I don't act as an accomplice to grave robbing. Go get someone else."

"I've got you."

She met his gaze. "No, you do *not*. You played me like a violin to get me here, but I won't be manipulated by you to do anything that's against my conscience. Violating a grave is high up on the list."

"Because you think of a proper burial as bringing someone home. That's what you've been working toward since your daughter died." His lips tightened. "I assure you that the person in that grave has not been brought there by loving, caring hands. It's not home, Eve."

"So you say."

"It's the truth. Look at me." His voice vibrated with the force of his words. "I'm telling you the truth."

She had to believe him. "Or what you believe as truth. If you were sure, you wouldn't have brought me down here to verify. And why couldn't you get someone to do DNA?"

"I have someone lined up to do DNA, but I have to have some sort of proof before he'll run the risk."

"Why?"

"Because any scientist who touched that skull would end up murdered in a most unpleasant fashion."

"By whom?"

"Ramon Diaz. You may have heard of him."

"I've seen photos in newspapers. Drugs."

"Yes. Drugs and vice and murder."

"Then you have a good deal in common."

"You may think so. I told Miguel that you'd never met Satan. If you'd ever run across Diaz, I wouldn't be able to say that. I have my moments, but Diaz is the master. He's set himself up in a castle and thinks he's a king and has a license to do anything he wants to do."

"And if a DNA expert's life would be on the line for examining the DNA, what about mine?"

He nodded. "It would be the same. Forensic sculpting isn't accepted in a court of law, but you know about the skull and that would be enough."

She stared at him incredulously. "You admit you brought me down here to risk my neck for your reconstruction?"

"Yes."

"You bastard."

"Yes, but not Satan. Remember the difference." He took another sip of coffee. "And, if I'd had time to work at it, I could have been completely honest with you and you would have still come. If the price is high enough, the risk is worth it. But I didn't have the time once I put the plan in motion. I had to strike while I had the opportunity. I took the chance that you'd cooperate once you were here."

"You're out of luck, Montalvo."

"We'll see. The only reason you came was because I offered you Bonnie. That reason still exists. You didn't know what you'd find here. Everyone was warning you what a bad man I was. Still you came."

"I won't become the criminal you are. I made something decent of my life after Bonnie was taken from me. I won't be dragged down again."

"What if I promise that you'll not be doing anything dishonorable? Your reputation and moral principles will remain pure as the driven snow." He grimaced. "The only thing that you'll be risking is your life. Sorry about that."

"Only my life? Well, then of course I'll ignore everything else and jump right on the bandwagon."

"You might if I'd caught you during those years after Bonnie's death. Not now."

She gazed at him, anger flaring through her. "You think you know me so well. You can't learn about someone from a dossier. You don't have any idea who I am."

"The dossier was only a start. I thought about you. I ran scenarios in my mind about you. Sometimes I even dreamed about you."

She felt a ripple of shock. "You're psychotic."

He shook his head. "When I first started to look for someone like you, I was very coolly analytical. Then when I stumbled over you and started probing, all that vanished. I knew you were meant to come here and do this reconstruction."

"Why?"

"Because I looked at you and saw myself." He pushed back his chair and stood up. "You've had enough to digest at one time. And I don't mean your breakfast. We'll talk later."

"You haven't told me anything that would make me want to continue this discussion."

"I had to break the ice. It's not the time for details."

"I want you to drive me back to that landing strip. I'll have Soldono arrange a flight out."

He headed for the door. "I believe you'll change your mind."

"You'll be wrong."

"You know, I never thought you'd take money for the reconstruction." He stopped at the door. "It was just an opening play. I knew from the beginning what would make you work with me. That gave me time to try to find something that would make you want to stay after you got down here. I had Miguel put a report on the desk in your bedroom. You might look at it before you make a decision."

"Report?"

But he'd already left the room.

She stared after him, filled with frustration and bewilderment. Jesus, what kind of man was he? Deadly, threatening, and yet the threats had been so matter-of-fact that she had not felt fear. There had

been a sort of bizarre companionableness, an intimacy, about the way he had talked to her.

I looked at you and saw myself.

"Chat finished?" Soldono was standing in the
doorway. "You don't look too pleased."

"I'm not. He doesn't even have the skull I'm supposed to reconstruct. He has to rob a grave to get it."

"And what did you tell him?"

"That I was going to ask you to arrange a flight
out for me." She stood up. "Will you do it?"

"I'll do my best." He added, "But if he doesn't want
to let you go, it may be useless. It would take an army
to get you out of here unless he gives the word."

"Just make the arrangements. I'll deal with
Montalvo."

Soldono nodded, frowning thoughtfully. "What
grave is he going to rob?"

"He didn't tell me. What does it matter?"

"Everything about Montalvo's movements mat-
ters. They have repercussions all down the line. You
might consider doing the job for him. It would make
your exit easier."

She stared at him in disbelief. "And your job easier
too, I suppose."

"Infinitely easier." He looked her in the eye. "I
don't care about disturbing the dead if it keeps you
alive and on your way back home."

Her anger ebbed away. "I don't have any right to
judge you. This is my responsibility. I knew when I
came down here that I was stepping into a spider's

web and I might have a hell of a time breaking out of it."

"A hell of a time," he echoed. "So do whatever you have to do to get all of us away from here with our skins intact."

"I'll think about it." She headed for the door. "But don't hold your breath."

Do whatever you have to do.

Soldono's words repeated in her mind as she climbed the steps to her room. Those words were easy to say, but she couldn't go along with that philosophy. Not when it came to her work. Soldono and the CIA made deals all the time and a good many of them were with criminals like Montalvo.

Even though she'd made a deal with Montalvo, she wasn't sure that she could countenance his deception, much less—

Miguel put a report on the desk in your bedroom.

Her steps instinctively quickened as she reached the top of the staircase.

A blue binder was lying on the desk.

She moved slowly toward it.

I knew from the beginning what would make you work with me.

She flipped open the cover of the binder.

Bonnie Duncan.

A picture of Bonnie taken the year before she disappeared.

A sheaf of papers over half an inch thick.

Oh, my God.

She sank down in the desk chair and started to go through the pages.

"They'll know we're coming." Galen looked down at the jungle below. "We can't get anywhere near that compound without Montalvo knowing that he has visitors."

"All we have to do is get somewhere near Montalvo's place, and be dropped off. Then we disappear into the jungle."

"Oh, is that all?" Galen asked. "My, my, and I thought you had something complicated in mind. Venable said that jungle is very well-patrolled and we might have to dispose of a few sentries."

"You don't have to go with me."

"Yes, I do. This has nothing to do with you. I have a job to do. I was hired to find out about Montalvo. This is as good a way as any. And besides, I happen to have a fondness for Eve. I just thought I'd bring up the difficulties because I have no intention of wasting my efforts without a plan of action. Are we to storm the Bastille? Or perhaps try guerilla warfare? We brought enough firepower for a minor war but it would be a little absurd since there are only two of us."

"We get close. We look for a weakness." Joe smiled grimly. "And I call Eve on my cell phone and get her to come out and play our game instead of his."

"Now that makes much more sense than storming

the Bastille." Galen sighed. "If a good deal less interesting."

"We may have to go back to one of your scenarios
if Eve doesn't answer my call. She warned me that she
might not."

"I think she will. Eve is a worrier. She'll be concerned that you're in dire straits and need her help."

"I am in dire straits." And Joe needed to know if
she was well and not over her head in trouble. He'd
been scared shitless since he'd left Atlanta after
Galen had told him about Montalvo's connection
with Diaz. It wasn't enough that Eve was dealing
with one scumbag. An even greater one was hovering
on the horizon. "And I'm not sure you're right. She
keeps her word and she said that she wouldn't answer the initial call."

"I'm right. I may not know her as well as you do
but I can stand back and observe with a more impersonal eye. You're not thinking as clearly as you might
at the moment."

"Tell me about it," he said sarcastically. "Of
course, you'd be perfectly calm and rational if the
same thing were happening in your personal life."

"No. I'd be as scared as you are. But it's not Elena
and Elspeth so I can preach to you. And be here to
strike a note of reason when you go off course.
Providing you listen to me."

Joe was silent a moment. "I'll listen to you. I don't
promise I'll pay any attention, but I'll listen." He
looked down at the vast stretch of jungle below him.

Venable had warned him that Montalvo's men knew that territory like the backs of their hands, but that didn't worry him. When he was a SEAL, he'd lived in jungles for months and played hit-and-run and still managed to survive. That was years ago, but it would come back to him. Getting Eve out was going to be the hard part. She was strong, and her determination and endurance could be incredible, but she had no training. Galen had been a mercenary at one time and would be able to help. "Thank you," he said haltingly. "I know I've been on edge with you, but you're being a good friend to Eve. I appreciate it."

"On edge? I hardly noticed. Of course, I've been bleeding from a hundred little cuts and I might be too faint to feel them anymore." He smiled slightly. "And I don't expect it to stop. You're hurting and you're a man who instinctively hits out when hurt. I happen to be the closest target. I'll magnanimously forgive you in the name of Eve."

"I don't believe 'magnanimous' is the word I'd use about your acceptance of my apology," Joe said dryly. "But I'll try not to use you as a punching bag."

"In the name of Eve?"

He looked back down at the jungle below. "In the name of Eve."

It was midafternoon when Eve finished the report and sat back in her chair. Stop crying. Stop shaking.

You have to go down to see Montalvo and you can't let him see this weakness.

Screw it. Give herself a little time. Accept the pain now while she was alone. Let the tears come. She closed her eyes and the tears flowed down her cheeks.

Bonnie.

Fifteen minutes later she got up, went into the bathroom, and washed her face with cold water. Her eyes were still a little puffy but she couldn't help that. She patted her face dry, grabbed the report, and strode out of the bedroom.

She almost ran into Miguel, who was leaning against the wall across the hall.

He straightened quickly. "You're ready to see him?"

"What were you doing camped on my doorstep?"

"He told me to stay here and bring you to him. He didn't want you to have to search for him. Are you ready?"

"Oh, yes." She went past him toward the stairs. "Where is he?"

"The library." Miguel caught up with her. "I'll show you. It's in the south wing downstairs." He went ahead of her down the staircase. "It upset you. I'm sorry. I asked him if it was necessary."

"You know what was in the report?"

"Yes, he talks to me sometimes. Not often. Not about things that are close to him. But he needed to talk to someone this time." He turned right at the bottom of the staircase. "It was my privilege."

"If you can call it that."

"I can." He opened a door on the left and smiled gently. "To share anything with the Colonel is a privilege." He stepped aside. "If I can help you, call me. That would also be a privilege."

"Come in, Eve," Montalvo called from across the library. "Miguel, see that we aren't disturbed."

"By all means," Eve said as she went into the room and strode toward the desk. She slammed the binder down on the desk in front of Montalvo and dropped into the visitor's chair. "We definitely have a few things to discuss."

"Coffee?" He poured steaming black liquid into a cup from a carafe on the desk. "You look as if you can use it."

"Not now."

He set the cup of coffee in front of her. "Because your hand would shake if you took the cup? I wouldn't regard that as a sign of weakness. Not in you."

"Not now," she repeated. She moistened her lips. "That was quite a report. Did it need to be that thorough? It started from the time Bonnie disappeared in that park and went into detail about every aspect of the investigation. Every sexual offender, every child molester the police interviewed, every word taken or written about the investigation. Every graphic description of the other little girls' bodies they found that they thought might be Bonnie. You did a complete background on Ralph Andrew Fraser, the man who was executed for the murders of those other children and assumed to have killed Bonnie."

"He didn't kill her," Montalvo said. "I think you thought that all along. That's why when another suspect appeared some years later, you were ready to believe he did it. Only her body wasn't where he told you it was going to be. That must have been a heartbreaker for you."

"Yes." She blinked back the tears. "A heartbreaker."

"But it didn't stop you. You never gave up hope."

"You talk as if it were some kind of virtue. Hope never gave me up. I couldn't do anything about it. Why did you go into such detail? It wasn't necessary."

"And it brought everything back and hurt you. I considered editing the report before I gave it to you but I couldn't do it. You had to know what I'd found out about the case. How deeply I'd probed to get answers."

"I'd have been satisfied with Section Three." She flipped open the report to the place she'd tabbed. "Where your investigators started to try to find Bonnie's murderer."

"They were amazing, weren't they? They were highly motivated. I offered them the million dollars you refused to dig deep and fast. They didn't manage to isolate a single suspect, but they narrowed it down to three."

She glanced at the three names on the list. "How?

You said something about leaks from prison inmates?"

"They interviewed prisoners who were in jail at the same time and facility as Fraser. No one knows what's going on in the underbelly like prisoners do. They talk a lot and most of them have no use for child molesters. There was a lot of talk on the prison grapevine about Bonnie's case. More speculation. Some actually claimed to have known the killer well enough for him to brag about it to them."

"Why didn't they come forward if they knew something? They could have cut a deal."

"Not without evidence. The state was very happy with the man they had on death row. The public had been clamoring for an arrest. They would have ignored the possibility of it being anyone else."

"My God." It was a moment before she got a grip on her emotions. "Paul Black, Thomas Kistle, Kevin Jelak. Are they still alive?"

"Yes. We've located Kistle. The others have disappeared from the radar, but we'll find them. I promised I'd do that for you, Eve."

"You could be lying about all this."

"I could. I'm not."

"Why did you give this report to me after I told you that I wasn't going to go through with the deal?"

"Hope."

She leaned back in her chair and rubbed her temple. "You're manipulating me."

"If you let me. It's all up to you. I'm at your mercy."

She snorted. "Not likely."

He smiled. "Or I thought I'd try a diversion to take your mind off my little deception."

"Little?"

"Not so little deception," he corrected. "And I thought you might believe what I told you and be willing to reconsider your decision."

She stared at him. He was smooth. He was complicated. He was silver-tongued. He was no doubt a very dangerous man. Yet she sensed in him a driving force she had seldom seen before.

I looked at you and saw myself.

And looking at him she could see qualities she knew she possessed. The same drive, the same energy, the same passion.

But passion for what?

"You said that I wouldn't be violating my principles if I did this job for you. Why not? I don't rob graves."

He relaxed with a sigh. "You're thinking about it."

"Why not?" she repeated.

"You wouldn't rob graves in the usual course of things. But what if your Bonnie were in that grave? Wouldn't you go after her?"

"I'd get a writ and have her exhumed. I wouldn't go slinking around in the dark."

"What if you couldn't get the writ? What if you knew she was there, but there was no other way?"

She didn't speak for a moment. "I'd go after her if I had to go to hell itself."

"And so would I," he said simply. "And that's what I'm doing. Going to hell itself."

"Stop being obscure. Spell it out for me."

"The cemetery is in the farm country controlled by Diaz. He's been searching for this grave for the last five years. And watching me to make sure I don't find it first. That's why Aquila showed up here. He was trying to bribe my men for any information he could get."

"So you killed him."

"Yes, I didn't know how much information he might have gathered. I was getting close to bringing you here. I only hope that he didn't get word back to Diaz before I took him out."

"You're saying you did it because of me? I didn't even know I was coming until the last minute."

"And I kept our negotiations extremely confidential. That doesn't mean he might not have picked up a kernel of information. Miguel found bugging and surveillance equipment in Aquila's camp in the jungle outside the compound."

"And what would Diaz have done if he did know I was coming?"

"He would have sent a man to Atlanta to kill you. Or he might have ambushed us on the way to the compound. Since neither event occurred, he may not know who I was bringing here or that you were definitely coming. But he might guess that I think I've found the grave."

"And who's in that grave?"

He was silent a moment. "My wife."

She stiffened in shock. "What?"

"Nalia Armandariz. She was the daughter of Antonio Armandariz, the rebel leader. I was fighting with the rebels when we met." He smiled. "What a tiger she was. Yet full of courage and ideals and a zest for life like I've never seen before."

"You loved her."

"Oh, yes," he said softly. "I was sick with bitterness and anger when I met her. She healed me. It was all joy with her. It sounds weird to say that, when she was a soldier like me. A fine soldier and her father's right hand."

"How did she die?"

"Diaz. She was probing too closely into his business. Her father was dealing with Diaz, who was very outspoken in his support for the rebel effort. He protected Diaz's coca growers from rival drug dealers and did a few other raids for him. When the military was becoming troublesome Diaz set the rebels to attack. He had Armandariz convinced that he was devoted to the rebel cause and tossed him an occasional bone of cash and weapons to prove it. But Nalia found out that he was double-dealing. He was paying off the government and funneling cash into their coffers as well to look the other way when he was exporting his drugs."

"She found proof?"

"She was looking for it when she disappeared."

"Disappeared? I thought he killed her."

"Your Bonnie disappeared. Do you have any doubt that she's dead?"

She slowly shook her head. "I wish I did."

"So do I. Diaz was very clever. He buried the evidence of his double-dealing and convinced her father that Nalia had stolen the latest payment Diaz had sent him and gotten on a plane for Australia."

She shook her head. "He couldn't have believed that of her. She was his daughter."

"He wanted to believe it. He was a fanatic and Diaz was helping his cause. Turning a blind eye to a little double-dealing was a cheap price to pay."

"Not so cheap. He lost a daughter."

"In his eyes he didn't lose her, she deserted the cause. She wasn't his daughter any longer."

"What did you do?"

"What do you think? I went after Diaz. I ended up getting away from his men barely alive and dragging myself to a friend's house to recuperate. It took almost a year to get well. By that time things had changed. Nalia's father wanted to have nothing to do with me. I'd attacked his benefactor and he couldn't accept that if he was going to continue with his self-delusion."

"Did you go after Diaz again?"

"No, I'd had time to simmer down and think. I didn't want to just kill Diaz. I wanted to bring him down. I wanted to destroy everything he'd built, everything he'd created in his little empire. But I couldn't do that without gathering together almost as much money as Diaz possessed. I needed money for bribes, to hire the kind of manpower Diaz had at his command. I was a soldier with only the clothes on my back and my rifle. So I set out to get that cash."

"By becoming a criminal yourself?"

He shrugged. "Weapons were the only thing I knew about."

"Are you making excuses?"

"No, I wouldn't make excuses to you any more than I'd make them to myself. I'm sure Soldono will be willing to tell you what a very bad boy I am. I'm only explaining what happened. I had to bring Diaz down. I didn't care how I made the money as long as it was there for me to tap. I did what I set out to do. I had cash to set up the compound so that Diaz couldn't touch me." He paused. "And the kind of big money that permitted me to hire investigators to find out where your Bonnie's killer might be found. I think perhaps you'll believe that expenditure to be worthwhile."

Damn him, he might not be making excuses but he'd managed to strike the one note that resounded in the depths of her being. "Go on."

"But I needed to do more than become some kind of Midas. I needed to find Nalia. I had to make her father admit she was dead and that Diaz had killed her. I started searching. It took me two years before I found out what he'd done with her body."

"The cemetery?"

"Christ, no. He threw her into a swamp to rot. I bribed one of his men who did it to go get her. But he double-crossed me and didn't bring the body directly to me. He buried her in an unmarked grave in the cemetery. He said he couldn't run the risk of Diaz knowing what he'd done. The damn cemetery is practically on top of Diaz's villa. Then Diaz found out that his man had been dealing with me and went after him." His lips tightened. "I got to him first. I couldn't have him telling Diaz where he'd disposed of the remains."

"You killed him?"

"Of course. Don't feel sorry for him. At least, I was quick. I guarantee that Diaz would not have been. Anyway, I was stuck with waiting until I could structure a way to get in and out of that cemetery with Nalia's body without getting my men killed."

"And getting someone to do the reconstruction."

He nodded. "Before Diaz finds out exactly what we're doing and sends out his full force."

"And then you want to show the reconstruction to Nalia's father? What good would that do now?"

"Do you remember how shocked you were when you opened the box I sent you? Imagine how a father would react, how Nalia's friends she'd grown up with would react. The rebels still have considerable firepower in these parts. If they turned that firepower against a single target, it could be devastating."

"You want to turn them against Diaz."

"I intend to turn them against Diaz." He held her gaze. "As soon as you give me my wife back."

After a moment she tore her eyes away from his. "She might not be in that grave. You could have been double-crossed in more ways than one."

"I realize that. I have to take the chance."

"And you want me to take a chance too. You've put me on the spot with Diaz. And you could be killed going after that skull."

"I've told Miguel to get you out of here if that happens. And I'll set up the mechanism to keep searching for Bonnie's killer even if I die. All you have to do is agree."

"Why should I believe you? You could be making up a fairy story."

"You do believe me."

She didn't want to believe him. She didn't want to feel sympathy or empathy for him. "Or you could be telling me part of the truth and twisting it to suit yourself. You're a criminal yourself. Why should I believe you want to destroy Diaz's operation? You could be throwing in that part of the story to convince me that what I'm doing is basically ethical."

"It's the truth." His voice vibrated with force, his gaze held her own. "Every word I've spoken. Yes, I've tried to manipulate you but only to get you here. I knew I'd have to lay the cards on the table."

"Why?"

"Because I couldn't cheat you. I felt your pain." He added quietly, "Because it was the same as mine. I loved my wife, Eve. Diaz killed her and then tossed her away like a piece of garbage. During those years when she was lost, I'd wake up from nightmares about trying to find her and never being able to do it."

Christ, she could feel tears sting her eyes. She had known that agony. It never went away no matter how much time passed. She stood up. "I have to think about this. I can't tell you—I have to think about it."

"Just do the reconstruction. I'll have you on your way back home a few hours later. You'll be out of it."

"I have to think about it," she repeated as she moved toward the door. "Dammit, you're asking me to trust you and I'd be a fool to do it."

"You might be a fool to risk doing the job but not to trust me."

She glanced back at him and for the first time she thought she glimpsed the emotions beneath that smooth facade. The haunted pain and hollow loneliness . . .

I looked at you and saw myself.

She tore her eyes away and almost ran out of the room.

He must be a magician to be able to play on her emotions like this. Maybe his wife was one of the lost ones but she mustn't identify her with Bonnie. She might not even be in that grave. It might be a false lead.

And how many false paths had she gone down in

hopes of finding her daughter? How many hopes had been crushed?

She was identifying again. Block it out. Think calmly and logically. She shouldn't let emotion influence her decision.

But, dear God, she was very much afraid she was going to do it.

7

She didn't go down to dinner that night and at seven-thirty that evening Miguel came to the door with a tray.

"You shouldn't have bothered. I'm not hungry."

"It's no bother." Miguel put the tray down on the low chest by the door. "It's just a sandwich and a salad. And it's my pleasure. Turnabout. You're going to help the Colonel. I'll help you."

"I didn't tell Montalvo that I'd help him. Everything's . . . changed."

He nodded. "And you're very upset about it. He knew you would be. Trust him. He'll try to keep you safe."

"'Try'? That's a little too uncertain for me." She sat down at the table and lifted the cover. "But you appear to trust him."

"Of course I do."

"Why?"

"Because he does what he says he's going to do. And he's always there when I need him." He poured her coffee. "He saved my life, you know."

"I didn't know. I don't know anything about any of you."

"That's right." He smiled. "But you'll learn more if you stay and help the Colonel."

And she needed to know more. She'd spent the afternoon torn between skepticism and hope. "How did he save your life? You're very young to be involved with a man like Montalvo."

He grinned. "That's what he says. He keeps trying to send me away. He tells me I need to go to school and learn to better myself. I'm pretty good just as I am. I'm a damn good soldier."

"Then join the army. Don't stay with a criminal. If he saved your life, he probably put it in danger to begin with."

He shook his head. "No, he killed my father."

She gazed at him in shock. "What?"

"My father was going to kill me. He'd already killed my mother. I was hiding in the forest and he was tracking me down. I was only thirteen. I wouldn't have been able to hide from him for long."

"Jesus, why would he do that?"

"The drugs. He distributed Diaz's drugs to the farmers as part of their payment for growing. He was a user too. When he was on the drugs, he'd beat my mother and one day he killed her. If I'd had a gun, I would have shot him. I took the drugs he had in the house and threw them down the well. Then I took off into the forest. He shot me before I could get very far. In the leg. I kept crawling but he caught up with me." His lips tightened. "I remember him standing over me and aiming his gun at my head to finish me off."

"And Montalvo shot him instead?"

"Yes. He'd come looking for my father and followed him into the forest. He thought he might be a weak link who could tell him something about the death of his wife." He smiled. "Was I not lucky? He killed the son of a bitch."

She shouldn't have felt that sense of shock at his words. The attitude was probably healthy. Fathers and mothers were only as sacred as their actions toward their children. She had run across many abusers in her life. She was glad that Miguel had survived and apparently managed to not be permanently scarred. "You're lucky if you take hold of your life and don't cling to Montalvo."

"He doesn't let me cling. He just gave me a home and a purpose. He says that purpose is important."

And Montalvo's purpose was revenge.

And finding his lost one.

And wasn't that her purpose too?

"I'll go now," Miguel said. "If you need anything, call me. I'll stay close."

"Wait."

He glanced back at her.

"Did Montalvo send you to tell me this?"

"No. He said to bring you supper." His lips

indented in a faint smile. "But he's very clever and knows me well. He might have guessed what turn the conversation would take."

"I'd bet on it," she said dryly.

"Please finish your sandwich. You need your strength." He opened the door and left the room.

Jesus, another Montalvo in the making, she thought. And Miguel had the same tenacity and determination as his idol, together with an appealing boyishness. She liked the kid.

She finished the last bite of her sandwich. Miguel was right, no matter what path she took she'd need strength and determination to get her through the—

Her cell phone rang.

She tensed as she saw the name on the ID screen.

No, Joe. Not now.

It rang again.

Dammit, she'd told him she wouldn't answer if he called her. Why was he—

It rang again.

She punched the button. "Joe, I can't talk to you."

"The hell you can't. You're doing it."

"To tell you that I'm fine and there's no reason for you to worry."

"How nice of you to offer me that scrap of comfort. You're not fine. Not as long as you're in that compound. And I'm going to worry until I have you out of there. What do you expect?"

She expected exactly what she was getting from

Joe. Anger and near-explosive frustration. "I expect you to respect my decision."

"Your decision? He swayed you like a snake charmer. He used Bonnie, dammit."

"Yes."

"Lies, Eve. You know it's lies. You knew you were following a ghost when you came down here. You just couldn't help yourself."

"You're right, I thought he might be playing me when I got on that plane. It didn't matter. I had to take the chance." She paused. "But after I got here I found out that there's a chance he wasn't lying. I have to stay until I can decide if it's worth—"

"No!"

"Don't tell me no. I'm the one who has to decide. I'll call you when I do."

"Don't hang up." He was silent a moment and she could feel him struggling for control. "Galen tells me that I'm blowing this. I can't afford to do that."

"Galen? He's with you?"

"He's more with me than I'd like. He keeps interfering."

She had a sudden suspicion. "Joe, where are you?"

"If I used my telescope, I could probably see you."

"Shit."

"My feelings exactly. You should be here with me, not in that compound."

"Go away, Joe. I don't want you here."

"It's mutual. I'm staying. And Galen insisted on

bringing everything from explosives to surveillance equipment so we can set up for the duration."

"Joe, Montalvo's a desperate man. And he has a damn army at his disposal."

"Then come out and save me."

"Joe, listen to me. Montalvo's promised me you won't be harmed, but accidents happen and I don't want one of his men to get trigger-happy and shoot you."

"How do I know you're not being held against your will? Maybe Montalvo's standing there with a gun to your head."

"Your imagination is working overtime. I told you—"

"I don't know anything without seeing you face-to-face. I'll leave when you leave."

"Joe, don't blackmail me. I'm not—"

"Blackmail is permitted in circumstances like this. I'll do anything I can do. And Galen says if you won't come out and save me, you can save him instead. Or make it a package deal and get double credit."

"I'm hanging up, Joe. When you call me again, I want to hear you're in Bogotá." She pressed the disconnect.

Jesus, it was exactly what she'd been afraid would happen. Admit it, what she'd known would happen or she would never have made Joe a part of her deal with Montalvo. Yet there had been the slightest hope that her actions wouldn't impact Joe.

She stood up and went over to the window and

gazed out at the dark jungle. He was there. Close. She was filled with panic and yet there was also a tingle of primitive joy. They were together. That was how it should be. Her mind had said to leave him, but there was no rhyme or reason where instincts were concerned.

Crush those instincts. Protect Joe. She could understand his doubts about her safety. Telephones were often deceptive and unsatisfactory. Yet if she tried to meet with Joe and convince him in person that he should leave, she might be tempted to go with him. She didn't know what Montalvo's reactions would be if she ran. She would have bet on violence before she'd come here. Now she knew him better and yet he'd become even more of an unknown quantity. He was a desperate man. Desperation could be even more deadly than ruthlessness.

"Quinn's here," Miguel said as he came into the library. "We have a report of a helicopter sighting this afternoon. We think it landed about twenty miles north."

Montalvo frowned. "You're sure it wasn't one of Diaz's? He's been making his presence known lately."

"We checked the number. Rented in Bogotá to a Carmine Valdez. The pilot was to drop the clients off and then stay in the neighborhood to pick them up when they called."

"Description?"

"Does it matter? Quinn would have hired someone to do the rental for him."

"No, it doesn't matter." Montalvo grimaced. "I
was hoping that I wouldn't have to face that problem
right now. I'm making progress."

Miguel nodded. "But she's an emotional woman.
She can be swayed by her feelings. I could see that
tonight. She wanted to reach out and comfort me."

"She'd do just as well to comfort a tiger cub."

"Tiger cubs can be very cuddly," he protested. His
expression sobered. "Do you believe Quinn is close?
We've had no report from any of our sentries."

"Quinn was in the SEALs. There's a good chance
our sentries wouldn't see him. If they did, they might
wish they hadn't."

"Do you want me to go out and find him?"

"No, I don't know yet what I'd do with him if we
found him."

"So what do we do?"

"We tell the men to be on high alert. We report any
sign of Quinn. And we don't touch a hair of his head
until I give the word."

"He could be an opportunity."

How many times had he said that? Montalvo
thought as he gazed at the boy. It shouldn't surprise
him that Miguel had thrown it back at him. An opportunity was to be grasped, never ignored.

"This particular opportunity could have a back-
lash. We'll wait and watch and see what he does."

"And see what she does?"

Yes, it all depended on Eve. Quinn would try to get in touch with her and his influence would be powerful. Which way would she jump?

It was almost midnight when Eve left her room. She saw Soldono crossing the foyer as she started down the steps.

He stopped. "It appears to be a late night for all of us."

"I have to see Montalvo."

"And I just came from having him grill me."

"Why?"

His gaze searched her face. "I think you know."

"Joe?"

He nodded. "Montalvo wanted to know if the CIA is helping him. He's here in Colombia."

It couldn't have been worse news. If Montalvo knew, they might be scouring the jungle for Joe right now.

Soldono's eyes narrowed on her face. "Just how near is he, Eve?"

"Too close. Did you help him get here?"

"Not personally. But there's a good chance Venable might have given him a hand."

"Then tell Venable to get him out of here, dammit."

"I don't give Venable orders. He's my boss."

"Then he shouldn't interfere in my business. I got

Gonzales out of here for you. You owe me. I won't have Joe killed."

"I'll do everything I can to—"

"Forget it." She strode past him. "I'll take care of it myself." She went into the library and slammed the door. "You promised me Joe wouldn't be hurt, Montalvo."

Montalvo turned away from the window. "He hasn't been hurt yet."

Yet. Ice shivered through her. "And he won't be. I have your word. If you do anything to him, I'll kill you myself."

"I'd be stupid to take out Quinn when I have you considering helping me. I've worked very hard to accomplish that coup. I don't want you angry with me. But he shouldn't have come after you. Accidents happen."

"Not to Joe."

"He's contacted you?"

She hesitated. "Yes."

"And you couldn't persuade him to let you make your own choice." He shrugged. "He's a stubborn man."

"He's not sure that you're not holding me against my will. He said that you could be forcing me to tell him everything's all right."

"A valid premise." He met her gaze. "Convince him. I can't keep him safe if he persists in getting in my way. My men are trained as soldiers. When attacked, they react instinctively."

"Then you can forget about my doing the reconstruction."

"Stalemate." He was silent a moment, thinking. "You want Quinn to leave. You don't want to be forced to make a decision, even by him. What can I do to help you get him away from here?"

Knock the stubborn idiot on the head and put him on a helicopter, she thought in frustration. "I need to see him face-to-face. He needs to know that I'm under no restrictions. I have to have time to talk to him and persuade him to leave. It's the only thing I can think of that might help."

"And what do you want me to do?"

"I want you to swear you won't follow me and that no one will hurt Joe while I'm meeting with him."

He studied her, his expression impassive. "And what if I give you my word and then you take off with him?"

"I'll promise I won't do that. If I go, it won't involve Joe."

He nodded slowly. "I believe you."

"Swear to me."

He smiled. "I swear on the grave of my wife that I'll not follow you or do harm to your Joe. When do you want to do this?"

"As soon as I can get in touch with him. Tonight."

"You want to go alone? The jungle's not safe at night."

"And I'd probably get lost. I'm not jungle-savvy. Give me Soldono."

"Miguel would be happy to—"

"Soldono."

"Very well. Understandable. Miguel is definitely loyal to me. Sometimes a little too much." He moved toward the door. "You make your call. I'll get Soldono for you."

She reached for her cell phone. She'd bought time for Joe. If she could convince him to go, then he might get away from here alive. Montalvo had not been reassuring.

She drew a deep breath and dialed Joe's number.

Please listen, Joe. Listen.

"It could be a trap," Soldono murmured as he guided her through the dense undergrowth. "Montalvo could rid himself of an encumbrance and still bank on forcing you to do the reconstruction."

"It wouldn't be his style." Her gaze was peering ahead into the darkness. She'd taken down the directions but she didn't even know how far they'd traveled in the last ten minutes. "And he could force me to do a job but not necessarily a good job."

"You appear to be getting to know him very well."

"I've had no choice. I need to—" She jumped as the bushes ahead parted.

"Take off, Soldono. I've got her."

Joe.

But not the Joe to whom she was accustomed. He was dressed in khakis and boots, his hair tied back by a bandanna. This was Joe the ex-SEAL, the man who could kill silently and efficiently. She had seen him like this before when they'd been together in the bayous of Louisiana.

"That's up to Eve," Soldono said. "I promised her I'd take her to you and then bring her back to the compound."

"Go wait at the turn of the trail," Eve told Soldono. "I'll be with you in ten minutes."

"The hell you will," Joe said as Soldono moved away. "You're out. You're going to stay out."

"I came for one reason and it wasn't to—"

"It's no use. He's turning a deaf ear." Galen appeared out of the darkness behind Joe. "Hello, Eve. Quinn's a bit upset. You really shouldn't have taken off like that."

"Shut up, Galen." Joe didn't look at him. "Go away. I don't need you."

"I was about to do that. I need to do a little reconnoitering to make sure that Montalvo's not planning a double cross."

"I've already done that," Joe said impatiently.

"I believe I'll do a second round," Galen said. "I wouldn't want Quinn to be dead meat, Eve. I've grown accustomed to his endearing nastiness. I might miss it."

"Montalvo's not going to ambush him," Eve said.

"I'll just take a look...." Galen disappeared into the shrubbery.

Joe's hand closed on her wrist. "We're going."

"Let me go, Joe. I promised Montalvo I wouldn't run."

"And I didn't promise anything." He smiled recklessly. "So I clip you on the chin, just hard enough to put you out, and you've kept your word and I've gotten what I wanted."

"You wouldn't do that."

"Look at me. I'd do anything to keep you safe. Anything."

She was looking at him and she didn't like what she saw. His eyes were glittering with savagery in his taut face. "You're enjoying this," she whispered.

"No, I'd enjoy it if I could get my hands on Montalvo. Are the juices flowing? Hell, yes. Do I knock you out or do you come with me?"

"Neither." She looked down at her arm held by his hand. "Don't threaten me, Joe. And you're bruising me. Every time I look at my arm, I'll remember those bruises came from you."

"Better bruised than dead." But his grasp loosened on her arm. "And I don't care if you remember me as a brutal son of a bitch. Not if you're still alive to remember."

He was just as hard and angry as she'd known he'd be. Don't argue. It wouldn't work. She'd come here to explain. Do it. "I have to stay, Joe. It's my chance. Will you listen to me? Montalvo gave me a report. It was about Bonnie and I didn't..."

·   ·   ·

Galen slid silently through the shrubbery, his gaze raking the trees and palmettos on either side. He could hear Eve's voice but couldn't make out any words. Her tone was urgent, persuasive, almost pleading as she talked to Quinn. He doubted if it was going to do any good. Quinn was on the edge and ready to fall off.

What the hell? Wouldn't he feel the same if it were Elena in the same spot? He could tell Quinn that he should handle Eve with diplomacy instead of reaching out and grabbing, but Quinn was a desperate man and primitive instinct was paramount now. Galen could only strike a balance and hope that Quinn didn't—

Something was moving up ahead.

He froze, listening.

An animal?

If it was an animal, the sound of its passage through the shrubbery indicated it was as large as a man.

Shit, it probably was a man. The direction of the movement was changing, cutting toward the path where Quinn and Eve were talking.

Galen started forward, his ears straining to hear the slightest sound.

Move fast.

Move quiet.

He had a fix on the location.

But the rustling had stopped, he suddenly realized.

Christ.

Screw being quiet. He took off at a run.

"The report could have been an elaborate fake," Joe said.

"That's what you said about the Valdosta report on Marty," Eve said wearily. "It turned out to be authentic."

"You know the saying: when you're about to tell a big lie, you pad the way with small truths. This could be the big lie."

"And it could be the truth. It could be the break I've been looking for all these years."

"You have the names. Let me go after them. You don't need Montalvo."

"Montalvo didn't need to give me those names. He trusted me to keep my part of the bargain."

"And after he has what he wants, he won't care what happens to you. Don't be blind. If he doesn't kill you, Diaz will. Opt out now while you have—"

"Eve! Down!"

Galen!

She heard Joe muttering an oath and then he was jerking her toward the ground.

A shot.

Pain streaked through her temple.

Darkness all around her. Fight it. Keep it at bay.

She was on the ground and Joe was covering her body with his own.

Another shot.

Joe's muscles jerked as the bullet entered his body.

No. No. No.

Her arms tightened around him.

Help Joe. Help Joe.

Darkness smothering her.

Help Joe. He was a dead load on her.

Dead. Don't think dead.

Help Joe.

Darkness swimming, increasing with every panicky breath.

Help Joe.

Oh, God, she couldn't even help herself....

8

M USIC.
Chopin, she realized vaguely. Beautiful...
She'd always loved it. More soothing than he
usually—

Joe!

Her eyes flew open to see Montalvo sitting by her
bed. She struggled to a sitting position. "Joe.
Where's—"

Montalvo was spinning crazily, the room was
whirling around her.

"Easy." Montalvo was there, gently pushing her
back on the pillow. "Quinn's alive. Galen's alive.
Everyone's being taken care of. Rest."

*The twitch of Joe's body on top of her as a bullet en-
tered him.*

"How the hell can I rest?" Her voice was shaking.
"You bastard, you *shot* him."

"I didn't shoot him."

"Then one of your men did it. You warned me that it might happen."

"Yes, I did. That's why I wanted to be the first one to talk to you when you woke." He stared her in the eye. "It wasn't me. It wasn't my men. I know that it's difficult for you to think right now but I'm asking you to try to use a little logic. The first bullet was aimed at you. Quinn pulled you down and sideways or it would have blown your head off. It was the second bullet that got Quinn. There's no way on this earth that I would have tried to kill you. Every effort I've made for the last year has been aimed at keeping you alive and able to work. Why would I want to blast all that work to kingdom come?"

"How do I know? I don't know anything about how you think."

"Yes, you do. You don't want to realize how close we already are." He handed her a glass of crushed ice with a straw. "Drink a little water. It will give you time to consider and ease that parched throat. You've been out for almost twenty-four hours. You had a hell of a concussion. I was getting worried when you didn't wake up."

She sipped the water. Her throat was dry and the cold water felt good as it went down. "Joe. Tell me about Joe."

"The bullet entered his back, hit a rib, and angled upward. It didn't strike a major organ but he did lose quite a bit of blood. He had to have a transfusion." He smiled. "I was the same blood type so Quinn is now cursed with a pint of my blood. I'm sure it will annoy him no end when he becomes aware of it."

"I'm sure too." Relief was flowing through her. "He's going to live. You're certain?"

"I'm certain. It will take him a couple weeks to get back to something like normal. But I've survived worse wounds than that and I'd bet Quinn is very tough."

"Yes. Yes, he is." She closed her eyes. Thank God. "When can I see him?"

"Right now he's pretty well out of it on pain medication. Probably tomorrow. Can you go back to sleep now? The doctor said that rest is the best medicine for—"

"No." Her eyes flew open. "Galen?"

"Galen is the one who saw the shooter and took him out. He wasn't hurt at all."

"Then I want to see him."

"I thought you would." He took the glass of water and put it on the nightstand. "I'll send him to you in three hours. No sooner. I want you to get that nap that Dr. Diego recommended."

"I want to see him now."

"Then you'll have to crawl out of that bed, search the house, and risk injuring yourself. In which case you'd be no good to Galen or your Joe." He started for the door. "We'll talk later after you finish being reassured by someone you trust." He glanced back over his shoulder as he opened the door. "Remember, the first bullet was for you."

"But it didn't kill me," she said bluntly. "And it took Joe out of the picture. That's what you wanted."

He shook his head. "I was hoping you wouldn't explore that path but I should have known you would, considering how clever you are. Ask Galen whether that bullet would have killed you if Quinn hadn't interfered."

"Don't worry. I will."

He smiled ruefully and inclined his head. "I expect nothing less of you, Eve."

He left the bedroom.

Damn him. She didn't want to lie here in this bed and be bombarded by worry about Joe. She wanted to see him. Galen would help her to see him. She lifted herself on her elbow and then fell back as pain shot through her head.

Maybe not now. Montalvo was right. She'd have to crawl out of this bed if she tried to get up.

Three hours. Montalvo had promised to send Galen in three hours. . . .

Galen.

He smiled down at her as she opened her eyes. "It's about time, luv. I was just going to give you a good shake."

"You would not." She tried to smile. "Or I'd have a very firm word with you. My head is very fragile at the moment."

His smile faded. "I don't doubt it. You had me

scared when I ran over there and saw the two of you drenched in blood."

"Drenched?"

"Well, perhaps not quite. But in my heightened state it appeared that way."

"I want to see Joe."

He nodded. "I suspected as much. He's better today. He's still going in and out of consciousness but he won't scare you like he would have yesterday when you first woke up."

She frowned. "Yesterday? I woke up three hours ago."

"I beg to disagree. Montalvo sent me in here yesterday but you weren't stirring. So I've been checking every few hours and waiting for you to wake up."

"It doesn't seem possible." But she did feel better. Her head was less painful, her thinking was sharper. "Did he drug me?"

"I wouldn't know. I wouldn't put it past him." He shrugged. "Or maybe it was just Mother Nature who put you out. You were pretty messed up." He gazed at her critically. "You still look weak as a kitten. Suppose I get Miguel to bring you some soup and then we'll make the attempt to see Joe. I have no desire to have you fainting and forcing me to lug you around."

"And I have no intention of—" But she still felt weak. "Okay, soup sounds fine. Thank you."

She watched him leave the room before she carefully sat up in bed. A little dizziness but it passed quickly and she swung her legs to the floor. Get to the bathroom, wash her face and brush her teeth.

Slowly.

Her legs felt like spaghetti.

But by the time she reached the bathroom she felt stronger. By the time she finished cleaning up she felt almost like a human being again.

"Eve?" Galen was knocking on the door.

"I'm okay." She threw open the door. "I feel better now."

"You look better." He handed her a pair of khakis, underwear, and a loose white shirt. "I rifled your suitcase. I'll help you dress when you finish your soup."

"That won't be necess—" Screw being independent. She had to get to Joe and she'd take any help that would be necessary. "We'll see." She dropped the clothes on the bottom of the bed and climbed back under the covers with a sigh of relief. She felt as tired as if she'd run the Boston Marathon. "For God's sake, it's only a glancing wound. But it doesn't feel that way."

"It's a head wound, and concussion isn't just a minor inconvenience." Galen tucked the covers around her. "And an inch to the left and we wouldn't be having this conversation."

"Could it have been a deliberate miss?"

"No, you were the target. And I hate to toot my own horn but if I hadn't tackled that son of a bitch at just that second you'd have been with the angels."

Or Bonnie. Her Bonnie.

"You don't look upset," Galen said. "It's the truth, Eve."

She shook her head to clear it. "I know, Galen. Tell me what happened."

"I was cruising around and I spotted someone moving toward the path where I'd left you and Quinn. He was kneeling and aiming his rifle, drawing a bead, when I got close enough to see him. I reached him in seconds but he got off two shots before I put him down."

"You weren't hurt at all?"

He shook his head. "But he wasn't easy and he was a professional. I might not have been able to save your necks if he hadn't been concentrating so completely on the shot."

"Montalvo's men are professionals."

He studied her expression. "You want that shooter to be one of Montalvo's men. Why?"

"It's not that I want it to be him. I have to question everything Montalvo does." Because too much was riding on whether she could trust Montalvo. "What happened after you spoiled that shot?"

"I broke the bastard's neck. Then I ran over to you to see if you were both still alive. By that time Soldono was there checking you out. He called Montalvo and got his guy, Miguel, and a team of men out there at top speed. They brought the two of you back to the compound and had their medics do emergency procedures. They sent for Dr. Diego, who lives in the village, and he was here within the hour."

"And the shooter?"

"Miguel thought he recognized him as one of Diaz's men. Paulo Duarte. Very lethal. Very nasty. Diaz saves him for special jobs that require—"

"How do you know Miguel is telling the truth?"

"A good question." Miguel was standing in the doorway with a smile on his face and a tray in his hands. "I would lie for the Colonel. There's no question about that being true." He came forward. "It's also true that I'm very happy that you're looking better. I was worried about you." He set the tray down on the bedside table. "So was the Colonel. He wouldn't leave your side until he was sure you were out of danger."

"I'm sure that wasn't entirely unbiased concern."

"No, of course not. But he does regard you highly. Even if you weren't useful I'm positive he wouldn't want you to be killed."

"How kind."

He chuckled as he handed her a napkin. "I've no way with words like the Colonel. He's always reproving me." He glanced at Galen. "You're going to take her to Quinn?"

"That's my intention. Any objections?"

"No, the Colonel said when I thought she was able that I shouldn't interfere." He headed for the door. "But I'd better check with the doctor. That would affect my decision."

"The hell it would," Eve said. "I'm seeing Joe."

"I have to ask the doctor," he repeated as he left the bedroom.

"Stubborn kid," Galen murmured. "But that kid commanded that troop of men who came after you like a seasoned veteran. Montalvo's lucky to have him."

"Not lucky for Miguel. He hero-worships Montalvo." She was eating the soup quickly. "And, as he said, he'd lie for him without a thought."

"He didn't lie about the shooter being Duarte. I rifled his pockets and didn't find any ID but I took a photo of him with my phone and sent it off to my contact in Bogotá. The ID came back six hours later. Paulo Duarte. He's been working for Ramon Diaz for the last three years. One ugly customer."

"And Diaz sent him to kill me."

"Presumably. Montalvo told me the reason why he'd have a motive to do it. You do get yourself in tight corners, luv."

And she'd gotten Joe into that corner too. He was lying in another of these palatial rooms fighting to survive because she'd waded recklessly into this mess.

"No one had to follow you, Eve," Galen said quietly, his gaze on her face. "You told us to stay away. So stop blaming yourself. We came because we couldn't do anything else. You didn't know what you'd be up against."

"I knew it could be bad." She finished her soup

and threw back the covers. "I need to see Joe. I'm still a little unsteady. Will you help me dress?"

"My pleasure." He smiled as he picked up the bra on the bed. "Turnabout is fair play. You've seen me naked."

Naked? Oh, yes, she'd almost forgotten that night in Louisiana. "Joe didn't get much pleasure when you told him, you devil."

"He needed stirring up." He helped her take off the nightshirt. "And I'm always willing to oblige...."

Montalvo met her at the door as she walked slowly down the hall toward Joe's bedroom. "It's good to see you on your feet." He nodded at Galen. "I'll take her in to see him."

Galen's brows raised. "Eve?"

She nodded curtly. "I don't care. I just want to see Joe."

"I'll deliver her safely back to her room, Galen." Montalvo opened the door for her. "She won't be long."

"Don't count on it." She went past him into the room that was dimly lit by a single lamp on the bed-side table.

Joe was lying in the massive bed across the room. For a big man he looked...small. Small and oddly helpless. It shook her. She wasn't accustomed to Joe looking anything but tough and totally pulled together.

She sank down in the chair beside the bed.

"He's just had his medication," Montalvo said behind her. "He won't be awake again for another couple hours. That's why I thought you might want to go back to your room after you assured yourself that he wasn't any worse than I told you."

"For once you were wrong about me." She took Joe's hand in both of hers. "I won't go anywhere until he knows I'm alive and with him." She leaned back in the chair. "So you might as well run along, Montalvo."

"Soon." He sat down in a chair a short distance away. "I'll keep you company for a time."

"I don't need your company. I have Joe."

"Who's not with us at present."

"He's always with me."

He was silent a moment. "Your history with Quinn must be extraordinary."

Joe holding her through the night in the time after Bonnie had been taken. Joe talking to her, trying to make sense out of the madness. Joe giving, taking, beside her through a thousand dawns and sunsets.

"You have no idea," she said unsteadily.

"No, but I wish I did. I had Nalia for only three years. We had the joy. We had no real time to bond as you did with Quinn. We were cheated of that." He stared down at the carpet at his feet. "And she was cheated of so much more. There was a whole world I was going to show her. She grew up in the jungle and only knew struggle and war. Yet she became...a wonder. Do you believe people are born with souls?"

"Yes."

"I didn't. Not before I met her." He paused. "Your Joe will be fine. I promise you."

Her hand tightened on Joe's. "I know he will. I won't let it be any other way."

He got to his feet. "And I had no part in hurting him, Eve. I gave you your chance. I didn't betray you."

She didn't answer.

"I know you're confused and you don't want to waste any time thinking about anything but Quinn. That will pass. Truth is important. We both realize that in the end there's very little as vital."

"Except your revenge."

"And your revenge." He headed for the door. "I'll have Miguel check on you during the next few hours. He'll get you anything you need."

"I don't need revenge right now. I need Joe to get well."

"I believe that will also pass after he recovers. And you might consider what Quinn's reaction is going to be. Revenge is a very basic desire. How primitive is your Joe Quinn?"

She remembered the Joe who had met her that night in the jungle. Primitive? Hell, yes. "I don't want to think about that right now. Go away, Montalvo."

He smiled. "Forgive me. I didn't mean to disturb you."

"No, with you it comes naturally."

"Perhaps. Or it could be that I'm eaten up with envy of your history with Quinn. But new history is formed every day. Sometimes you just have to put the old history behind you."

She frowned. "What the devil are you talking about?"

"Something you don't want to hear. Good night, Eve. I'll see you in the morning. Or if you want to talk to me, I'm always at your disposal."

She watched the door close behind him. As usual, he was being maddeningly enigmatic, and she didn't want to deal with him right now. She had enough on her plate and she needed to concentrate all her attention on Joe.

Jesus, he was pale. Montalvo had said he'd lost a lot of blood and there was clear evidence that was true.

Wake up, Joe.

Look at me. Let me see that you're going to be fine. Just wake up . . .

"Eve?"

Eve's lids flew open. Joe was awake and looking up at her.

"Hi," she said softly as she leaned forward, her hand grasping his. "You're being very boring lying there sleeping. I must have dozed off."

"Sorry." His gaze was on the bandage on her temple. "Are you okay?"

"I'm fine."

"How fine?"

She should have known Joe wouldn't accept a pat answer. "The bullet grazed my temple. It was a little too close and I ended up with a concussion. It put me out for a time or I would have been here sooner."

"Montalvo was here. I asked.... He said you were alive and well." His lips tightened. "Liar."

"No, I was as well as could be expected. He didn't want you to worry."

"Is that why they kept giving me drugs?"

"No, they gave you drugs because you were in pain. You got the worst of the attack. You covered me with your body."

"Not in time. You were still hurt."

"In plenty of time. I'm alive. According to Galen, I wouldn't have been if you hadn't jerked me down. The bullet was aimed at my head."

"*Damn* him." He was silent a moment. "Then it probably wasn't Montalvo. He wouldn't mind me dead. But he wants you alive and functioning."

"Galen checked his ID and the shooter was named Duarte and he works for Ramon Diaz. Diaz must have sent him to make sure I didn't do the job I was brought here to do."

"He came close." Joe's eyes were once again on the bandage on Eve's temple. "Too close."

She didn't like the hard edge she heard in his voice. She had heard it before and it usually meant anger barely leashed. "It didn't happen, Joe."

"He *hurt* you."

"Not nearly as much as you were hurt."

"And you think Diaz isn't going to come after you again? You're caught in the middle between him and Montalvo. He's going to keep on coming until he puts you down."

"That's not going to happen. Stop thinking about it. Concentrate on getting well. That's what's important right now."

He nodded curtly. "Damn right, that's important. I'll be out of this bed by the end of the week."

"Not likely."

"Entirely likely." He closed his eyes. "Tell Galen I want to see him, will you?"

"Hey, are you trying to get rid of me?"

"Hell, no." He didn't open his eyes but he squeezed her hand before releasing it. "I'm just making sure no one else does."

How primitive is your Joe Quinn?

Montalvo's words came back to her as she looked down at Joe. She hadn't even wanted to consider the answer to a question that would have opened a whole can of worms. Yet she knew it had been in the back of her mind. There was no one who was more protective or more vengeful than Joe if the occasion warranted it.

Jesus, and this occasion definitely warranted it.

"Stop fretting and get me Galen," Joe said.

"I'm not fretting. I want to shake you."

He opened his eyes and smiled faintly. "The way I

wanted to shake you when you wouldn't come back to Bogotá with me? Don't argue. I'm not listening."

Her hands closed in frustration as she stared at him. "Joe, this isn't the—"

"Galen," he said again.

She jumped to her feet. "I'll get Galen because you're hurt and I don't want you upset." She strode toward the door. "But this isn't the end of this discussion." She jerked open the door. "What the devil am I talking about? You won't even let me argue you back to some sort of reason."

"I'm being perfectly reasonable. It's the oldest logic in history. Cause and effect. Action and reaction."

"Logic, hell." She slammed the door behind her. Then she leaned back against it and tried to get her breath. Dizzy.

And angry.

And scared.

"Are you well?" Miguel was beside her. "May I help you?"

"I'm okay." Not well. Definitely not well. "Yes, you can help me. Go get Galen and tell him to go and see Joe."

"After I help you back to your room."

"I'm not going back to my room. Where's Montalvo?"

"His bedroom. It's after three in the morning. He's retired for the night."

"Where's his bedroom?"

Miguel nodded to a room at the end of the corridor. "I could wake him and send him to you."

"No, you go find Galen. Joe will probably get out of bed and try to go after him if he doesn't show up in his room soon. The idiot doesn't know his limitations."

"Neither does the Colonel. That's why he often succeeds in doing impossible things. Perhaps Quinn is the same?"

"Impossible attempts can kill you." She started down the hall. "And you're as bad as all the rest of those blasted macho men in this place. All for glory and revenge. It doesn't matter that the odds are—"

"You're sure you don't want me to wake the Colonel for you?"

"No, I'll do it. Didn't you hear him? He's always at my disposal."

"I'm sure he will be. However, I should warn you he does sleep naked."

"So?"

"Nothing." He turned away and headed down the hall. "Just a random piece of information I thought might hold some interest. Galen will be with Quinn in fifteen minutes. I hope that will please you."

"No, it doesn't please me. Not one bit. But it's not your fault." She knocked on the door of Montalvo's room and then threw it open. "I need to talk to you, Montalvo."

"By all means. Come in."

It was dark, but she could dimly see the outline of

his body in the huge bed across the room. "Turn on the light."

"As you wish." He turned on the bedside light. "As you can see, I wasn't expecting guests." He smiled. "Although I'm sure that nudity doesn't bother you."

"No, it doesn't." But he was a magnificent specimen, she thought. Big, muscular, and the epitome of the totally adult sensual male.

He sighed. "I didn't think so. One can but hope." He pulled the sheet over the lower half of his body and sat up. "Your 'history' is too hard to overcome at the moment."

"Good God, you'll try any ploy to get your way, won't you?" She sat down in the chair by the window. "Sex is not a weapon I use or accept. I'd think you'd be intelligent enough to realize that."

"Oh, I do. I'd never use it as a weapon. But I'm a lonely man and it's seldom I come across a woman who pleases me mentally as well as physically." He smiled. "And there's a certain closeness between us that would be interesting to explore." He held up his hand as she opened her mouth to speak. "But since you didn't come here on an exploratory mission we won't discuss it. It must be urgent if it wouldn't wait until morning."

"Urgent enough."

"Would you like something to drink?"

"No," she said impatiently. "I told you I need to talk to you."

"I'm listening."

"Joe is going to go after Diaz."

"I thought it likely. I'm sure that if you'd allowed yourself to consider the possibility that you would have come to the same conclusion. Are you certain?"

"Do you mean has he told me that's what he's going to do? No, but I know him and there's no doubt in my mind. He asked to see Galen. He wants information and maybe his help. He's going to work like hell to get back on his feet and then he's going after him." Her folded hands clenched together on her lap. "He's angry and he wants to protect me. There's no way I'm going to be able to talk him out of it."

"What do you want me to do? Drug him? Lock him in his room?"

"No, Joe would find a way to get free. He's very smart and savvy."

"That leaves you very few options, doesn't it?"

"You know damn well it does."

"Then tell me what you're going to do."

"Are you mocking me?"

"Because I'm smiling? I'm smiling because I believe I'm going to be made a very happy man. Am I right?"

"I'll do your reconstruction. Go after the skull. Bring it here."

"The conditions?"

"You keep your word about finding Bonnie. And you go after the skull immediately, no waiting for just the right moment. I want to be able to start working on her tomorrow night."

"Why?"

"I believe you know why. The sooner I get her done, the sooner you're able to go after Diaz. Joe can't possibly be in any kind of shape to tackle Diaz for another week or two. By that time, with any luck you'll already have blown Diaz and his scumbag cohorts to hell."

"What a charming plan." He chuckled. "But you've set me quite a tight timetable. How do you know I can meet it?"

"You came damn close when you set yourself that deadline with Marty. You like challenges. This is one you've been preparing to meet since your wife was killed. I imagine you've been going crazy twiddling your thumbs, waiting for your chance."

"At first. But I've learned patience. It was forced on me. Just as it was with you, Eve."

"I'm not going to be patient about this. Joe's not going to go after Diaz. He said I was caught in the middle between you and Diaz, but it was my choice to come down here. I won't have Joe caught in the cross fire." She leaned forward, her voice lowered to steely softness. "I'll give you what you want and you'll keep your promises, Montalvo. You'll move and move fast. Not one hair of Joe's head is going to be singed while you two tear each other apart. Do you understand?"

"You couldn't be more clear." He threw aside the sheet and got out of bed. He bowed slightly and started for the bathroom. "Speed you shall have. And

I'll try to have Diaz taken out before Quinn can totter from his sickbed."

"Not 'try.' You'll do it." She shrugged. "Use one of your damn missiles if you have to."

"My, how violent you can be when your emotions are involved. Quinn isn't the only one who's protective."

"It goes with the territory."

He smiled over his shoulder. "Or the history? I told you past history was a strong foe to overcome." He disappeared into the bathroom and shut the door. A moment later she heard the shower.

It was done. She was committed. She'd spurred Montalvo to kick his attack on Diaz into high gear. Not that he'd needed kicking. She'd seen how passionately eager he could be when he wanted something.

How would that eagerness translate in bed?

She felt a ripple of shock at the thought. It had come out of nowhere. She couldn't remember the last time she'd even had a sexual thought about a man other than Joe.

It meant nothing, she assured herself quickly. She was a woman who'd spent the last fifteen minutes in a room with a strong, virile, naked man. She was not a nun and it was natural that instinct would rear its head. It didn't mean that she loved Joe less or that she would ever act on that instinct. It was like watching Brad Pitt in a movie and thinking maybe it wouldn't be so bad to—

Dismiss it. She had gotten what she wanted from Montalvo and it wasn't a quickie in that monster of a bed. Joe would be safe. She might have a chance at finding her Bonnie.

If everything went well for Montalvo and his men tonight. It all rested on him being able to fade into that village and snatch the skull before Diaz knew he was there.

She stood up and started toward the bedroom door.

A big if, she thought worriedly. A terribly big and forbidding if.

9

When Eve reached the hall, she met Galen coming out of Joe's bedroom.

His gaze went beyond her to Montalvo's door. "A late-night rendezvous or an assassination attempt?"

"Neither. And you're not being funny. What did Joe want with you?"

"You have an idea or you wouldn't be cozying up to Montalvo in the middle of the night."

"Joe wants information. He wants your help when he's able to go after Diaz. Anything else?"

"He wants me to keep you from involving yourself any further with Montalvo while he's incapacitated."

"He's asking a hell of a lot from you."

"No, he's not." He smiled gently. "My friend Eve Duncan was shot and almost killed. Everything Quinn asked I would have done anyway."

"I'm not going to let him go after Diaz." She met his gaze. "I'm not going to let you go after him either."

"How are you going to stop us?"

"I'm turning Montalvo loose on him. It's his bat-tle. Hell, it's his war. Soldono says that he has no compunction about letting these criminals kill each other."

"But I believe you don't quite think of Montalvo on the same level as Diaz."

"That's because I know him. Diaz is still a mystery. It doesn't change the principle."

"Then I should have no trouble convincing you that you should shy away from Montalvo. Right?"

"Wrong. I'm going to do the reconstruction. He'll be retrieving the skull tonight and I'll do the work with as much speed as I can."

Galen gave a low whistle. "Quinn's going to have a relapse."

"No, he's not. Because you're not going to tell him anything. As far as he's concerned, you're doing what he asked you to do." Her lips twisted. "Including keeping me away from Montalvo. I'm only telling you what's happening because I know that you'll find out anyway. I can keep Joe in the dark for a lim-ited time because he's going to be tied to that bed for a while. I just hope it's long enough for Montalvo to persuade the rebels to move against Diaz."

"Don't count on Quinn's recovery going along with your timeline. He asked me to bring him some hand weights so that he won't lose strength while he's lying in bed. He says that with my help he thinks he can get out of bed in the next two days."

"Shit."

"Even if he makes it out of bed that doesn't mean he's going to have the strength to stay on his feet. It could be days before he's even mobile."

"And it may be much sooner. I know how determined Joe can be. He's an irresistible force when he's focused on anything."

"Then you'd better work very quickly indeed. I've learned one thing working with Quinn during the past days. He won't be stopped unless you put another bullet in him."

"How comforting."

"I'm not sure I want to comfort you. I'm leaning toward going along with Quinn on this one. You believe what Montalvo told you but that doesn't mean either Quinn or I do. How do you know he's told you the truth about anything connected with that skull? It might be better for Quinn and me to go after Diaz ourselves." He shrugged. "We're not greedy. We don't have to take down Diaz's entire operation as Montalvo wants to do. We'd be happy with putting a neat bullet hole between his eyes. That's possible for a two-man job."

"Damn you, Galen. You know how dangerous it would be to get that close to Diaz."

"But we wouldn't have to depend on someone we have no idea we can trust. That's also very dangerous."

"You're saying I can't count on you?"

"You can count on my help. I'm not saying how that help will be given."

She took a deep breath to smother her anger and frustration. "Tell me what I can count on. Are you going to tell Joe that I'm doing the reconstruction?"

"No. I think you'll be telling him about that. Unless you're not planning to visit him in his sickbed, you're not going to be able to hide that you're working. Not from someone who's as intimate with you as Quinn. I've watched you doing a reconstruction. You're not even in the same world."

She hadn't thought about that. Galen was right. "Maybe not right away. I'll try to build in a delay."

"And work with the speed of light. Quinn doesn't need a spur to prod him."

"You don't believe in pressure, do you?"

"You always work better under pressure, luv."

She shook her head. "But why do you want me to work faster? Which side are you on, Galen?"

"I haven't decided." He grinned. "Elena says I'm like a cat on the proverbial hot tin roof. I jump whichever way seems best at the moment."

"Bull. I know you make commitments."

"But how I execute them is my choice," he said gently. "Now run along and get to bed. I'll stay with Quinn. I don't believe you want to see him right now. You're too full of plots and plans and you'll be trying your best to keep from shaking him and telling him to do what you say. Not good for a patient in his condition."

"Neither is trying to get out of a sickbed before he should. You're aiding and abetting him in doing that."

"Touché." He turned to the door. "But I won't shake—" He broke off as Montalvo's door opened.

Montalvo was dressed in khakis and army boots, the ever-present pistol holstered on his hip as he strode quickly toward them. He nodded at Eve. "Is this quick enough for you? We're not on our way but I'm in full throttle at making plans. We should be ready to leave by eight tonight." He went past her and ran down the staircase.

"You certainly lit a fire under him," Galen murmured. "Or should I say a bonfire. You could almost warm your hands at it."

She knew what he meant. Montalvo's excitement and urgency were almost palpable. "He's been waiting for this. He used to be a soldier and he likes a challenge. He's going to love every minute of going after that skull under Diaz's nose."

"Yeah." Galen was still looking after him. "It's kind of addictive."

Good God, Galen actually sounded wistful, she thought in exasperation.

Men.

"He'll be lucky if he comes back with his own head, much less that skull," she said curtly.

"He seems to have a well-trained team. He has a good chance."

"According to Montalvo, Diaz knew he was close

to finding her body. Maybe he knows more than Montalvo thinks about where the grave is located. We'll see if he manages to deliver that skull to me tonight." She turned and started back toward her room. She was weaving a little and concentrated on trying to steady herself. She was exhausted and her head was pounding. She needed sleep to heal and she had to heal. She had a strenuous couple of days ahead if Montalvo delivered the skull to her tonight.

She glanced back over her shoulder and saw Galen at last turning away from staring after Montalvo and opening Joe's door. Galen was proving as difficult as all the other men here at the compound.

Cat on a hot tin roof, indeed.

"Duarte hasn't reported since Tuesday, two days ago," Nekmon said. "We know he was in the area and monitoring what was happening at the compound. He made no mention of Eve Duncan. We know that a doctor was called to the compound from the village also two days ago. He's still there."

Diaz frowned. "Then, if Duarte did manage to take his shot at Eve Duncan, he botched it. Dead women don't need doctors."

"We're not sure she was at the compound."

"Because the man we sent to Atlanta could find no record of her leaving? Don't be a fool. Montalvo could find a way of sneaking her over any border."

Nekmon nodded. "And Joe Quinn did leave Atlanta for Bogotá. But after that we lost track of him."

"You seem to be losing track of a good many people," Diaz said sarcastically. "Aquila, Duarte, and you can't even locate Eve Duncan, much less lose her."

"If Duarte took his shot, there's a chance that she's dead. He was good."

"Then why call the doctor?"

Nekmon lifted his shoulders in a slight shrug. "Quinn? Montalvo himself?"

"Guesses. God, I'm tired of guesses. I want answers. I want this problem resolved." He scowled down at the wine in his glass. "Montalvo has been a thorn in my side for too many years. He should have been killed when he came charging after me when we got rid of the Armandariz woman."

"We did our best," Nekmon said. "We thought we'd put him down for a good two years after that time. He became a damned phantom. And after he turned to selling weapons we would have had to deal with that little battalion he kept around him. You said yourself it was better to watch and wait."

"Because I need that damned woman's body. I should have burned it and scattered the ashes to the four winds. I won't have it surface and spoil the sweet deal I have with Armandariz. I still need him. It's not every man who has an army at his command."

"May I suggest that need may be obsolete? You

have enough money to move your operations to another country."

"Another country? Are you mad? Here I'm king. I take what I want and who I want. If I go to another country, I'm only considered a lowlife who must be crushed." He smiled grimly. "I do the crushing here. No one stands in my way."

"Only a suggestion."

"That's the trouble with you, Nekmon. You settle for the safe berth. That's why you'll always be working for a man like me."

"There's only one Ramon Diaz. There's certainly no one like you."

The asshole was flattering him, Diaz realized. Or maybe he was insulting him and thought he wouldn't catch the drift. Nekmon with his college education and his smooth ways was beginning to annoy him. He was valuable on the accounting end and he was an excellent front man, but he could be replaced.

But not right now. He needed no change in the men around him while he was dealing with Montalvo. The bastard was getting too close.

"Should we send someone else to check out Duarte?" Nekmon asked.

"If you haven't heard from him, he's probably captured or dead. Can't you do any better than that?"

"There's a possibility I may be able to lure someone in Montalvo's camp over to us as an informant.

I've been working on it for some time. He's been holding out for more money."

"Then give it to him." He frowned thoughtfully. "My sending Aquila and Duarte to Montalvo may act as a trigger. He'll know that I suspect something is going to happen and am trying to find a way to dodge it. He may not realize that I know about Eve Duncan but it's going to put a burr under his tail to bring her that fucking skull."

"If he doesn't have it already."

"He doesn't have it. If he had it, he wouldn't have waited years to make a move. I've been watching him like a hawk since I found out he got that son of a bitch to dredge up her body." His scowl deepened. "That body is somewhere near here. I know it. That bastard didn't have a chance to get far before I found out he was dealing with Montalvo. No, Montalvo knows where she is but he hasn't got hold of her yet."

He stood up and wandered over to the high arched window to look out at the rolling hills of coca lying before him. Such a sleepy, sunny scene. Nekmon would never know the thrill it gave him every time he stared up at those hills. There was more power invested in one of those fields of coca than most men would know in a lifetime of wheeling and dealing. The power to destroy, to twist minds, to lift a sucker to the heights and then take it away if it suited him. The fact that drugs had made him a very rich man was only secondary. It was the power that counted.

And he wasn't going to let Montalvo take one bit

of that power away. He'd beaten him once. He'd beat him again.

"You're going to do nothing?" Nekmon asked.

Yes, he'd definitely have to replace Nekmon at the earliest opportunity. "I didn't say that. You'll increase the surveillance of the compound. You'll make sure that the security here is tight."

"And?"

He smiled. "Why, we'll wait and watch and scoop him up when he tries to retrieve his beloved bride."

The bedside clock read 6:35.

Eve shook her head to clear it of sleep. She'd slept as if she'd been drugged, not Joe. The moment her head had hit the pillow she'd been lost to the world.

The skull.

She swung her feet to the floor and headed for the bathroom. Montalvo had said that he'd be leaving at eight. She had to get downstairs right away. He might leave early and she had to—

She stopped short. Why was she in such a hurry? Why did she have this sense of urgency to see him before he left?

She slowly went into the bathroom and turned on the shower. Her entire being was alert, wired, expectant.

Expecting what?

And then she knew.

And there wasn't much time.

She quickly stepped beneath the spray.

Thirty minutes later she was running down the staircase. The first floor was a turmoil of activity. Men dressed in khakis and trail boots, all fully armed, were everywhere. She caught sight of Soldono near the front door.

"Where's Montalvo?" she called from the landing.

"Outside on the ramparts, I think," Soldono said. "He's been in and out all afternoon." He gave her an appraising glance. "You look surprisingly healthy considering that blow to the noggin you took. When I first saw you lying underneath Quinn, I thought you were dead."

"I'm okay." She passed him and went through the front door. It was almost dark but there were lanterns everywhere and she caught sight of Montalvo almost immediately. He was coming down the steps from the rampart talking to someone behind him.

"Montalvo."

He smiled as he turned to look at her. "Ah, you've come to bid me good-bye. Do you have a favor to give me as I ride into battle?"

"No. That's not why I came."

His smile faded and he gave a sigh. "I was afraid of this. I was hoping that you were too wounded and light-headed to react in the most characteristic manner for you. Evidently my hopes were to no avail."

"I'm going with you."

"Not possible."

"I'm going with you."

"Eve, we're moving fast and you'd get in our way."

"I'm not saying I want you to give me a gun and let me go after that bastard Diaz. I'm not stupid. I leave the fighting to those who are trained to do it. But I'm going to be there when you dig up that skull."

"No!" Soldono was standing behind her. "Eve, this is foolish. You'll get yourself killed. Why would you insist on going?"

"It's a matter of trust." Montalvo's tone was mocking. "The trust she does not have in me. Isn't that correct, Eve?"

"Of course it's correct. You spun me a fine tale of a lost love and a monster who sits in his castle like a fat gargoyle and smears his poison on everything he touches. What if you're lying? What if you have this skull hidden away somewhere and you take your men out and come back a few hours later with the skull? Only maybe it's not your wife's skull. I've been lied to before. Maybe the reconstruction is to be of someone else. Or maybe this body is buried somewhere else other than Diaz's territory and I'm violating a grave. How do I know?"

"A matter of trust," he said. "Catch-22."

"I won't do that reconstruction unless I'm at least marginally certain that you've been telling me the truth."

"How marginally?"

"I want to see the cemetery for myself. I want to see that castle you said Diaz lives in that towers over the village. I want to see you dig up that skull."

"Eve," Soldono said protestingly. "It's a mistake."

"I've made a lot of mistakes lately." She stared Montalvo in the eye. "But I won't compromise my ethics because of gullibility. That's one mistake I won't make."

She heard Soldono mutter a curse behind her but she ignored him. This was between her and Montalvo.

"You can't keep up with us," Montalvo said. "You could hardly get out of bed yesterday."

"Then find a way to make sure I will keep up. Use your ingenuity."

"You won't change your mind?"

"I won't change my mind."

He was silent a moment. "You'll slow us down. That won't matter going in but it could be fatal getting out."

"I don't want anyone dying because of me. Position me somewhere so that I can see what's happening. Once I see the skull in your hands you can send me back ahead of your team. Then you can move at your own pace."

"If everything goes right."

"I've got to make sure that you're telling me the truth."

"Don't let her go, Montalvo," Soldono said. "You know what Diaz will do to her if he catches her."

"Oh, yes. Kill her, throw her in a swamp. And someday someone will find her skull and wonder who would be so foolhardy." Montalvo shrugged.

"But that won't be me. Because I won't let it happen again. Therefore, I can't let him catch her." His gaze shifted back to Eve. "Go upstairs and get back in the shower."

"What?"

"Wash off all the lotion and soap residue. You smell very pleasant but I could tell you were coming from yards away. Some of Diaz's men have the same commando training."

She nodded. "Anything else?"

"Miguel will give you some standard-issue mosquito repellent." He checked his watch. "You have forty-five minutes."

"I'll be here." She was already moving quickly toward the front door.

"I'm afraid you will."

Soldono caught up with her as she reached the staircase. "This is crazy."

"I don't have time to argue with you. I'm going to do it. Leave me alone, Soldono."

"I can't leave you alone. You're my job. I'm supposed to be here to offer you protection." He frowned. "If you go, I go."

"Montalvo won't let you go. You're a CIA agent and he wouldn't run that risk." She was taking the steps two at a time. "I can't waste any more time talking to you. I want to see Joe before I hit the shower."

"Perhaps he can talk you out of it."

"Joe's not going to know about this." She glared

at him over her shoulder. "Do you understand, Soldono?"

"I think someone should—" He broke off. "I understand."

"Good." She'd reached the top of the steps and tore down the corridor past the guard to Joe's room. She opened the door quietly. She'd expected to see Galen there but the room was empty except for Joe. She moved across the room to stand beside the bed. Joe's eyes were closed and at first she thought he was asleep.

"Eve?" He opened drowsy eyes. "I thought it was you. That gardenia body lotion . . ."

"Too much? Evidently I should tone it down."

"No, I've always liked it. It smells clean. . . ."

"From yards away," she repeated Montalvo's words dryly. She gently touched his hair. "Are you still in pain?"

"Not much. They keep giving me those damn drugs to ward it off. Tomorrow I'm going to tell them to go to hell." He took her hand. "You didn't come to see me today. I missed you. Was it because you're pissed at me?"

"It was because I practically fell unconscious when I went to bed."

"You look fine now." His gaze raked her face. "You're flushed and your eyes are . . . I don't know." His own eyes were closing. "You look . . . good."

"Thank you."

"I think . . . it bothers me."

Jesus, if he hadn't been under the drugs he would have been able to read her without effort. She bent over and kissed his forehead. "I'm fine and you're going to be fine too. And, yes, I am pissed at you. That wouldn't keep me from coming to see you when you're ill. That's not how it works. Not when you love someone."

"Glad...I knew that, but sometimes I forget..."

He was asleep.

She gave herself another moment to hold his hand, look at him, stay with him.

Then she carefully put his hand on the counterpane and glided toward the door.

She had less than thirty minutes remaining of the time Montalvo had allotted her and she had to hurry.

Miguel was waiting outside the door. He handed her a bar of soap and a small bottle of mosquito repellent. "You're being unreasonable. The Colonel isn't happy."

"Sorry. I know that's a major crime in your eyes."

"Yes. But I will not treat you as a criminal unless your lack of reason causes harm to the Colonel." His glance was cool as he turned away. "That's not acceptable."

"Not to me either." She headed toward her room. "I don't want anyone hurt." She slammed the door behind her. She was tired of arguing and this was difficult enough. Take the shower and wash her hair, rid herself of this blasted scent and then get down to the yard.

She was running down the stairs twenty minutes later. The hall was now clear, she noticed. Everyone must be assembled outside and ready to go.

She was right. Two jeeps with engines running were parked in front of the house but she could see a truck loaded with men already pulling out of the gates.

Montalvo was talking to someone in the shadow of the far jeep and she walked toward him.

"I'm ready. No scent as you spec—"

Galen.

He smiled at her. "Hello, luv."

Montalvo turned away from talking to Galen. "Good. Get in the jeep. I'll see you at the village, Galen." He was striding away toward the jeep in front. "Or if we're lucky, I won't see you there."

Eve whirled to face Galen. "What the devil are you doing here?"

"It appears I'm going to help rob a grave."

"I told you that I didn't want you to—"

"That was before you decided to risk your neck to make sure that Montalvo's not lying to you." He grimaced. "And I have a hunch that I piqued this move on your part. I asked you last night how you knew that Montalvo was on the up-and-up about this grave-robbing scenario."

"I would have probably thought it through and known I had to verify it myself. It was in the back of my mind anyway. I was just too exhausted to make the connection. You have no responsibility about—"

"Hush. You have to have someone guarding your back and you gave Soldono his walking papers."

"Soldono ran to you and asked you to do this?"

"He didn't have to beg and plead too hard." He helped her into the jeep. "Even if you hadn't been involved I might have tagged a ride to the party. It looked like my kind of shindig."

"I don't want you coming, Galen."

"Too late."

"Someone has to be here to take care of Joe."

"I designated Soldono to hold his hand." He started the jeep. "Not that he's needed with a doctor in attendance. And you talk as if we're going to be gone for days. Montalvo is estimating six hours."

She looked at him in exasperation. "How did you persuade Montalvo to let you come?"

"My reputation isn't pure as the driven snow like Soldono's and he saw I could handle myself. It frees one of his men from babysitting you. It wasn't too difficult to convince him that I was a good addition to his merry band." He glanced at her as he followed Montalvo's jeep through the compound gates. "Now, wouldn't it be more beneficial for you to stop arguing and discuss what Montalvo and I decided would give you what you want and still keep all of us alive?"

There was no budging him. "Okay, tell me what's going to happen."

"The hill overlooking the cemetery is heavily wooded. We can park the jeep on the road, climb the hill, and stay there and watch Montalvo and his men do the deed. When you're satisfied, then we take off and hightail it out of there."

"It sounds very simple and efficient."

"Oh, did I forget to tell you that we don't use the lights for the last four miles to the hill and we might end up in a ditch? Or that Montalvo has sent scouts out to make sure there aren't any snipers on this side of the valley but he's only eighty-five percent sure that one might not have slipped by?" He glanced at her. "Do you still want to go?"

"Yes." She stared out the windshield at the taillights of Montalvo's jeep ahead of them. "I have to go."

"It should be up ahead." Galen peered through the windshield. "Christ, it's like crawling through a dark tunnel. Montalvo said there should be moonlight tonight. Where the hell is it?"

"Evidently Montalvo can't control everything. Clouds do come."

"Well, evidently he controlled the sniper situation. We got this far without being—There it is." He swung the wheel and the jeep skittered off onto a side road. A hundred yards farther he turned the jeep around.

"Out. Montalvo and his men should be ten minutes ahead of us. It took longer than I thought to crawl along that road. If you want to see the show, we've got to hurry."

"I definitely want to see the show." She'd already jumped out of the jeep. "Which way?"

"There's a path to the left." He grabbed her arm. "There it is."

She moved up the path behind him. "How far?"

"Sorry. Montalvo wasn't that precise. He said to climb to the top of the hill."

The hill was steep and the shale path slippery underfoot. She slipped twice and righted herself. Her breath was coming hard by the time they'd been climbing only five minutes or so.

"Okay?" Galen whispered.

"Hell, no. I'm still wobbly from that concussion but I'll make it."

"I don't have the slightest doubt you will. But if you could use a hand feel free to tell me."

"As an alternative to falling at your feet, you can be sure I'll yell," she said grimly.

"Well, don't yell. That might arouse any snipers Montalvo missed accounting for. But a gentle tug would—I think we're there." He reached behind him and pulled her the last few feet to the crest of the hill. "There's Diaz's kingdom."

If this was a kingdom, the castle on the hill across the way did justice to the concept, she thought. The moon was still behind the clouds and the castle was the only structure that was brightly lit and easily discernible in the darkness. It was a Spanish-Moorish mansion on the grand scale. Turrets and massive arched windows were sprinkled throughout the exterior of the castle and as far as she could tell the grounds were equally impressive.

Her gaze shifted from the castle to the village directly below her. Darkness. She could barely make out the roofs of the houses but nothing was distinct. "I didn't come here to see the castle. I can't see anything but those lights on the—"

The moon came out from behind the clouds.

"Right on cue," Galen murmured. "Maybe Montalvo does have influence on the higher plane."

She barely heard him. Her gaze was searching the village below for some sign of—

"There it is." She dropped to her knees and lifted the binoculars to her eyes. "The cemetery is behind that small church to the left. Jesus, it's on the edge of the village, in the open. There aren't any houses around it to shelter it. If Diaz's men looked down from that monstrosity of a castle, they'd see everything that's going on."

"Then Montalvo had better hope they're not looking down. Do you see him and his men yet?"

"No."

"The grave should be two-thirds back to the right of a large stone tomb."

"Montalvo told you that?"

"I didn't want to waste time."

She scanned the cemetery in the direction he'd indicated. The large tomb ... "Got it. It's not large, it's enormous. It doesn't look like it even belongs in a country cemetery."

"Oh, it belongs. It's the final resting place of Rosa Maria Diaz, Ramon Diaz's mother."

"And Montalvo's wife's body was buried almost on top of it? Not very smart. The area around it must be the best-tended site in the cemetery. Not to mention the fact that Diaz must come there frequently."

"It was actually a very smart choice, according to Montalvo. The area isn't tended at all. Diaz hated his mother. He's rumored to have caused her demise. She turned him in once to the police when he was just starting out."

"Then why bury her here where she'd always be with him?"

"Perhaps some sick badge of triumph to gloat over. He was the king on the hill and his stupid, interfering mother was moldering in that vault at his feet."

"I'm at a wrong angle. I have to move." She started shifting to the left. "That's better." She stiffened. "Montalvo's already there. He's digging. Two other men are digging too."

"Good. The more manpower, the quicker we get out of here." He lifted his head and looked back at the path they'd taken. "Things have gone too smooth. I don't like—"

"Nerves?" She lowered her binoculars. "Do you have any concrete concerns?"

He shook his head. "Nothing is concrete about this job. I'm winging it. May we leave now?"

"In a minute." She lifted the binoculars to her eyes again. "When they find the skeleton."

"Then I hope he didn't bury her deep."

"So do I." She went still. "I think they've reached it. Montalvo is jumping into the grave and Miguel is handing him a box." Her hands tightened on the binoculars. "He's got it. He's climbing out and they're running through the—" She turned to glance at Galen. "That's all I need. We can—"

Galen wasn't there!

Panic. Her heart leaped in her chest.

She whirled and started down the path at a run.

Stop. Slow is better. Be cautious. You don't know what's happening.

"Eve."

She jumped as Galen appeared out of the bushes beside the trail. "You scared me."

"Good. We may need a little adrenaline right now." He grabbed her arm and took off at full speed. "We've got to get out of here."

"Why? Where did you go?"

"I did a little backtracking. I had a feeling..." He was glancing on either side of the path as they flew down it. "I ran into one of Diaz's sentries who was on the trail behind us. I took care of him but I don't know if he notified anyone we were here."

"What about Montalvo?"

"He's on his own. He's not going to do anything differently if he knows Diaz is coming. He expects it. He may get lucky. We're providing a diversion." They'd reached the jeep and he jumped into the driver's seat. "Come on." He started the engine. "Let's get out of here."

She was already in the passenger seat. "You flicked on the lights. We'll be seen."

"I'd rather risk being spotted than end up in a ditch if Diaz's men are going to come pouring down that hill." He pressed the accelerator. "Four miles and we're out of Diaz's territory and into Montalvo's jungle. They can still follow but we'll be safer. Montalvo and his men know that jungle like the backs of their hands."

The jeep was bouncing over the rutted dirt road and she held on tightly to keep from being tossed against the seat belt. "Four miles isn't that far. We may—"

A bullet shattered the corner of the windshield.

"Down."

She released the seat belt and leaned down in the seat. The jeep was weaving back and forth on the road like a serpent on a sand dune.

Another shot.

"A miss," Galen muttered. "Same weapon. One sniper. If we can get out of range we'll make it. Idiot didn't aim for the tires...."

How far was it to safety? Eve wondered desperately. He'd said four miles but they were moving fast. Three? Two?

Another shot.

"He's out of range," Galen said. "Hold on. I have to keep zigzagging in case there's another sniper up ahead. Another minute and we'll be out of Diaz's territory."

"*You* hold on. And don't you dare get shot, dammit."

"I'm doing my best." He grinned down at her as he swerved back and forth on the road. "And that's pretty damn good. Admit it."

"I admit it. Superior. Stupendous. Now get us back to the compound."

"Home free." He made a sharp turn and they were suddenly enveloped in darkness. "You can sit up now."

She sat up and looked around.

Jungle. The thick, pervading darkness was caused by the overhanging foliage blocking out the night sky. "It's not what I call home." She gave a sigh of relief. "But it will do for now. Let's call Montalvo and check and see if he ran into the same trouble."

10

"Montalvo's phone is off," Galen said. "That could mean that he's not in the clear or that he's been captured by Diaz."

"Or that he's dead," Eve said.

"Don't be pessimistic." He paused. "Or maybe it's optimistic. That would end your obligation to do a job you don't want to do."

And it would end a chance to find Bonnie.

"You're not answering," Galen said.

"He didn't lie to me. I saw everything just the way he described it. I think what he told me about Diaz and his wife's skull was true."

"And that means you want him to live."

"Our aims aren't so far apart." She thought about the Montalvo she had come to know. "And I think he deserves to bring his wife home."

"And to blow Diaz out of the water?"

"Hell, yes. He almost killed Joe."

Galen chuckled. "And that deserves every punishment under the sun. For a complicated woman, you have a very simple code, Eve."

"I'm not complicated."

"No more than Lucrezia Borgia mixed with Mother Teresa."

"Call Montalvo again."

He dialed the number and this time Montalvo picked up.

"Ah, you're alive and kicking," Galen said. "We were wondering if you were dead. We had an interesting conversation on the pros and cons of your demise. Yes, we're out of the line of fire. Where are you? Oops." He hung up. "He started cursing. Can't blame him. I heard gunfire in the background. He probably only picked up because he wanted to know if you needed help."

"Evidently he's the one who needs help."

"We can't go back. He's on his own. He'll either get out or not." He glanced at her. "It's not our fault. As I said, if anything, we were a distraction. He had a plan, he has trained men. I think he'll wriggle out of it."

"I hope you're right. How close are we to the compound?"

"Not too far. Who knows? Montalvo may meet us at the gates."

Montalvo didn't meet them at the gates. It was Soldono who came toward them when they stopped the jeep in the courtyard.

"It's evidently not been a stress-free jaunt." Soldono's gaze was fixed on the bullet-splintered windshield. "Is either of you hurt?"

"No." Eve got out of the jeep. "But I don't know about Montalvo and his men. Have you heard from them?"

Soldono shook his head. "But I'm not someone in his confidence. He'd have no reason to report to me. Is there any reason why he shouldn't be?"

"Gunfire." Galen came around the jeep. "That's usually a pretty good sign of trouble, don't you think?"

"Perhaps." He shrugged. "But I can't pretend to be concerned. I've told you how I feel about gang wars, Eve. I don't see why you risked your neck when you should be trying to walk away."

"You don't have to see. It was my decision. Did you check on Joe?"

"Once." He held up his hand as he saw her frown. "It's only been four hours since you left."

"Four hours?" She checked her watch and he was right. It was still hard to believe. Those hours had been crammed so full with tension, it seemed as if days had gone by. "Montalvo estimated six hours."

"He's not always right. He must have built in time for disturbances like the one he ran into." He started up the steps. "I had the cook make a pot of coffee and bring it to the front parlor. I imagine you could use a cup."

"Not now." She sat down on the top step. "I think I'll wait for Montalvo."

Soldono shrugged. "Suit yourself." He disappeared into the house.

"Want company?" Galen asked.

"No, go check on Joe. I'd go myself but I believe he sensed something wrong when I went to see him before I left. He can read me even half knocked out with drugs."

"That doesn't surprise me," he said as he went inside the house.

Her gaze was fastened on the gates. Where the devil was Montalvo? If he hadn't been caught, he shouldn't be that far behind them.

Five minutes passed.

Ten minutes.

Fifteen.

Another ten minutes passed before she heard the roar of the truck engine. Two minutes later the truck and jeep entered the courtyard.

Relief poured through her. She jumped to her feet.

Jesus, the truck looked like it had been through a grenade attack in Iraq. Bullet indentations spiked the doors and hood, the passenger door hung half off its hinges. The jeep driven by Montalvo appeared to be in almost as bad shape.

"What happened?" she asked as Montalvo stopped the jeep and jumped out. "Galen said he heard gunfire."

"We got out of the cemetery and through the

woods to the vehicles okay." He grimaced. "Well, almost okay. We were intercepted by a troop of Diaz's
men and had a few tight minutes. We got out of it,
but they radioed ahead and more were waiting for us
on the road. They followed us into the jungle and we
got out of the vehicles and staged an ambush at the
tower."

"What tower?"

"There's a crumbling ancient tower used for reli-
gious ceremonies by the Chibcha Indians about forty
miles from here. They probably threw down sacri-
fices from the top of the battlements. At any rate, the
windows offer great views for snipers."

"And?"

He shrugged. "We're here, aren't we?" He reached
into the jeep and pulled out a muddy leather con-
tainer. "And we got what we went for. Nalia." He
handed her the box. "She's in your hands now."

Nalia, his wife.

His voice was without expression, as was his face.
No, not quite, she noticed. There was an almost in-
discernible twitch at the corner of his mouth. His
shoulders were squared and tense as if carrying a
burden.

Burden? My God, he had yanked her skull from
the grave with no care, no reverence. How would she
have felt if she'd been forced to do that to her
Bonnie?

"She'll be in very respectful hands," she said

gently. "I'll treat her as if she were my friend. She'll be my friend before this is over."

"Thank you," he said jerkily. He turned on his heel and went into the house.

"It was hard for him." Miguel had gotten out of the jeep and was standing beside her. "It's good that you gave him comfort."

"I only told him the truth." She stared down at the box. "He did it himself, didn't he?"

"Yes. He wouldn't allow anyone else to touch her." He held out his hand. "Would you like me to take the skull to the library for you? The Colonel had me set up your equipment this afternoon. You should be ready to start tomorrow."

She ignored his outstretched hand. For some reason she didn't want to release the skull to anyone else. "I'll start tonight."

His brows rose. "Tonight?"

"Tonight." She started up the steps. "I can do a lot tonight. She's got to be cleaned up and I can start the measuring. Bring me a pot of black coffee."

"You must be very tired. You're not well."

She didn't feel tired. She felt alive and tingling with the excitement and drive of the project ahead. She had a purpose again.

Nalia, we have you safe. We're going to bring you home.

She repeated, "Black coffee."

·   ·   ·

It was three in the morning when Montalvo came into the library. "Go to bed. This isn't necessary."

She didn't look up. "This is what you brought me here for. Now let me do my job."

"I have every intention of doing that. I just don't want to have to pick you up off the floor if you pass out."

"I won't pass out." She arched her back to ease it. "It doesn't happen when I'm working. No matter how bad I feel, it goes away when I'm working."

His lips twisted. "Divine intervention?"

Divine? Bonnie?

"I never rule any help out." She looked back at the reconstruction. "But purpose and determination can also work miracles."

"I don't want miracles from you. Just a good job. Go to bed and get some rest."

"I will. I was almost ready to stop. I just wanted to get her cleaned up and see what I have to work with."

"And what do you have to work with?"

"All the bones are intact. That's a big help. She's Caucasian, a mature woman." She reached down and handed him an object in a small Ziploc bag. "A tooth. There should be a chance for a DNA match if you have any of her intimate belongings. I suppose you couldn't get her father to give you a DNA blood sample?"

"No way on this earth."

"Well, the tooth may be enough for definite proof."

"He'll think I bribed the lab. I'm relying on your reconstruction to break through to him."

"Don't count on it. I'll do the best I can but I'm not perfect." She glanced at him. "And this may not be your wife. What if it's some other woman that Diaz murdered? What if the man who dredged her from that swamp was just trying to score big money?"

"He would have been too scared to betray me."

"He wasn't too scared to bury the skeleton instead of turning it over to you."

His lips set. "It's Nalia."

"Because you want it to be?"

"God, no. I want her to be the crook her father thinks her and basking on a beach somewhere in Australia. I want her *alive*." He started to turn away. "But it was Nalia in that grave."

"We'll find out."

"When? How long?"

"A few days." She paused. "You don't have to come in here while I'm working. I don't need you."

"But I need to know what's happening." He stopped, gazing at her. "Why shouldn't I come? Will I bother you?"

"No, once I end the preliminary measuring I won't even know you're in the room. But it will bother you. Her skull is going to look like a voodoo doll while I'm working on it."

"Christ, you're talking to a man who tore her skull from her skeleton tonight," he said harshly.

"I'm talking to a man who hasn't looked once at his wife's reconstruction since he walked into the room," she said quietly. "And I'm telling you that you don't have to see it again until I've finished. You don't have to go through that pain."

He stood looking at her for a moment. "Is that why you were in such a hurry to clean her up?"

"Maybe." She glanced back at the skull. "And maybe I thought she wouldn't like to be such a mess. I gather she was a very special woman."

"Yes, she was. Beautiful." He cleared his throat. "And very fastidious. What are you calling her? I know you never assume your reconstruction's identity."

"I'll call her Nalia."

"Because you believe me?"

"No, because it seems right to me. If I don't have any photos or descriptions, a name isn't going to throw me off." She wiped her hands on the towel on the workbench. "She'll be what she will be."

"But you do believe me or you wouldn't have started the reconstruction."

"I believe what my eyes saw tonight. You could have embroidered the background story."

"You don't think that."

She wearily shook her head. "No, I don't believe that you told me fairy tales. I hope I'm not wrong."

"I know you won't trust any pat assurances on my part. I guess time will tell." He left the library.

She stood there for a moment, gazing at the skull.

"We're beginning, Nalia," she whispered. "He wants to bring you home. I want to bring you home. What happened to you was terrible but I hope there's peace for you now. There's no peace for him...."

No peace. No end to the anger. No end to the hurt. She knew that chaos of feeling.

But he might have reached the end of his search in this skull before her. She hoped it was true.

"I'll see you in a few hours, Nalia. I have to get some sleep." She started toward the door and then impulsively turned and went back to the dais, grabbed a drop cloth, and tossed it over the reconstruction. "This is his library, Nalia. He'll probably have to be in here for some reason or other. You wouldn't want him to see you until you're at your best."

She moved across the room and turned out the light before closing the door.

Exhaustion hit her like a club. It was always like that once the day's work was completed. The weariness that had been held at bay was released.

Divine intervention.

Strange how Montalvo had used those words that had struck that note and had reminded her of Bonnie, she thought as she started to climb the stairs. Perhaps not so strange. Montalvo and she, who were so different, were on the same plane in some ways. She had felt very close to him in the library.

Mistake.

She was identifying too much with him and it could cloud her judgment. His personality was too strong to ignore and she felt as if she knew him. She was beginning to hurt when she thought of his loss.

She'd reached the top of the stairs, and hesitated. She hadn't meant to go to Joe. She didn't want to wake him because she was feeling disturbed.

Oh, what the devil. She needed him. She'd make sure that her presence didn't bother him. She strode toward the bedroom door and quietly turned the knob. A moment later she was at the bed, crawling in beside him.

"Eve?" he said drowsily.

"Shh." Her arms slid around him. "Go back to sleep. I just wanted to hold you for a while. I won't be here long. Okay?"

"Better than okay..."

Yes, it was better than okay, she thought. It was good and solid and treasure-bright.

Her arms tightened around him. "Yes, it is, Joe."

She was gone. It was as if Eve had never been in this bed with him.

Joe gazed at the indented pillow next to him that was the only evidence that she'd been here. But the memory of her was very clear even through that haze of heavy medications.

And there was something else. A familiar scent

drifting to him from that pillow. Not perfume. Almost acrid and—

"Good morning." Galen came into the room, carrying a tray. "You're awake, I see. I brought your breakfast. Eggs, bacon, toast, and coffee. Lots of protein and enough caffeine to make you get up and walk out of—"

"Where's Eve?"

"Still in bed, I think." He set the tray on the bedside table. "How do you feel?"

"Hazy. No more drugs."

"The doctor says there may still be considerable pain."

"Screw it." He took the coffee Galen handed him. "I want to see Eve."

"I'm not going to wake her up. I'm sure she'll drop in to see you."

"She dropped in to see me twice last night. Both times I was so drugged out I barely knew she was here."

"Did she? How disappointing for you. Eat your breakfast."

Joe's gaze narrowed on the indentation in the pillow next to him. That maddeningly familiar scent was still drifting up to him.

Then he recognized it.

"Shit." His cup crashed down in the saucer. "She's doing the reconstruction."

"You almost broke the cup." Galen rescued the

cup and saucer and put them on the tray. "And such fine china."

"She's doing the reconstruction, isn't she?"

"What makes you think that?"

"The smell of that alcohol on the hand towels she uses. When she's working, it clings to her like a second skin. I've smelled it a thousand times when she's working on a reconstruction. Her pillow is still smelling of it." He picked the pillow up and hurled it violently at Galen. "Now stop bullshitting me and tell me what's happening."

"I didn't bullshit you." He tossed the pillow back on the bed. "I was merely being evasive."

Joe tried to control his temper. "Galen, you're going to either tell me why she smells of—or I'll get up and go ask her myself."

"She wouldn't like that." He dropped down in the chair beside the bed. "And she wouldn't like me to confide in you either. But she deserves it since she tipped her hand by coming to see you and giving away the show."

"What show?"

Galen poured himself a cup of coffee. "Actually, it went off quite successfully. I didn't mean to go along, but it was an interesting…"

The skull was gone.

Diaz started to curse as he stared down at the skeleton.

"It seems Montalvo is on the move," Nekmon said as he shone the flashlight into the grave. "You think the forensic sculptor is still alive?"

"Montalvo wouldn't have come after the skull if he hadn't been sure he had someone to do the reconstruction."

"He took a big risk."

"Evidently not so big," Diaz said sarcastically. "When he invaded my territory and managed to steal this skull in the shadow of my mother's tomb."

Nekmon gazed down at the skeleton. "It's the Armandariz woman?"

"How do I know? She's just a pile of bones. But Montalvo must think she's Nalia Armandariz or he wouldn't have gone to the risk of claiming her skull."

"Can you get DNA from a skull that's been in the swamp for years?"

"I'd bet on it. They're doing all kinds of recovery with DNA lately." He turned away. "But that's not why he wanted the skull. He knows how difficult I could make it for any lab that ran the tests. No, her father is an emotional son of a bitch and Montalvo wants to stir him up against me."

"What do we do?"

"What do you think? We toss dirt into this damned grave and then we go after that skull."

"At his compound? You said it was too well-armed to attack."

"I *want* that skull. I'll do whatever I have to do to get it."

"We'll have to get more men from Bogotá."

"You fool. There's no time. Of course we'll send for more men but we have to move quickly now. He wouldn't have brought that woman down here to cool her heels after he got the skull. She'll be working on giving that skull a face now. We have to buy time." He strode toward the cemetery gates. "No more mistakes. We have to take out Eve Duncan."

Eve was just out of the shower when there was a knock. She threw on a robe and opened the door.

"Quinn knows," Galen said. "You blew it."

"Damn. How?"

"He says you paid him a late-night visit smelling of those alcohol towels you use when you're working on a reconstruction."

"Stupid," she said in self-disgust. "Lord, I was stupid. I should have known he'd recognize that smell. He wasn't that far out of it. He even commented on my body lotion earlier in the evening."

"It wasn't bright," Galen said. "Couldn't you wait until today to see him?"

"Of course I could." She grimaced. "But I didn't want to wait."

"Because you were feeling a little bit as if you'd betrayed him by doing the reconstruction?"

She stiffened. "I'm trying to save his life."

"Very laudable motive." His eyes were narrowed on

her face. "But weren't there a few other reasons why you wanted to do the reconstruction?"

"All right, I wanted it for me too. Montalvo gave me hope and I ran with it. There's nothing wrong with that as long as no one else is hurt. I did everything I could to keep Joe out of it."

"I'll testify to that. But you should have been more devious if you wanted to fool Quinn. Now you've got damage control."

"I'm not good at devious." She nibbled at her lower lip. "How did he take it?"

"He's royally pissed off. What do you expect? He tried to get out of bed and go to see you. Then he got grim and quiet."

She knew that mood. Joe was at his most dangerous when that first anger ebbed away. "I'll go to see him before I go to the library." She turned away. "Thanks for warning me."

"I tried to take some of the flak but he still has plenty of ammunition left for you. I don't blame him. I'd probably feel the same way. You had your reasons and they may have been good ones. But he doesn't like the idea of being protected and he doesn't like being left out."

"Too bad. This is my problem and I won't have him suffering for it. He's already gone through too much."

"But now you have another problem. Keeping him from exploding like a live grenade and blitzing all of us." He started down the hall. "I've already had a little taste of that and I'm not willing to stand still for it again. I'm patient, I'm not a martyr. Fix it, Eve."

Fix it, she thought in exasperation as she tossed on her clothes and ran a brush through her hair. How was she supposed to fix anything when every minute of her time, every iota of her mind, was going to be absorbed by the reconstruction of Nalia Armandariz?

The only thing she could do was be honest with him. She didn't have some sort of magical sticky glue to bond together all the pieces that seemed to be splintering. If she couldn't make him see her point of view, then she had to blast right through the situation in the only way she knew.

Ten minutes later she was opening the door to Joe's room. He was sitting up in bed and his expression was not encouraging.

"I had to do it, Joe," she said quietly.

"That's what I hear from Galen." His tone was cold. "It would have been nice to hear it from you."

"You would have argued with me."

"Considering the length of time we've lived together I believe that's my privilege."

"Maybe." She wearily shook her head. "I'm tired of arguing, Joe. We haven't been doing anything else since this business began. You're not going to change my mind. And evidently I can't change yours either. Stalemate."

"I can't accept that. I *won't* accept it."

"Then you'll have to suck it up and deal with it,"

she said bluntly. "I'm going to do the reconstruction and turn it over to Montalvo. Then I'm going to go home to Atlanta and wait for Montalvo to pay me back. I can't do anything else. I need to see if he'll go through with his promise. I need him to do that, Joe."

"Do you also need Diaz to cut your throat? That's what you're setting yourself up for."

"I'll take the risk. It's worth it to me. I'm close, Joe. I haven't been this close to finding Bonnie for years."

"You're blind."

She smiled shakily. "Possibly. But you've known that for a long time." She turned and opened the door. "I'm not going to change."

"I won't sit back and let you do this. I'm going to get out of this bed and I'm going after Diaz. I don't care what Montalvo is planning for him. He's going down."

She didn't look back at him. "And I'll try to stop you." She tried to steady her voice. "I guess that makes the situation very clear."

"Eve."

She stopped in the act of closing the door. "What?"

"Why did you come to me last night?"

"Why not? I always come to you when I'm hurting." She drew a shaky breath. "But I guess I can't do that anymore."

She shut the door.

Jesus, her eyes were stinging. She wasn't accustomed to Joe being that hard and cold. Not with her. She felt . . . bereft.

"Not a happy visit?"

She looked up to see Montalvo coming down the hall.

"A lousy visit." She cleared her throat to ease it of aching tightness. "I hurt his pride. I hurt him. Sometimes I wonder why he stays with me."

"I don't." He smiled. "And I thought he was not that foolish either. It gives one hope."

"Don't play games, Montalvo. I'm not up to it right now."

"Games are for business, not the personal." He nudged her gently toward the stairs. "Go get something to eat. Miguel is waiting for you. I don't want you to go to the library until you have something in your stomach."

"I'd no intention of not eating. It's painstaking work right now. The end of a reconstruction is a different matter. That's all instinct and flow. . . ."

He nodded and then said quietly, "Thank you for covering the reconstruction last night before you left. It made it easier to go in there this morning." His lips twisted. "I had no idea I was such a coward. I was actually dreading it."

"I know." She started down the stairs. "But you shouldn't. Come to peace with her." She stopped on the landing. "Any word about Diaz?"

"Ripples from my informants in Bogotá. He's calling for reinforcements."

"Attack?"

"Probably."

"Can the CIA help you?"

"Why should they? The CIA considers me as troublesome as Diaz. I'll handle it. What do you want me to do about Quinn?"

She hesitated and then made the decision. "He's going after Diaz. I don't want you to let him do it. Stop him."

His brows rose. "He's not going to like you for asking this."

"Then he'll have to dislike me. I can't have him dead." She continued down the stairs. "If we're lucky, he may be too weak to make a move but I have to take measures in case he tries."

"And I'm the measure?"

"I can't watch him day and night. I'm going to be busy with your Nalia. You keep him safe."

"An exchange of caretaking of one significant other for another?"

"Yes, but my significant other is alive and I want to keep him that way." She saw Miguel hurrying toward her across the hall as she reached the bottom of the steps. "Will you bring me a sandwich and soup right away, please, Miguel? And another pot of black coffee in about two hours."

A few minutes later she was closing the door of the library behind her. The tears were gone but the sadness remained. She had a feeling that the rift that was widening between Joe and her was becoming more frightening with every spoken word.

She moved over to the dais and took off the drop cloth over the reconstruction. "You're causing an awful lot of trouble, Nalia. You remind me of one of those women from the court of Camelot who had all the knights fighting over her. Only I'm one of the knights who are trying to bring you—"

Camelot.

Jane had been talking about Camelot at the art show. Camelot and MacDuff's Run.

Jane.

Panic surged through her. Of course she was okay. Montalvo had promised to protect her family.

Screw it. She needed to talk to Jane, to hear her voice. She reached into her pocket for her phone and dialed Jane's number.

No answer. No voice mail. Nothing.

Keep calm. Try again later.

She turned back to the reconstruction. Concentrate. Don't let nerves keep you from thinking logically. There could be a reason why Jane wasn't—

Her cell phone rang.

No ID.

"Hello."

"I hope Montalvo's paying you well." It was a man's deep voice, the English slightly accented. "Funeral expenses can be exorbitant these days."

"Who is this?"

"But I'll be glad to take care of that for him. You can share the grave with the bones of his wife."

"Diaz?"

"Yes, Ramon Diaz, you bitch. You're playing on the wrong side. Shall I tell you what I'll do to you if you continue to give Montalvo what he wants?"

"I'm not listening to your threats, Diaz."

"You'll listen. I'll keep you around for a week or two to amuse my men. Then I'll kill you, slowly. Very slowly."

"And will you throw me into the swamp as you did Nalia Armandariz? That was pretty stupid. She's come back to haunt you." She kept her voice cool and steady. "I'll haunt you. I'll bring her back and there's nothing you can do about it."

"Oh, but there is something I can do. You lost one daughter. Are you prepared to lose another?"

She went rigid. "What are you talking about?"

"Such a beautiful girl. Not to my taste. I prefer my partners younger and less independent. But there are many whorehouses that specialize in breaking the spirit of the women I send them."

"You can't *touch* Jane. I'll kill you if you lay one hand on her."

"Ah, that frightened you, didn't it? I can always find a way to reach out and get what I want."

"You slimeball."

"You're making me angry. You don't want to do that. Stop what you're doing and go back to your country. Your daughter may survive if you do that right away. Though I don't promise. It's hard to stop when you've set a plan of action in motion." He hung up.

Eve's heart was beating so hard she couldn't get her breath. Her finger was trembling as she pressed the disconnect.

Bastard. Slimy son of a bitch.

Jane.

She dialed Jane's number again.

No answer. No voice mail.

Oh, God.

She hung up and ran to the door.

Miguel was coming toward her carrying a covered tray. "I've brought your food. I hope—"

"Get Montalvo," she said through her teeth. "I want to see him *now*."

Miguel took one look at her expression and set the tray on a chest beside the door. "At once. Is there anything I can do?"

"Just get Montalvo."

He turned and moved swiftly down the hall.

She tried Jane again.

Same result.

Let her be safe. Please, let her be safe.

"What's wrong?" Montalvo was hurrying down the hall toward her. "How can I help?"

"You said you'd protect my family. You promised me."

"Yes, I promised." His gaze was searching her face. "Tell me what's wrong."

"Oh, nothing. Except Diaz said that he was sending my daughter to one of his pet whorehouses."

He stiffened. "He phoned you?"

"Yes. Now tell me that my daughter is safe and that bastard is lying."

"She's safe. He's lying."

She stared him in the eye. "Now prove it. I can't reach her by phone."

He reached in his pocket and drew out his phone and dialed a number. "Montalvo. Let me speak to Jane MacGuire." He handed Eve the phone. "Proof."

"Eve?"

It was undoubtedly Jane's voice. Eve sagged back against the wall. "Thank God. Are you okay, Jane?"

"I'm fine. I'm getting a little stir-crazy. I wish you'd finish up that job and get back here."

"Where are you?"

"Some safe house in Tucson that Venable set up. It's pretty nice and they supplied me with canvases and paints to keep me occupied."

"Venable?"

"Didn't you know he was handling it?"

"No."

Silence. "Are you okay, Eve?"

"I was worried about you."

"I'm fine. But next time you take an internationally sensitive job, I want to go along. I'm bored silly."

"Sorry." She cleared her throat. "I'll be through here as soon as possible. I'll call you. Take care, Jane. I love you."

She hung up the phone and turned to Montalvo. "The CIA?"

He nodded. "I made a deal with them."

"What kind of deal?"

"I promised Venable I wouldn't sell weapons to a certain dictator on his hit list. He promised me they'd keep your daughter and mother safe. Would you like to call your mother? She's in a safe house in Griffin, Georgia."

"How did Venable persuade them to go underground?"

"They love you. He told them it would be safer for you if they were safe."

"How long have they been in safe houses?"

"Since the night Quinn and you were shot. I decided it would be better to take precautions."

"Why the CIA?"

"You'd trust them. Your daughter and mother would trust them." He shrugged. "I don't particularly trust them, but I have my own people watching the houses. And I do trust them."

"Why couldn't I reach her cell phone?"

"Venable didn't want to risk having her phone traced. I'll give you the number of the safe house. Satisfied?"

She nodded slowly. "I was frightened."

His lips tightened. "That's what Diaz wanted. What else did he say?"

"That if I didn't stop working on the reconstruction, he'd make sure I shared a grave with Nalia

Armandariz. After suitable pain and degradation, of course."

"Of course." His gaze narrowed on her face. "That's enough to frighten anyone. Did he convince you?"

"He convinced me that I'd better finish this job quickly. I want that son of a bitch to go down. He's threatening people I love." She turned and started back into the library. "Now leave me alone so that I can start to work."

"In a moment." He picked up the tray Miguel had shoved hurriedly on the chest and carried it into the library. He set it on the table by the leather couch. "Miguel was very upset when you summoned me with such grimness. He'll feel much better if he picks up an empty tray a little later. Won't you oblige him?"

She nodded. "I told you, I'll eat. I'll take care of myself. It's part of the job."

He smiled faintly. "See that you do that part as well as you do the reconstruction." He turned toward the door. "Call me if you need me."

She sat down and took the cover off the tray. "I believe I've demonstrated I'm not in the least hesitant about that."

She heard him chuckle as he left the library.

11

"We can't find Jane MacGuire," Nekmon said when he came into the office. "She disappeared from her hotel in Phoenix a few nights ago."

Diaz muttered a curse. The response he'd gotten from Eve Duncan last night on the threat to her adopted daughter had been the strongest lead he'd had. Montalvo had probably known of that weakness and hurried to reinforce his position. "Find her."

"We're looking." Nekmon paused. "Sendak is here."

"He brought it?" Diaz asked.

"He says he has." Nekmon shifted uncomfortably. "I didn't verify."

Diaz smiled maliciously. "Coward."

"Shall I send him in?"

"By all means." He leaned back in his chair with a tingle of anticipation. Jane MacGuire wasn't the only arrow to his bow. Eve Duncan was sitting behind those high walls thinking she was safe. She would never be safe.

Montalvo would learn Diaz wasn't to be stopped.

The next evening Galen met Eve in the hall when she was going upstairs to shower and have dinner before she came back down to work.

"You've emerged from your cave at last," he said. "Miguel hasn't let anyone in to see you all day."

"I didn't tell him to do that. But I'm grateful that I wasn't interrupted. It's essential that I concentrate to get all the measurements exactly right."

"Have you seen Quinn today?"

"No." She looked away from him. "We agreed to disagree and I don't feel welcome to just drop in. I checked with Miguel and he said he had a good night."

Galen gave a low whistle. "I thought that Quinn had been prodded to move at top speed."

"Is he?"

"He was on his feet this morning and again this afternoon. Before dinner he sat in the chair by his window quizzing me on the details of Diaz's setup."

"And you told him?"

"He'd find out with or without me. I'd rather he have accurate information."

So would Eve, but the news that Joe was beginning

to move at his customary top speed was filling her with panic. "How long do I have?"

"With any other man I'd say maybe four days. With Quinn . . ." He shrugged. "Like I said, he's motivated. How's the reconstruction coming?"

"Not fast enough, evidently. I'll have to put in longer hours."

"It sounds to me as if you're overdoing it now. How much sleep did you get last night?"

"I don't know. Four, maybe five hours. Enough."

"You said you had to be absolutely accurate. You have to have a clear head for—"

"I have a clear head, dammit. What do you expect me to do? Get a solid eight hours of sleep when Joe could—" She stopped and drew a deep breath. "I'll sleep when Nalia's finished." She started up the stairs. "Now let me get cleaned up and eat. I need to get back and start working."

Christ, Joe on his feet. Joe gaining more strength by the hour. Lord, it was ironic that ordinarily she would have been overjoyed at his progress. Not now. She had to worry about him pushing himself too hard and having a relapse. On the other hand she was in a panic that he'd be able to take action before she was finished with the reconstruction.

He wouldn't be able to do the latter if she kept working at lightning speed, she assured herself. She'd allow herself the minimum rest and give Montalvo his evidence before Joe got his chance at Diaz.

"I wanted to see you, Eve." Soldono rose from the bench opposite her room. "And Miguel wouldn't let me into the library."

"Miguel must have been very persuasive. Evidently there must have been a queue outside the door."

"If you can call a gun persuasive."

She stared at him in disbelief. "He pulled a gun on you?"

"No. He only glanced down at that gun he has in his holster and said he was ordered to use any means to keep you from being disturbed."

"He was bluffing."

"I've seen him in action. I wasn't going to call his bluff." He continued on, "I just wanted to tell you that I think I've found a source to get you away from the compound when you say the word." He made a face. "I just wish I'd been able to tap that source when Montalvo was holding Gonzales. It might have prevented all this mess."

"I don't deal in might-have-beens, Soldono. It didn't happen and I'm walking another path now." She opened her bedroom door. "And as long as Montalvo keeps his word about keeping my family safe, I'll finish the reconstruction and hand it to him wrapped up in pink ribbons. So far Venable seems to be doing a good job."

"Venable?"

"You didn't know Venable made a deal with Montalvo to protect Jane and my mom?"

"He's my boss and he often doesn't share every aspect of his cases with me. I'm just a peon." He shook his head admiringly. "That crafty bastard. Montalvo had every base covered, didn't he?" He turned away. "If you change your mind, let me know. Try to give me a little notice. It may take a bit of doing."

"I can't see that giving notice will be an option if I have to leave in a hurry." She shut the door behind her.

Don't think about Joe.

Don't try to second-guess the decision she'd made because Soldono had found a way out.

Just focus, move quickly, and get the reconstruction done.

Ten minutes later she was out of the shower and dressing hurriedly.

Call Jane and talk to her before she went down?

No, she'd called Jane and her mother this morning before she'd started work. Everything was fine and they'd only worry if she acted too anxious. She'd eat something and then get back to work.

Miguel was on guard in front of the library when she reached it. "Good evening." His smile was sunny. "I have a steak waiting to go under the broiler. How do you like it?"

"Medium well-done." She opened the door. "And you seem to have done a little roasting of my friends today as well."

"No threats. Just implications. I didn't have to do that with Galen. He understood."

"I'm sure he did."

"And I let them talk to you after you came out of the library." He turned away. "Please don't get too involved with your work before I have a chance to bring you your steak."

She smiled faintly as she watched him hurry away. Miguel was a strange and fascinating individual and she was growing to like him more every day. She closed the door and turned on the lamp. Darkness had fallen since she'd left the room a short time ago. She moved over to stand before the dais. She'd draped the reconstruction with the black drop cloth as she always did when she left the library. She reached up to take it off the skull. Montalvo had not mentioned the practice after that first time but it only took her a second and if it held his pain at bay then it was worth—

Teeth sinking into the cloth.

Brown triangular head lunging at her.

She jumped back and dropped the cloth.

The snake turned and launched itself at her.

It missed her by an inch.

The snake launched again.

Kill it. Kill it. Kill it.

She ran across the room, grabbed the brass lamp, and hurled it at the snake.

The shade hit the snake but it kept gliding toward her.

She darted toward the door.

It was thrown open before she reached it.

Montalvo took one quick look at the serpent and shoved her aside. "Jesus."

The snake sprang toward Montalvo.

He shot it in the head.

"My God." He was breathing hard as he stared down at the snake. "Damn close."

"He kept coming. He just kept coming." She was shaking uncontrollably. "He was under the drop cloth with the reconstruction. He sprang at—"

"Did he bite you?"

"I don't think so. I didn't feel—"

"Don't think. Tell me." He grabbed her arms and looked closely at each of them. "I don't see any marks."

"He bit into the cloth. I . . . dropped it." She shook her head dazedly. "But he didn't stop. I've never . . . He kept coming at me."

"They can be very aggressive."

"Ugly. I . . . don't like snakes."

"It's over. Stop shaking."

"Soon. I can't seem to—"

"God." He pulled her into his arms and held her. "It's okay. Don't fight me. I didn't want to do this. It could interfere." He rocked her back and forth. "But I can't stand you—"

His body was warm and strong and she clung instinctively to that strength. "I'm sorry," she whispered. "I wasn't expecting that to—it frightened me."

"It should have frightened you." He stroked her

hair with rough gentleness. "Shh, it's going to be fine. Nothing's going to hurt you. I won't let it."

She didn't move for a few moments. It was good to stay here and share his strength. She'd move soon. She'd just give herself a short time to get over the shock of those dark frantic minutes.

"What happened here?" Miguel was standing in the doorway and staring at the remains of the snake on the floor. "Another emergency? I'm beginning to think you'll do anything to avoid eating one of my meals."

She stepped back out of Montalvo's arms. "I guarantee I wouldn't go to these lengths." She tried to steady her voice. "Would you please . . . get rid of it? I don't believe I can concentrate with that . . . thing lying there."

"Of course." Miguel was studying the snake. "What is it, Colonel? I don't recognize it. You could have left the head so that I—"

"No, I couldn't. It was a black mamba."

Miguel shook his head. "I don't think so. They're not common to this area."

"Exactly."

"Mamba," Eve repeated. She knew she had read about them somewhere but she couldn't remember any details. "Poisonous."

"Extremely." Montalvo said to Miguel, "Search the room and make sure it didn't bring a friend. Be careful."

"Don't worry. I want to live to a ripe old age." He smiled slyly. "Like you, Colonel."

"You won't live another year if you keep jabbing at me." He pulled Eve out into the hall. "Stay here until he's finished. I don't believe there's another one but it doesn't hurt to check."

"I'm not arguing. I can wait." She tried to stop shivering. "I wouldn't want to run into another snake like that again anytime soon."

"I'll see that you don't. After Miguel finishes the library, I'll send him up to your bedroom."

She moistened her lips. "I take it you don't think this was a stray serpent that wandered in from the jungle."

"The odds are astronomical against it. Mambas are found almost exclusively in Africa. We have poisonous snakes here, but not anything as deadly as the black mamba."

"It's not black, it was sort of brown-gray."

"The inside of its mouth is black. I'm surprised you didn't notice."

"I wasn't color-oriented at that moment. Just how deadly is it?"

"It's the most dangerous snake in the world. If given a chance, it will slither away, but if it feels it's cornered, it will strike over and over. When you pulled off the cloth, it felt under attack. You were almost face-to-face with him. Its venom attacks the respiratory system and is almost a hundred percent fatal unless you can quickly get to a hospital that has the antivenin."

"Jesus," she whispered. "How does anyone survive a bite from one of them?"

"Most people don't. Particularly if they're bitten on the throat or anywhere on the upper body. The poison is closer to the vital organs and travels fast. Too fast to get to medical help that might save them." His eyes were narrowed on her face. "You're still pale. Sit down." He pushed her into a chair by the door. "I'll get you a drink."

"Coffee. Just coffee." She leaned back in the chair. "That snake should have struck my upper body. He was almost on a level with me. He must have been curled beneath the reconstruction." She shuddered as she remembered that triangular head darting toward her. "I didn't know I put my arm up to protect myself but that might have saved me. I had the drop cloth in my hand..."

"And the mamba bit into the cloth instead of you." He handed her the coffee. "Thank God."

She felt like echoing that sentiment. "How did it get there? The French doors?"

"Probably. But not under its own steam. Someone carried it into the library and placed it under the drop cloth."

"One of Diaz's men?"

He shook his head. "My security is too tight to permit one of his men to wander in out of the jungle and drop off a package like that."

"It happened."

"Not that simply. It stinks of a payoff."

"He bribed one of your men?"

"I hope I'm wrong." His expression was grim. "I don't believe I am. I can't see any other explanation."

"No other snakes." Miguel came out of the library. "The mamba was very large, over fourteen feet and probably carrying a big load of venom. Sendak?"

"I'd bet on it. He delivered the snake to Diaz's mole inside the compound to be tucked under the drop cloth."

"Who's Sendak?" Eve asked.

"An Ethiopian who sells his serpents for very high sums. I've run into him a few times over the years. One of his little friends killed a customer who was proving difficult for a rival of Diaz's. I'm sure Diaz was intrigued by the possibilities."

"I'll go up and check her bedroom," Miguel said as he started for the stairs. "We wouldn't want her to have a strange, exotic bedmate."

"No, we wouldn't want that." Montalvo's intent gaze was on her face. "You're frightened. That's what he wanted. He meant you to feel unsure of my ability to protect you."

"A mamba hurling itself at my throat would have a tendency to do that," she said dryly.

"How badly are you frightened? What's my damage-control ratio going to have to be?"

"You're impossible." She got to her feet. "Screw your damage control. I don't like snakes attacking me but I'm not going to be scared off by Diaz. You take care of my family and you find the snake charmer who put that mamba under that cloth with Nalia. I'll handle my part."

"I'm sure you will." A faint smile indented his lips. "And you can be sure that I'll know who the Judas is in my camp in short order. He won't bother you again."

That last sentence had an ominous ring. "I didn't tell you to kill him. I just want to be able to keep on working with no threat hovering over me."

"I can't promise you that will happen anytime soon. There will be a threat until Diaz is gone."

"Montalvo."

"Yes."

"You know what I said about how ridiculous you were to wear a gun in the house?"

He nodded.

"Erase it from your memory. I was damn glad you were wearing it tonight."

"So was I." He turned and walked away from her.

She drew a deep breath, braced herself, and went back into the library.

Everything in the room was as neat and orderly as if the incident had never happened, she noticed. Miguel had been busy. The remains of the snake had vanished. The lamp she had thrown at the serpent was back on the desk. Even the drop cloth had been whisked away.

She went over to the dais and gazed at Nalia.

Coffin-shaped, triangular head lunging toward her.

She tensed and instinctively took a step back. Christ, she couldn't work with that memory hanging over her.

All right, play it over so that it couldn't sneak up on her. She closed her eyes. Black mamba striking at her. The drop cloth falling from her hand. The lamp hurling through the air. The snake coming. Coming. Coming. Montalvo shooting the snake. The snake was dead. Nothing to fear. Nothing to fear.

Gradually the panic faded away and she opened her eyes. It might return but not with the same force. "It's gone, Nalia. We worked our way through it. But you'll have to help me keep it from coming back."

Get to work. Do your job. She examined the work she'd done that day. She couldn't see that any of the depth markers had been disturbed by the snake but she'd have to recheck them to make sure they were still accurate.

"Okay, here we go again," she murmured. "It was ugly using you that way. You had enough ugly things happen to you. You didn't need this."

She carefully began to measure.

"I hear you had a nocturnal visitor," Galen said when she came down the stairs the next morning. His expression was sober. "You were lucky. I ran into one of those snakes in Africa while I was on a job once. Nasty."

"I hope you don't mean that literally. If you did, Montalvo was lying about how deadly they are."

"He's not lying. The mamba slid into one of my men's bedroll. It bit him in the throat. He didn't have a chance."

"It didn't happen to me. I don't want to think about it any more." A sudden thought occurred to her. "How did you find out?"

"Miguel. He told Soldono and me last night after he searched your room. He thought we should check out our own rooms in case you weren't the only target."

"Does Joe know?"

He shook his head. "I didn't want to drive him nuts. I searched his room myself after he went to sleep. He's having enough problems getting himself in shape without having that to goad him on."

"How is he?"

"Why don't you go and see for yourself?"

"So that we could argue? No thanks. I'm having enough trouble concentrating."

"I wonder why. I don't imagine it's every day you have a black mamba popping out of one of your re-constructions."

And he didn't even know about Diaz's threat to Jane, she remembered. "No, it's not a common occurrence."

"Have you had breakfast? I thought I'd grab a bite before I took a tray up to Quinn."

"Miguel brought a tray to my room." She smiled

faintly. "He said that it seemed the only way he was sure I'd eat something."

Galen gazed at her appraisingly. "You do look a little fine-drawn. Are you sleeping enough?"

She'd gotten three hours last night. She'd been on edge and excited and her mind wouldn't stop functioning. "Enough. I can sleep later." She started down the hall toward the library. "She won't let me sleep right now. I'm getting too close."

"'She'?"

"The work. The reconstruction."

"It sounded much more intimate."

"I feel intimate when I'm working on a skull. It's a human being, for God's sake."

"How close are you?"

"I should start the finish work either tonight or tomorrow." She stopped at the door of the library. "Can you keep Joe from making a move until then?"

"I'll try. No promises."

"It's only one more day."

"But you never can tell when you're going to run into another pesky reptile. That could cause a delay."

"Montalvo says that there won't be any more problems. He promised that he'd find out which one of his men took a bribe to bring the snake to the library."

"I'm sure he's doing everything he can. Miguel said Montalvo was going to work all night going over the personnel records and trying to discern the weak links. Everything will be fine if he can isolate the snake he took to his bosom." He smiled. "Did you ever realize how many phrases there are that pertain to snakes? Our culture seems to be obsessed with them."

And she wasn't sure she'd ever hear one of those phrases without remembering that moment when the mamba had lunged toward her. "I'd just as soon ignore them from now on."

"I can understand that." Galen turned and headed for the breakfast room. "But Montalvo won't be ignoring what happened and neither will Quinn if he finds out."

She didn't want Montalvo to ignore the incident, she thought as she opened the door. She wanted protection from interruption during this critical stage in the reconstruction and it was his job to give it to her. But she hoped to God that Joe wasn't told about what had happened. Joe was the—

She stopped.

Montalvo was sitting in the desk chair, staring at the reconstruction. "Good morning, Eve." He didn't take his gaze from the skull. "It's exceptionally gruesome, isn't it?"

"Not really. But I suppose it appears that way to most people."

His lips twisted. "But I'm not most people, am I? I loved her. I've spent years trying to avenge her. Yet I look at...this and I can't muster any tenderness. It looks like the cover of a horror DVD."

"If she were alive and horribly scarred, would you feel like that?"

"No."

"It's the same. She's not with us any longer but your memory of her is here. A reconstruction isn't pretty during the initial stages. That's why I didn't want you to see it until the end. I didn't have a drop cloth or I would have covered it last night."

"I told Miguel not to give you another one."

"Why would you—" Then she understood. "The snake. You thought that every time I took it off her that I'd remember the snake."

"A natural reaction. You didn't need the drop cloth. I did. So I thought I'd come in and meet her face-to-face again."

"You're not meeting her. You don't understand her. This isn't who she is." She sat down on the edge of the desk and stared at Nalia. "Let me explain her to you. Those little sticks that make her look like a voodoo doll are tissue-depth markers. There are more than twenty points on the skull for which there are known tissue depths. There are anthropological charts that give a specific measurement for each point of a Caucasian woman of average weight. After I have the tissue depths right, I take strips of plasticine and apply them between the markers, then build up to all the tissue-depth points." She delicately touched the nasal cavity. "The nose is always very difficult. I have to make sure the measurements are precise on the nasal spine and the opening. They dictate everything, the length, the angle of the nose. But it's all there if you work hard enough. The bones tell us what we need to know if we listen. *She's* telling us, Montalvo. There's nothing horrible about her. She's the woman you loved. We just have to strip away the veil."

"And then what happens after you finish measuring?"

Her gaze shifted to see that his intent stare was no longer on the skull but on her own face.

"Then I start the final phase, the actual sculpting. That's when instinct takes over from intellect."

He was silent a moment. "I'd like to be here when you reach that point. If you don't mind."

"I don't mind. I probably wouldn't know if you were in the room. But don't expect me to let you know. Sometimes it doesn't work that way."

"You just go with the flow?"

"That sounds very pleasant and lazy. This particular flow is more like a lava flow after a volcano eruption."

He stood up. "I'll let you get to work." He smiled. "I'll check in on you periodically and gauge your lava output." He headed for the door. "Thank you, Eve."

"For a lecture on forensic sculpting?"

"No, for trying to make what she's become easier for me."

"And did I do it?"

"Yes. I'm not big on spirituality. I've always lived in the physical world and I had to come to terms with this." He said quietly, "You're a very special woman, Eve."

"Damn right." She got up to stand before the reconstruction and checked the mid-therum marker. "But you're better at snake demolition."

"It's amazing she's able to continue working," Miguel said as he met Montalvo in the hall. "Nerves of steel."

"No. She's frightened but she has a purpose," Montalvo said. "And that will keep her going no matter what happens." He strode down the hall. "But I'm not going to have her contend with anything more than finishing that reconstruction. That snake incident shouldn't have happened."

"I'm sorry. I'll make no excuses."

"For God's sake, I'm not blaming you. You're not responsible for everything that goes wrong in the compound."

"What a relief. Not even the stopped-up toilet in the armory?"

"Miguel."

He smiled. "A little humor."

"Very little. Have you gathered the names of any of the possibles who might have been bought by Diaz?"

"Fascquelo, Ramierez, Gomez, and Destando. All of them are comparatively new men with you. They seemed all right when we took them on and I've no proof they're not." He paused. "I'm leaning toward

Destando. He plays a lot of poker in the barracks and he owes money. He's never talked against you but he's surly."

"I can't shoot him for that. Find me proof."

"I'll work very hard on doing that." He looked back at the closed door of the library. "I, too, believe in the power of purpose, Colonel."

"Sendak's mamba didn't kill her," Nekmon said. "She still managed to work last night. Our man in his camp says she may be getting close."

"If he managed to get close enough to plant the serpent, then he should be close enough to kill the bitch. I paid him enough."

"You didn't pay him enough to stop him from being frightened."

"He wasn't too frightened to slip the snake into the library." Diaz added sarcastically, "You wouldn't even look in the cage when Sendak had it here."

"I don't like snakes," Nekmon said. "And taking overt action is different. Montalvo has her guarded every moment of the day. No one is going to be able to walk up and shoot her."

"Poison?"

"Miguel Vicente prepares her meals."

Diaz muttered a curse. "If Duarte hadn't blundered, she would have been dead and we wouldn't be having this problem. Luck has been on Montalvo's side since this began."

"Luck can change. All we need is an opening," Nekmon said. "I've called Phoenix and they say that they're questioning the local hotel people. Jane MacGuire can't have just disappeared into the sunset. Someone must have seen the car. Perhaps gotten a license number. All I need is a number and we can call that senator you have in your pocket and ask him to send a tracer through the highway patrol and try to locate the car."

"In the meantime Eve Duncan finishes the reconstruction."

"Not necessarily. The parking garage has video cameras. If they used the garage, we may have her. I have someone working on that angle right now." His lips tightened. "It's much cleaner and more efficient than using that African snake shaman. I knew it wouldn't work."

"It could have worked." Diaz scowled. "And I dislike people who tell me 'I told you so.' You might remember that, Nekmon."

"No offense. Shall I continue hunting for Jane MacGuire?"

"Of course. Do everything you can," Diaz said. "I'm getting very tired of being bested by that son of a bitch. I think I'll have to make an example of Jane MacGuire to show the Duncan woman who has the power here."

"An excellent idea. As you wish."

"You're damned right. Everything is as I wish. That's as it should be." He went to the window and gazed down at the cemetery in the village. The moonlight was glimmering on the tomb where his mother was buried. What a fool she had been. She had never understood how special he was. From the time he was a small child she had told him to listen to the priests, to be humble and he would grow in stature and glory. She didn't understand a man had to grab both for himself. He would have made a queen of her if she'd realized that his destiny was not to be trifled with. Instead, she had betrayed and tried to destroy him.

And he'd had to destroy her.

You see, Mother? I'm a king now and I take whatever I wish. I kill who I wish. I'm above the priests, above your God.

And I'm alive and you're dead and moldering in the earth.

"You're smiling," Nekmon said. "Did I miss something?"

"I was just wondering when I get my hands on Eve Duncan if I should make her do a reconstruction of my dear mother. Do you think my sweet *madre*'s skull would be a nice decoration for my desk?"

12

She heard the door of the library open and then close but she didn't look up from the reconstruction. "I'm still doing the basic work, Montalvo. I won't be ready for the final for another few hours. You're wasting your time."

"I have time to waste."

Joe.

She whirled to see Joe carefully seating himself in the chair next to the door. He was fully dressed in khakis and a dark shirt. He appeared thinner and he was pale but other than that he looked almost normal. "What are you doing out of bed?"

"It was time." His jaw tightened. "Past time. It was my first journey and I made it. Though those stairs were a bitch."

"They'll be worse going up."

"Then I'll have your guard dog outside give me a hand. All I needed to know was that I could make it."

"You should be in bed."

"And you should be at home doing reconstructions for local police departments. Neither of us are doing what we're supposed to do. So we're canceling each other out." His gaze fastened on the reconstruction. "It's going fast. She's not difficult?"

"Not so far."

"And you believe she's Montalvo's wife?"

"You know I don't allow myself to believe anything. She could be Nalia."

"What if she's not? Are you going to stay here until he finds another skull, and then another?"

"I haven't thought that far ahead."

"Because you want her to be Nalia Armandariz. She's the key to all your dreams." He pushed himself forward and then with difficulty started to pull himself up out of the chair.

She instinctively moved forward to help him but was stopped by his sharp "No!"

She kept coming but halted in shock at the icy glance he gave her. "Let me help, Joe."

"I have to do it myself." He pulled himself to his feet. "This afternoon will be better. Tomorrow I'll be almost well."

"Bullshit."

"Your confidence is inspiring."

"You're a stubborn asshole and you're scaring me to death."

"Not enough to get you out of here."

"I need to finish this—"

"Is everything okay?" Montalvo had come into the library and was staring warily at Joe. "Miguel was concerned when he saw you come into the library, Quinn. You didn't look well."

"But he didn't try to stop me. I understand from Galen that he's the guardian at the gates."

"Naturally he wouldn't attempt to do anything that would hurt you."

"Because I'm not able to defend myself?"

Montalvo smiled. "He wouldn't make that mistake. As I said, he was just concerned." He turned to Eve. "You look worried. Is there anything I can do to help?"

"No."

"Then I'll leave." He met and held her gaze. "But you know that you only have to tell me and it will be done."

She nodded jerkily. "I know that." Her glance shifted back to Joe and she found his narrowed eyes going from her to Montalvo and back again. "Joe and I will work out our own problems."

"Certainly. I only thought I'd offer." Montalvo turned and headed for the door. "Call me if you change your mind."

"Yes, I'm sure she will," Joe murmured as the door closed behind Montalvo. He moved toward the door. "I'll let you get back to work. I wouldn't want to disturb you."

"You did disturb me. How could I help but be disturbed? You scare me, Joe."

"Good. At least, you don't pity me. That would drive me nuts."

She flinched as the door slammed behind him. His response had been every bit as volatile as she'd known it would be. He was walking on the edge and might fall off at any step. She had ached to help him, soothe him, but the price was too high. She would have had to give up her chance for Bonnie.

She turned and went back to the dais. The only way she could help either one of them was to finish the reconstruction and move on. If she worked fast enough, she might be able to save them both before their relationship became tattered beyond repair.

"We're going to go for the big prize soon, Nalia," she whispered. "I'm getting ready for it and I hope you are. I'm going to need your help...."

"Need a shoulder to lean on?" Galen was standing at the bottom of the staircase when Joe came out of the library. "That's a lot of stairs for a crotchety bloke like—" He broke off and gave a low whistle. "Just joking, man."

"It wasn't funny," Joe said through his teeth. "I *won't* be helpless. I won't be weak." He started up the staircase, clinging to the banister with one hand. "And I can make it up by myself."

"Whatever." Galen was slowly climbing the stairs beside him. "But if you don't mind, I think I'll come along to pick up the pieces if your legs give out."

"They won't give out."

"I believe you. Whatever happened in that library gave you a massive shot of adrenaline."

"You bet it did."

"I saw Montalvo come out before you. Did you argue with him?"

"Hell, no. He's too clever to quarrel with an injured man." He didn't look at Galen as he said between his teeth, "Why didn't you tell me he was trying to get Eve into bed?"

"Is he?"

"Don't give me that bullshit. You notice everything. There's something going on between them that a blind man could see."

"I haven't seen them together very much."

And Joe wished he hadn't seen that last interchange of glances between Montalvo and Eve. It had not only been full of understanding but also intimacy. No, it was good that he had seen what was happening even if it hurt. Eve would never be unfaithful to him because of a sexual attraction. With Eve it would have to involve all the emotions and it hadn't reached that point with Montalvo yet.

But, my God, they were on their way.

She might not even realize that she was circling toward Montalvo like a moth to a flame. They shared a common tragedy and the desire to find a way to bring closure to their lives. It was a strong bond and would open other facets, other doors of a relationship. Christ, he thought with disgust, he had it all figured out. Except how to stop it.

He had reached the top of the stairs. As Galen had said, the adrenaline had been coursing and he'd scarcely paid attention to the weakness and pain. That's how he had to function from now on. Ignore the weakness. Ignore the pain. Montalvo was strong and well and Joe had to be on equal ground. Pity might temporarily hold Eve, but that wasn't going to happen. He wouldn't be able to go on patching a relationship with that kind of Band-Aid.

"Do you need help to get to bed?" Galen asked.

"No, I'll do it myself." He paused at the door. "But I might need help from you later. Can I count on you?"

Galen was silent a moment. "If you can prove to me that you have a plan that will work. I'm not into suicide missions."

"Neither am I." He opened the door. "I'm not trying to make a grandiose statement. I want to take Diaz out and not give Eve any reason to stay here one minute longer."

"I brought your dinner." Montalvo came into the library and set the tray down on the desk. "If you choose to take the time."

"I'll take the time." Eve wiped her hands on a damp alcohol towel. Choice. Joe would have dug in his heels and insisted she break for a meal. Montalvo had put the decision in her court. Perhaps because he really wanted her to continue to work and the meal was a token goodwill gesture. "I don't know long it will be until I get around to eating again."

He sat down across from her. "The reconstruction doesn't look much closer to completion than the last time I saw it."

"She's closer." Eve bit into her sandwich. "And what's even more important, I'm closer. I'm almost ready to begin."

He glanced away from her. "I was afraid that disturbing visit from Quinn might slow you down. Did I interrupt anything?"

"Nothing important. We weren't covering any new ground." She made a face. "I was almost glad you came."

"You wanted to get rid of him."

"No," she said instantly. "Never. I just had to get back to work and I was beginning to—" She sighed. "I can't get through to him. He thinks I've gone off the deep end and wants to save me from myself."

"Perfectly logical." He smiled. "You have gone off the deep end. I pushed you there. But I'll also be the one to save you if you need saving."

"Joe wouldn't like that."

"How regrettable. Try that lemon pastry. You'll need the sugar for energy. It may be a long night."

She chuckled as she took a bite of the pastry. "Lord, you and Joe are different. He'd tell me to eat a hearty meal and go off to bed. You want me wide

awake and alert so that I can finish your reconstruction."

"That's right. I'm a selfish bastard." His smile
faded. "But it's what you want too. Remember, I told
you that when I look at you, it's like looking in a mirror? That hasn't changed. The only reason I can read
you is that I've seen you shining in the darkness of
my mind."

"Darkness?"

"We're both creatures of the dark right now. We
come out into the sunlight occasionally but then
we're drawn back."

She grimaced. "You talk as if we're a couple of
vampires. Speak for yourself, Montalvo."

"Not vampires. But we're closer to the dead than
the living. That's all we think about, all we care
about. If that weren't true, you wouldn't be here." He
paused. "And you wouldn't have wanted to send
Quinn away from you."

"I didn't want to send Joe away."

"Yes, you did. He represents the sunlit, normal
part of your life. But he has no role when you're involved with the darkness."

"You're wrong. Joe always has a role in my life."

"Think about it."

She didn't want to think about it. His words were
striking a note that made her uneasy. "Screw your
darkness. That's not what I want from my life."

"Yet that's what you chose. And I made the same
choice. In the best of all possible worlds, it's not a

choice I would have made." He shrugged. "Perhaps someday I'll be able to walk away from it."

"And yet you don't hold out the same hope for me."

"Oh, but I do. You have all my hopes for coming out of the dark." He was holding her gaze with mesmerizing intensity. "If I get there first, I'll hold out my hand and help you out."

"Thanks." She couldn't seem to look away from him. "But I don't need your help. I do very well on my own."

"On your own. I notice you don't mention Quinn."

"I'm an independent woman. Joe is not my keeper."

He didn't answer. He just sat there looking at her.

"Stop it. This conversation is absurd."

"Are you afraid I'm hitting too close?" He leaned forward. "Darkness doesn't have to be terrifying, Eve. There are all kinds of wonderful things that happen at night. It's the time when most births occur. Everything appears sharper, more exciting. Yet it blurs reality and makes it bearable." He paused. "And it's the time for passion."

He was sitting there relaxed in the easy chair with the light from the lamp pooling over him. He was talking about darkness yet the warm glow of life seemed to surround him. The intimacy in the room was almost unbearable in intensity. She had a sudden impulse to reach out and touch him.

"No." He was reading her expression. "I feel the

same way but it's better that we wait. I want you, but I want you with no regrets."

Shock rippled through her. Jesus, she had been feeling, not thinking. She tore her gaze away from him. "It's not you. I'm always at an emotional high at this point in a reconstruction."

"I see." He smiled faintly. "Remind me to be sure to be around whenever you reach that point. It appears to be eminently rewarding."

"And there would be regrets. I don't do one-night stands."

"Do you think I don't know that? That's one of the problems. It would be much simpler if you could compartmentalize."

"As you seem to be doing."

"I only live in the past part of the time. Sometimes something so good comes along that you have to stop and let it happen." His smile faded. "And I don't mean sex. Sex can be had anywhere. The moment I started studying you I realized that you were going to be something special in my life."

She nodded. "I was going to be the woman who brought your wife home."

"Yes. Was that a slap on the knuckles? I loved my wife. I'll probably love her for the rest of my life. She was joy. The first love of my life. Before Nalia there were only sexual encounters. She taught me the difference. Nalia would be the first to tell me to find that joy wherever I could. What are you going to be in my life? I don't know. But I want to find out. I have an idea it could be earthshaking." He stood up. "I'll leave you now. You did quite a good job with that meal. Though I imagine you didn't even realize you were eating it. May I still come back while you're working on Nalia?"

"As I told you, I probably won't even know you're in the room."

"The ultimate insult for a man. Yet I wouldn't have it any other way." He headed for the door. "Bring her home and I might someday find that sunlight we were talking about."

"Montalvo." When he looked over his shoulder she said, "I love Joe. Whatever I feel for anyone else, that won't change."

"I know. But there are always degrees of feeling. Sometimes emotion changes from moment to moment, hour to hour, year to year. If I haven't learned anything else in these last years, I've acquired patience. We'll see how it goes." He left before she could reply.

Bizarre. Those last moments had been like something from an opium dream. Hazy, soft-focused, sensual, and yet with flashes of hard reality and truth. Darkness and sunlight.

Was he right? Could it be the reason she had been drifting away from Joe was because he wasn't part of the darkness? He lacked that final understanding that no one but someone who had experienced that loss would have.

She didn't know, she thought wearily, as she rose

to her feet. Maybe she was just as damaged as she'd told Joe. Perhaps she was tired of having him suffer for her sake. Maybe she was looking for a way to free him.

And maybe she was lusting after that sexy son of a bitch who had all the appeal of the new and the mysterious. He was like the Phantom of the Opera with all his talk of darkness. He was the Beast who lured Beauty back to his castle. He was a challenge to be met. An experience to be tasted.

And a betrayal to be enacted.

It wasn't going to happen.

She moved across the room to stand before the reconstruction. "I can see why you took him as your lover, Nalia. He's pretty hot stuff. He says you taught him joy. I hope you found it too." She began to smooth the line of the cheek. "It's time to start. Are you ready? Let's bring you home...."

Smooth.
    Pat.
    A little deeper indentation around the lips.
    Smooth.
    Forehead broader.
    Smooth.
    Carve.
    Help me, Nalia.
    Her fingers were working feverishly now.
    Smooth.

Carve.

Sweep the cheekbones higher.

The mouth.

Always difficult. Sometimes impossible because there were no visible clues.

Tell me.

Skip it. Come back to it.

The mid-therum area.

Carve.

Smooth.

Get it right. For God's sake, get it right.

No, for Nalia's sake. For all her pain and desolation. Come home, Nalia.

Smooth.

Go back to the mouth.

Easier now.

Her fingers flew over the visage. Small nose, straight, no upturn at the end.

I hope it's right, Nalia.

Smooth.

Work faster. Make it come faster.

Carve.

Smooth…

She stepped back from the reconstruction and closed her eyes.

"Is it enough, Nalia?" she whispered. "It's the best I can do."

The final touch.

Her eyes opened and she turned to the table and opened her eye case.

"May I do it?"

She looked up to see Montalvo standing beside her.

He was looking down at the glass eyes in the case. "May I?"

She nodded jerkily. "If you like."

He took two brown eyes from the case. "Thank you." He carefully put the brown eyes in the empty sockets. "And to answer your question." His voice was unsteady. "It's more than enough. It's Nalia."

"I felt it was. Sometimes I have no idea. But this time I felt sure." She gazed at the reconstruction. "She's very beautiful. I wasn't sure about the mouth...."

"I know. You had to go back to it."

"How long have you been here?"

"Hours." He didn't take his gaze from the skull. "First I found it fascinating. Then I began to be drawn into the whirlpool."

"Whirlpool?"

"Memories. I imagine I've relived every moment Nalia and I spent together during those last hours." He reached out and touched Nalia's cheek with infinitely gentle fingertips. "I couldn't say good-bye to her until I said hello, welcome back into my world."

"I can understand that."

"I know you can." His eyes were glittering with

moisture as he stepped back from the dais. "And now
that I've said it, it hurts like hell."

"Closure doesn't come overnight."

"It won't come for me at all until I make sure Diaz
is dead and that kingdom he's set up explodes into a
thousand pieces." He started to turn away. "And I'd
better start working on making that happen."

"Not until I'm finished with her."

"Finished?" He stopped to look at Eve. "She
couldn't be more finished. It's *Nalia*."

"The actual sculpting is finished but I have to
photograph the reconstruction, put it on the computer, and compare it to photographs of Nalia. I
need those photographs from you."

He frowned. "All that's not necessary. I have what I
want."

"But I don't have what I want. I do every job with
the same thoroughness. I'm a professional and I
won't cheat Nalia or myself by skimping. Give me
those photos."

He hesitated and then went to the desk, unlocked
a bottom drawer, and pulled out a large envelope.
"Letters. Photos. Anything else?"

"I'll see." She opened the envelope and drew out
the photos. They were snapshots of a young woman
in her twenties. One photo showed her in a skirt and
blouse sitting at a table in a bar. In another she was
dressed in pants and khaki shirt and smiling mis-
chievously into the camera. The woman was undoubtedly the Nalia of the reconstruction. She

looked so vital and alive that Eve could almost expect to see her walk out of the photo. "No, that's all I need."

He took the photo from her and gazed down at it. "You did a brilliant job but you missed one thing. The laugh lines around her eyes. She used to say those tiny creases made her look old. I liked them. They were part of her." He handed the picture back to her. "You couldn't know about that."

No, Nalia, or whatever instinct drove Eve during those reconstructions, hadn't told her about those creases. "I can't add them now. It wouldn't be ethical or professional."

He nodded jerkily. "And there wasn't anything for her to laugh about at the end anyway. Please hurry with your final wrap-up. I've got to get going on making arrangements to do mine."

And his arrangements were for death and mayhem.

"You'll have to make arrangements to send Joe and me back to the States too."

He stiffened. "When?"

"This afternoon or tonight. I'll finish the computer work within a few hours. I want to get Joe back to Atlanta as quickly as possible."

He was silent a moment. "I'd rather you stay until I'm sure Diaz can't get to you. He's very big on revenge."

"He's not the only one."

He inclined his head. "True."

"Send me home. Joe and I will take care of ourselves." She met his gaze. "And I'll be waiting for you to make good on your promise."

"Don't worry, I'll keep it. I'll be coming to Atlanta just as soon as I take care of business here."

After he left the library she went over to the window and stared out at the night sky. It was beginning to take on a rainbow-soft glow like the black pearls Joe had given her for Christmas a few years ago. It would be dawn soon.

It's almost over, Joe. We can go home and try to forget what happened here. If that's what you want. I owe it to you.

But perhaps it would be better if she didn't forget. She had learned a few things about herself that she hadn't known before. Jesus, you'd think after all she'd been through that she'd know every facet of her personality. But along came Montalvo and she'd discovered she'd barely scraped the surface.

When I look at you it's like looking in a mirror.

But the image was dark and twisted and not what she wanted from life. She wanted Joe.

Well, with any luck she still had him. And if she could keep him with her when Montalvo came to Atlanta as he'd promised, to help her find Bonnie and Bonnie's killer... the situation then would be tense and very, very dangerous. Yet she could not do anything else, she thought wearily. This was what she'd worked for, what she'd risked the happiness she'd had with Joe for. She'd made a decision before she'd left Atlanta that what Montalvo had promised was worth any risk. She wasn't going to back out now. The price had been too high.

She opened the door of the cabinet beside the French doors and pulled out her duffel with her cameras and equipment. Get the job done and get Joe back to Atlanta where he'd be safe. Worry about the search for Bonnie later. She had waited for all these agonizing years. She had to be patient and take care of the people she loved.

She began to set up the cameras.

"May I come in?" Soldono's hesitant knock was followed by the opening of the library door. "Since Miguel isn't standing guard in the hall, I take it that you've finished?"

"Yes." She rubbed the back of her neck. "I've just finished making the computer comparisons. I've been packing away the cameras." She glanced at him. "And, no, you don't have to sneak me out of here. Montalvo's sending us home."

"Is he?"

She stiffened. "Is that supposed to mean something?"

"He may be sending you home, but I'm not sure about Quinn." He paused. "That's why I dared break in on you."

"Soldono, what the devil are you talking about?"

"I'm trying to tell you. I think Quinn took off last night."

Her heart jumped in her chest. "He couldn't. I saw him yesterday afternoon and he could barely function."

"Well, he must have garnered the strength from somewhere." He was looking at her sympathetically. "I'm sorry, Eve. I checked his room an hour ago and no Quinn. I followed up and went to Galen's room and Galen isn't here either."

"Galen went with him?" She wanted to murder both of them. Why couldn't Joe have waited one more day? But no, he had to go off on his own. Not quite his own, thank heavens. Galen at least was strong and healthy and might strike the balance. "You're sure about this, Soldono?"

"Unless they're both hiding out in Montalvo's armory. I can't quite see that scenario as being realistic."

"Neither can I." No, they'd be going after Diaz to take him out. She had a sudden memory of that castle on the hill. It might be grandiose, but it represented massive power and she was scared to death that power would be leveled at Joe and Galen. "I have to see Montalvo. Do you know where he is?"

"He was out in the courtyard fifteen minutes ago." Soldono had gone over to the dais and was looking at the reconstruction. "She was very beautiful. Is it a good likeness?"

"Very good." She was moving toward the door.

"Except for a few little things. No reconstruction is perfect."

"This one must come pretty close. Montalvo should be pleased."

"Yes, but that's not important right now." She strode out of the room and a moment later she was out in the courtyard.

"Eve, are you finished shooting those photos?" Montalvo looked up from talking to Miguel. "I can't wait much longer for—"

"Did you know about Joe?"

"Quinn?" He asked warily, "What was I supposed to know?"

"Soldono says Joe is gone. He and Galen left some-time last night."

"And I'm supposed to have kept this from you?"

"I find it odd that you'd not know what was going on in the compound. And how would Joe manage to get out of here without you knowing about it?"

Montalvo turned to Miguel. "I also find that strange. Miguel?"

He shrugged. "He and Galen left at three this morning. They went over the west wall. I was very impressed. I wouldn't have thought that a wounded man would be able to make it."

"*Damn* you," Eve said. "Why didn't you stop him?"

"He was in the way," he said simply. "The Colonel didn't want him here, but he wouldn't send him away. This way he didn't have to do it. Quinn did it himself."

"You should have told me, Miguel," Montalvo said.

"But that would have spoiled everything. An opportunity was presenting itself. Neither of us had to kill him. He has a chance of surviving if he's as good as we've heard." He smiled. "It seemed very sensible."

Eve stared at him in disbelief. Sensible to serve up Joe to Diaz? The total ruthlessness of the boy was incredible.

"It was wrong, Miguel," Montalvo said. "And we'll have to make it right. That may not be easy."

"For God's sake, you're talking to him as if he were a two-year-old who'd used a crayon to scribble on the furniture. He let Joe leave. He'd probably have given him a boost over that wall if he'd needed it."

Miguel nodded. "But he didn't need it. As I said, he was impressive."

"Go get him back," Eve said through her teeth. "He's alone out there."

"He has Galen," Miguel said. "But I'll go if the Colonel wishes it." He checked his watch. "It's been over ten hours. Quinn was a SEAL and I don't believe I'd be able to track him."

"You know where he's going," she said. "Diaz."

Miguel nodded. "But if I interfere with the Colonel's plans for Diaz, he won't be pleased."

She swung on Montalvo. "Tell him."

"I will," Montalvo said. "But I'm not going to order him to go retrieve Quinn. One, that might trigger the kind of action you're trying to avoid. Two men with guerilla training have a much better chance of surviving than a whole unit trooping through Diaz's territory. Two, if Quinn is as good as I've been told, then they'd be able to avoid Miguel and anyone I sent with him."

"Then what the hell are you going to do?"

"Send Miguel to Diaz's village and have him ask questions and do a little surveillance. Miguel lived there most of his life and he still has contacts. Everything that goes on at the castle is known in the village. They'll know if Diaz captures Quinn and Galen."

"And if he does?"

"Then I'll have to get Nalia's father moving very quickly before Diaz cuts Quinn's throat." He added, "Though if he doesn't know you've completed the reconstruction, Diaz might use him as a tool to make you stop."

"You still don't know who he has in your camp that might tell him?"

"I'm leaning toward Destando, a man who hasn't been with me as long as others. He's being carefully watched." Montalvo turned to Miguel. "If you'd been watching Destando instead of following Quinn around, I'd be better pleased."

Miguel shrugged. "I was only doing as you taught me. It was an opportunity." He turned away. "I'll leave right away for the village. I'll let you know as soon as I hear something."

"Immediately," Montalvo said. "And, dammit, be careful, Miguel."

"Of course." Miguel smiled back at him over his shoulder. "It would cause you much grief if anything happened. Where else would you find such a fine son as me?"

Eve watched him leave with a mixture of anger, frustration, and concern. "Will he be in much danger?"

"Enough. For a spy there's always danger. But he's gone back to the village and gathered information for me before. Miguel will get out if he sees a threat."

"But you're letting him go."

"He knew that he was disobeying orders. It doesn't matter that he thought the result would please me. He has to learn he can't run the show."

"Even if it kills him."

Montalvo didn't answer directly. "He made the mistake, he has to make it right."

"I'm angry as hell at him, but I don't want him to die."

"Neither do I." He was gazing after Miguel. "If I love anyone in this world, I think it's that boy."

"Then call him back. Send out—"

"It's done." He turned away. "Everything I said was sound and this is the best way to handle it. Now have you finished with the reconstruction?"

"Damn the reconstruction."

"I can see how you'd feel that. Is it finished?"

"Yes, you single-minded bastard."

"Then I'll go pack it and get ready to take it to Armandariz." He started for the front door. "And, yes, I am single-minded. However, you might consider that the sooner I can turn Armandariz against Diaz, the sooner Diaz will be rendered helpless to hurt or kill your Joe."

"If he doesn't open that wound and bleed to death before he gets to him."

"Somehow I don't think Quinn will let himself die before he gets within shooting distance of Diaz. I was watching him when he was in the library. He was very...focused."

"Christ, I should have said something to him. Though I don't know what I could have said that would have stopped him." Her hands clenched into fists at her sides. "Why did he do it? He knew I was close to completing the reconstruction. If he'd only waited one more day. He's not an idiot. It was almost over. Why did he—"

"He knew that I'd try to hold you here," Montalvo interrupted. "He's a perceptive man. He guessed that I'd need you to take the next step."

She frowned. "What are you saying? You agreed to make arrangements for us."

"And I would have done it. If there had been no other way." He grimaced. "But I was going to try to persuade you to stay and help me."

"What?"

"I have the reconstruction and that will be pretty convincing. The shock value will be enormous. But a man in denial like Armandariz needs more than a jolt. Three days ago I sent him your dossier. It's impressive. Your honesty and professional ethics are above reproach. I gave him time to check you out on his own."

"And what if he throws my dossier in the trash without even looking at it?"

"He hasn't done it. I still have friends among the rebels and they say he read it. If he did his own check, he'll know that you're credible."

"A person in denial believes everyone lies."

"That's why I want you to come along to his camp."

Her eyes widened in disbelief. "What?"

"I want you to explain the process as you did with me. I want you to tell him how you did it. How you never look at a photo before the end."

"And he's supposed to believe me?"

"It's my best chance. You're an honest woman, Eve. It shines out of you. I'm probably the most skeptical bastard on the face of the earth and the first time I met you, I'd have believed you if you'd told me black was white."

"You didn't part with him on good terms. If you push him, he might shoot both of us."

"He'll know that I wouldn't come into camp without backup in the area." He paused. "But we'll have to go in alone."

"I don't have to go anywhere."

"No, you don't. You've done what I asked you. I'm

sure Soldono would say that you should let the vermin destroy each other."

"Yes, he would."

"I don't think you'd go along with that philosophy now. You have a vested interest in Nalia and what happened to her." He stared her directly in the eye. "You want her father to know he was wrong about her. You want justice for Nalia."

"And you equate justice with revenge."

"Yes, and so do you. In your heart of hearts." He added, "And that would have been my argument before I knew Quinn had gone. Now the situation has changed."

"You mean, you have an ace in the hole." She smiled sardonically. "Are you sure you didn't tell Miguel to let Joe escape?"

"No, but he reads me well. I'm feeling some guilt," he said. "Yes, you do have more reason now."

"How quickly will Armandariz act if he decides that Diaz has been betraying him all these years?"

"I don't know. I'd like to tell you that he'll rush out and start burning down coca fields but I can't do that. Armandariz is an emotional man but he's a soldier and he'll do what's best for his troops and his cause."

"Then I may be taking a risk for nothing."

"It won't be for nothing. But I have to be honest with you. There's a chance it may not help Quinn."

"Jesus." She felt the panic rush through her. She had two choices. She could sit here and wait for

Miguel to find out something about Joe. Or she could take an action that might be totally futile. "I'll have to think about it."

"I'm setting up a meeting for tomorrow afternoon. Think fast." He went into the house.

Nothing like applying a little pressure, she thought bitterly. There was one other option she could check before she made that decision. She followed Montalvo into the house and went to find Soldono. He was coming down the hall from the library.

"Can Venable or you find a way to locate Joe and get him away from here?" she demanded.

"I'll call Venable but the situation would be... delicate."

"You're the CIA. You should be able to do something."

"We walk a tight line between the military and Diaz."

"You mean you play both sides on occasion. Sweet."

"We can't take overt action."

"It sounds like you can't take any action."

"I know you're upset but you have to understand that the CIA today relies a good deal on negotiation."

"Heaven forbid you'd make an enemy of Diaz by saving Joe." She pushed past him and headed toward the library. "Forget I asked."

"You're going with him to Armandariz?" Soldono asked. "It's not a good move, Eve."

"At least I'm going to make a move. I'm not just spinning my wheels and hoping everything is going to be fine."

"That's not fair," he said quietly. "I'm doing everything I can."

"I don't feel like being fair. I feel like getting Joe back in one piece."

Montalvo was carefully placing the reconstruction into the leather box when she came into the room. He looked up and then stopped in midmotion. "Well?"

"I'm going. What else can I do? It's the only positive response I can make in this mess."

"Good." He closed the lid of the box and fastened it. "Then I'll call Armandariz's camp and set up a meeting."

13

"We've located the car that picked Jane MacGuire up in that parking garage," Nekmon said. "It was spotted at a grocery parking lot this morning in Tucson and the driver was a man in his late forties."

"Did they follow him?" Diaz asked.

Nekmon nodded. "Of course. We think we've found the safe house. The driver of the car went to a house in the Sunset View subdivision and unloaded a few sacks of groceries."

"'Think' isn't good enough. Has anyone seen her?"

"Not yet. But the house seems well-guarded and the chances are good she's there. I told them to get close enough to confirm her presence but not to risk getting caught. We don't want to blow our hand."

"I want men ready to move in the minute I say the word. No mistakes, Nekmon."

"With all due respect, I seldom make mistakes."

"Once is too much. I need to—" The ringing of his

phone interrupted him and he picked it up. "Diaz." He listened for a few moments and then hung up. "She's finished the reconstruction and Montalvo has it."

"Should we move on the girl?"

He thought about it. "Not yet. There's another possibility emerging now that may be quicker and more effective."

"That's the third checkpoint," Eve said as Montalvo started the jeep again. "Armandariz certainly doesn't play around with security."

"That's why we arranged a formal meeting and didn't try to infiltrate his lines," Montalvo said. "He may be a bullheaded father, but he's a damn good soldier or he wouldn't have lasted this many years."

"How far away from the camp are we?"

"Five minutes." He glanced at her. "Nervous?"

"Of course I'm nervous. I'm supposed to talk a neurotic man into the fact that he's betrayed his daughter and his cause at one and the same time. Even if he believes me it doesn't mean that he'll admit it."

"We have a decent chance. He's going to be surrounded by men who knew Nalia most of her life. A few of them were like brothers to her. They'll recognize her from the reconstruction and they may carry Armandariz along with them."

"Did she have any brothers?"

"No, that's why Armandariz raised her like a son. He needed someone to share his dream and Nalia was his only family."

"But she violated the dream."

"So he thinks." His lips tightened. "She died for his damn dream. She believed in it as much as he did and was trying to protect it from being betrayed." He pulled over to the side of the road. "We walk from here." He got out of the jeep and grabbed the leather box. "Let's go."

She got out of the jeep. "Give me the box."

"Why?"

"If I'm here to do a job, I'll do it my way. Armandariz resents you. The minute he sees you carrying the box he's going to get defensive. You may get some pleasure out of opening the box and saying 'I told you so,' but it's not going to be productive."

"I wouldn't do that."

"Not in so many words. The moment you show up with the box, it's an immediate implication."

He hesitated. "True." He handed her the box. "But I do the initial explanation."

"By all means." She kept her eyes on the path ahead. "I've no desire to do any more talking than I have to do. I don't even want to be here. I just want to have this over and find a way to get Joe out of here."

"I know that. I'm grateful that you—" He broke off as the bushes ahead parted and a dark-haired, thirty-something man appeared. "It seems the show's about to start." He stepped ahead of her. "Manuel, it's been a long time. I wasn't sure you were still alive."

The man he'd called Manuel smiled faintly. "But I knew you were alive and exactly where you were. When my belly was empty, I thought about you sitting all fat and rich behind your high walls."

Montalvo shrugged. "A man has to survive. Armandariz called me a liar and threw me out of the camp."

"You survived very well." Manuel's smile faded. "And he isn't going to change his mind." His gaze went to the box in Eve's hands. "Is that it?"

"That's her," Eve corrected. "And Armandariz will change his mind."

"Eve Duncan, this is Manuel Estevez. We knew each other for a long time before I became a pariah." Montalvo nudged her forward. "And I assume you're going to take us to Armandariz?"

"Yes." Manuel turned on his heel. "I have to warn you that he's ready to laugh in your face. It's not going to do any good."

"Encouraging," Eve murmured as she followed Manuel. Well, she hadn't expected this to be easy. She wasn't even sure that it would be successful. Montalvo hadn't given her any false hopes.

They abruptly emerged from the forest into a large glade dotted with a score of tents. The large tent to which Manuel led them was on the outskirts of the camp and he lifted the flap and gestured them inside. "Good luck," he said to Montalvo. "If you deserve it."

"I deserve it," Montalvo said. "Are you coming?"

Manuel hesitated and then shrugged. "I'm a little curious. Why not?" He followed them into the tent. He nodded at an older man sitting in a camp chair at a table. "May I stay, Antonio?"

"I've no objection." Antonio Armandariz was a thin, handsome man somewhere in his sixties with a mane of gray-white hair and magnificent dark eyes. "You were always too fond of Montalvo. You need to see him as the fool he is."

"Nalia loved him," Manuel said. "She usually didn't make mistakes about people."

Armandariz's eyes glittered with anger. "Don't defend her. She made the biggest mistake anyone could make. Why won't you understand that?"

"I try," Manuel said. "Because you're an honorable man and you believe it." He sat down in a chair in the corner. "Maybe Montalvo will convince me how wrong I've been to doubt you, Antonio." He gestured to Montalvo. "Entertain us, my friend. Let's see what you have to say."

"He has no friends here," Armandariz said. "He almost destroyed us with his wild actions against Diaz." He stared coldly at Montalvo. "Talk and then get the hell out of my camp."

"That's my intention." He nodded at Eve. "This is Eve Duncan. You read the dossier on her I sent you?"

Armandariz barely glanced at her. "I read it. Probably lies."

"You know better than that," Montalvo said. "And

you've done a check on her yourself. I know you. You wouldn't be able to help yourself. I'm sure that you only wanted to prove to yourself that I was lying and she was a complete charlatan, but it didn't turn out that way, did it?"

Armandariz didn't answer.

"You didn't like the fact that she was reputable and totally honest and had no axe to grind. It must have been difficult for you."

"Not difficult at all." His gaze shifted to Eve. "She can be corrupted like everyone else. Nalia was honest and she betrayed us."

"May I talk now?" Eve asked. "This is bullshit, Montalvo."

"In a minute." Montalvo reached into his jacket pocket and drew out an envelope. "Nalia died trying to prove that Diaz was playing games with the militia and betraying you. She didn't find that proof before she was caught and killed. Diaz buried it and it took me years to unearth it." He tossed the envelope on the desk in front of Armandariz. "Along with a few more-recent documents that prove that Diaz is still double-dealing whenever it suits him. He's being very careful but when the prize is worth it, he's selling you out."

"Proof?" Armandariz's face was white with rage. "You come and bring me these forgeries. Diaz is a friend to us. We would have had to disband if it hadn't been for his help."

"No forgeries." He glanced at Manuel. "Don't let

him destroy them before he checks. It took me a hell of a long time and a small fortune to find that evidence."

"I'll do what I please." Armandariz's voice was shaking. "Lies. You tell me lies."

Montalvo stepped back. "Eve?"

That's right, infuriate the man and then leave it up to me to convince him, she thought in frustration. "I don't know anything about those papers. Montalvo didn't think it best to share them with me. I wouldn't have wanted to be involved anyway." She put the leather box on the table. "This is the only part of the business I wanted anything to do with." She unfastened the box and lifted the lid. "I wanted to bring your daughter home."

"My daughter is in Australia."

"Your daughter was murdered and thrown into a swamp," she said bluntly. "By the time Montalvo was able to find her body, there was no body. Only a skeleton. He was lucky to find those bones intact, considering the passage of time and the water and wildlife in that kind of habitat."

"She's in Australia."

"Your daughter's skull is in this box."

He looked away from the box. "No."

"I don't have the slightest doubt about it." She carefully lifted the reconstruction from the box and set it on the table. "Now, dammit, look at her. You gave life to Nalia. Don't you dare reject her."

"My daughter is not dead."

"Look at her."

He slowly turned his head. She could see him flinch as his gaze focused on the skull. "A pretty statue. You could have carved it from a likeness in a photo."

"But I didn't. I measured the depth points and then I built up the face around them. Only after I finished did I ask for a photo. I took three-dimensional shots of the reconstruction and then superimposed them on the photo." She pulled out a disc and crossed to the computer in front of Armandariz and popped in the disc. "Every feature aligned perfectly. Watch it happen."

"I've no wish to—"

"Watch it. I didn't bring her home to have you turn your back on her. Watch the image as it covers the reconstruction."

"I don't want to—"

Manuel stepped closer. "Don't be a coward, Antonio. Watch it happen."

"Shut up," he said harshly. "This is my concern."

"It's all our concern if it means we've been betrayed. I'm willing to fight and die, but I won't go blindly. I've been at your side for twenty years. But you shouldn't expect that of me."

Armandariz hesitated and then swung his gaze to the computer screen. "Show me."

"I don't have to do anything. The program does it all." She watched the slow superimposition. Even after all these years it always amazed her. It was rather

like a ghostly hand blending the two images together. "The similarity ratio is ninety-six percent.
That's exceptional."

Armandariz didn't take his gaze from the screen.
"Not if you were looking at the photo as you did the
reconstruction."

"But I wasn't looking at it." She paused. "I told
Montalvo you'd believe what you want to believe. I
can't make you see anything you don't want to see."
She pointed at the superimposition on the screen.
"That woman is Nalia. She died trying to help all of
you. It's not right for you to throw everything she did
away. Her life should mean something. Her death
should mean something."

"She's not dead." His gaze never left the screen.
"She's not dead."

"It's Nalia, Antonio," Manuel said gently. "I know
that face. Her cheekbones are just like yours. The
eyes are deep-set like yours. I've watched the two of
you together since she was a child." His eyes glittered
with moisture. "For God's sake, I grew up with her.
It's Nalia."

"Proof," Armandariz said hoarsely. "We have no
proof."

"Montalvo sent a tooth off for DNA confirma-
tion," Eve said. "It will take time. He hoped the reconstruction would convince you. Diaz has found
out I was doing the reconstruction and will be
moving."

"Convince me without proof?"

"Look in the mirror. Your friend is right. Your bone structure and Nalia's are very similar." Her lips twisted. "Do you want me to reel off the probable tissue depth of every point in your skull? I could do it. I became so accustomed to working on Nalia that she seemed part of me. She became ... my friend. It's a pity you weren't a friend to her." She took out the disc from the computer. "Do you ever dream about her, Armandariz?"

"No."

"You will from now on." She turned back to the reconstruction. "Because you know you're wrong. You're not going to be able to lie to yourself any longer." She picked up the reconstruction and started to put it in the box. "Let's go, Montalvo. I can't do—"

"Stop." Armandariz was staring at the skull. "Leave her."

She went rigid. "I can't do that. She's in my care."

Armandariz looked at Montalvo. "I'm keeping her, Montalvo."

Montalvo's gaze narrowed on Armandariz's face. "Why?"

"I'm keeping her."

"That's not good enough."

"Leave her." Manuel stepped forward. "I'll see that nothing happens to her. I'll consider it my duty."

"We need to bring her to a final resting place," Eve said. "She's not a card to be traded about."

"I know." Montalvo was studying Armandariz's

expression. "Very well, we'll leave her for the time being. I'll come back for her tomorrow."

"Screw you," Armandariz said. "I'm keeping her. You took her away from me once. I won't let it happen again."

"Tomorrow." He took Eve's elbow and urged her toward the entrance. "Don't argue, Eve."

"Don't tell me that." She glanced angrily back over her shoulder at Armandariz. "This isn't a pretty statue of your daughter. This is part of her body. If you can't believe that, then give me the reconstruction."

Armandariz didn't answer, his gaze once more fastened on the skull.

"He does believe it," Manuel said as he stepped closer and placed his hand on Armandariz's shoulder. "Give him his time with her."

Eve hesitated, studying the older man's expression. His lips were tight, his face pale and strained, and his eyes... She whirled and strode ahead of Montalvo out of the tent.

"Is he right?" she asked Montalvo as soon as they were a few yards away. "Does Armandariz believe us?"

"You wouldn't have left that tent if you didn't think so," Montalvo said. "You did a great job, Eve."

"How soon before you can talk to him about going after Diaz?"

"As Manuel said, give him a little time with his daughter. He has to come to terms with her death and his own mistakes that hurt his precious cause."

"I don't have time. I need to help Joe."

"And you will. I'll get in touch with Miguel when we get back to the compound and see what he's found out."

"I'm still not sure Armandariz believed us."

"I am. He called the reconstruction 'her,' not 'it.' And he was as possessive as he always was with her. He hated the idea of her marrying me. He thought I stole her away from him."

"Did you?"

"Yes, I was a possessive bastard too. But now neither one of us has her."

She shook her head. "Now you both have her. As long as you love her memory."

He was silent a moment. "Maybe you're right."

"Of course I'm right." They had reached the jeep and she climbed into the passenger seat. "God knows I'm not right about a lot of things. I seem to be blundering on all sides these days. But I'm right about this."

Armandariz had not spoken for the last ten minutes. His gaze was focused on the face of the reconstruction.

"It wasn't your fault." Manuel sat down in the camp chair beside him. "She shouldn't have taken the chance she did. She should have waited until she could convince you that Diaz was crooked."

"She never waited for anything," Armandariz said.

"I taught her to make a decision and then act on it. That's why she was such a good soldier." His fingers gently touched the line of her cheek. "I forgot how beautiful she was. I made myself forget. She does look like me, doesn't she?"

"Yes."

"I lied to that Duncan woman. I do dream about Nalia."

"It was none of her business."

"I dream about her when she was a small child, when she was mine. Before Montalvo came and took her away from me."

"Nalia always loved you. She kept Montalvo here because she knew he was valuable to the cause, valuable to you, Antonio."

"I know she loved me." His face twisted with pain. "But that bitch was right; I wasn't a good friend to her. I didn't want Montalvo to be right. I didn't want Nalia to be right about Diaz. I wanted her to trust my judgment as she had before she was married."

"Everyone makes mistakes," Manuel said. "Nalia was my friend. I should have questioned you and told you that perhaps we could be wrong." He grimaced. "But you're not often wrong, Antonio. I've gotten out of the habit of standing up to you." He paused. "What do we do about this?"

Armandariz shook his head. "I don't know. I don't know anything right now." His voice was uneven. "I don't want to think. I only want to sit here and look at my daughter who's come home to me."

.   .   .

Eve's cell phone rang after they were only a few miles from the encampment.

"Where are you, Eve?" Diaz asked when she answered. "I understand you've become involved in Montalvo's negotiations. Have you met with Armandariz yet?"

"How did you know that I was going to see Armandariz, Diaz?"

Montalvo's hands tensed on the steering wheel as his gaze flew to her face.

"I have people in Montalvo's camp. Did you doubt it when you met my little reptile friend? You're not safe from me wherever you are."

"Empty threats. You've tried to kill me twice and you didn't succeed."

Silence on the other end of the line. "You're making me angry. That's not a smart thing to do."

"Why are you calling me? If you know we're going to Armandariz's camp, then you must know I've finished the reconstruction." She paused. "And there's no doubt it's Nalia Armandariz."

"There's always doubt. Shall I tell you what you're going to tell my old friend Antonio? It's all a big lie. You sculpted the face that Montalvo told you to create. The skull was not that whore."

"Why should I do that?"

"Because it will please me. Armandariz will believe you because he wants it to be true. He likes our cozy relationship and he wants to keep it flourishing. All you have to do is tell him what a liar Montalvo is and he'll be very happy."

"But I don't want to please you."

"Of course you do. You don't care anything about Montalvo. He's nothing to you but a fat fee. I can match his money." His voice lowered. "And I can give you something he can't."

"What?"

"Your lover. Do you want to see Joe Quinn alive again?"

She stiffened as panic jolted through her. Christ.

"You're bluffing."

"I'd let you talk to him, but my men were a little rough when they captured him, and he's unconscious."

She tried to keep her voice steady. "How convenient."

"Of course, perhaps it's not their doing. It could be that nasty wound my man Duarte inflicted. Perhaps it's opened and he's bleeding to death. Should I ask my men to check?"

"You bastard."

"No curses. You must be polite to me. You wouldn't want to have a guilty conscience if I became so angry that I forgot about Armandariz and decided to punish you." His tone became terse. "If Armandariz makes any move on me, Quinn dies. If I talk to him and he seems to be waffling in his loyalty to me, Quinn dies. If Montalvo attacks me, Quinn dies. Is that understood?"

"You're being very clear."

"Good. Then understand this. After you convince Armandariz what a cheat and liar you are, I want you to bring the reconstruction and turn it over to me."

"You know Montalvo won't let me do that."

"Then steal it. I don't care how you do it. You're obviously a clever woman. Find a way to give me that skull. I won't let Montalvo use it as evidence against me. I have the skeleton. I must have that skull."

"So that you can throw it back in the swamp?"

"No, I've learned my lesson. This time it will be ashes tossed to the four winds."

"I won't do it. I don't have any proof that you have Joe."

"Oh, I'll give you proof. By the time you reach Montalvo's compound it will be waiting for you." He hung up.

Keep calm. Don't panic. Don't fall apart.

"Quinn?" Montalvo asked quietly.

She nodded jerkily. "Diaz says he has him. That he couldn't speak because he was unconscious."

"It could be a lie."

"That's what I told him." She rubbed her temple. "No proof. He said it would be waiting for me at the compound."

"What did he want for Quinn?"

"Damage control. I'm to tell Armandariz I counterfeited the reconstruction. I'm to turn the skull back over to Diaz so it can't be used as evidence."

"Otherwise Quinn bites it."

"Yes. It could be a lie. Call Miguel and see if he knows anything."

He nodded, reached for his phone, and dialed. After a moment he shook his head. "No answer." He put the phone away. "I'll try a little later. He may be in a place where the sound of a ringing phone might not be safe."

It wasn't the answer she had hoped for. Nothing was going right, she thought desperately. "Hurry. I need to get back to the compound."

"I'm hurrying." Montalvo's foot pressed the accelerator. "It will still take another hour."

It was an hour that was going to seem a century. She gazed blindly out the window. "I'm not sure I want to know what his proof is."

"Yes, you do. You don't hide your head. You'll face it and then we'll find a way to skewer the bastard."

She felt a surge of warmth that banished a little of the chill. It was good not to be alone with fear. "Right. That's exactly what we'll do."

Montalvo got a call when they were just minutes away from the compound. He exploded after listening only a moment. "Shit. No, don't do anything. I'll be right there." He clicked his phone shut. "It was Soldono."

"What's wrong?"

"I think Diaz delivered your proof." The gates of the compound loomed ahead and there were several men milling around outside the gate. "Damn him to hell."

He stomped on the brake and jumped out of the jeep as Soldono came toward him.

"Where?" Montalvo asked harshly.

"Around the corner, the west wall," Soldono said. "I don't know how long—" He broke off as he ran after Montalvo.

Eve jumped out of the car and followed them. She could see the beams of several flashlights as she went around the corner of the compound. They were all focused on the wall several yards away. What the devil were they—

She stopped in her tracks. "Oh, my God."

Miguel.

Horror tore through her. She could dimly hear Montalvo cursing as he reached the wall but everything seemed surreal, lost in the hideous vision before her.

Miguel was nailed to a makeshift cross leaning against the wall of the compound. A leather strap gagged his mouth but his eyes...

Agony.

"Get him down," she said. "He's alive. Look at his eyes."

"I sent them for a ladder," Soldono said. "They

should be—Here they are." He stepped aside as Montalvo grabbed the ladder and flew up the rungs.

"Two of you get below him and lift him, take the weight off." Montalvo tore the gag from Miguel's lips. "We'll have you down in a few minutes. You're going to be fine."

"Hurts," Miguel gasped. "Hurts."

"I know," Montalvo said unevenly. "It will stop. I promise."

"I . . . failed you."

"No, it wasn't your fault."

"Yes, it was. I'll . . . make it up to you, Colonel."

"Yes, you will. By getting well." He called down, "Did you call Dr. Diego, Soldono?"

"As soon as I phoned you," Soldono said. "He should be here anytime. How else can I help?"

"We've got to get him into the house but I don't want to take those spikes out myself. I don't want to damage his hands any more than they are now. You and a few men get a stretcher and we'll take down the crucifix and carry it and him on the stretcher." He glanced at Eve. "Get a room ready for him. I want him close to me."

"I'll give him Joe's room." Eve turned and flew around the corner and through the front gates. She was glad to have something to do that might jar her from the horror and pity that was surging through her.

Jesus, that poor boy.

Proof.

Rage seared burning through the horror as she remembered Diaz's words. He had sent her this hideous message to frighten her. It was beyond belief that anyone could be this cruel.

He was a monster.

And that monster had Joe.

14

How is he?" Eve asked as Montalvo came out of the bedroom. "What did the doctor say?"

"He's going to live. He's lost some blood. He's getting a transfusion now. Soldono is his blood type," Montalvo said. "He's going to need surgery on both hands. I'll send him to a specialist for that. He's lucky that his arms were draped over the cross and bore some of his weight. He *is* going to be okay. I'll see to it. He has two broken ribs. Diaz had him beaten before they put him on the cross. No internal damage other than that break." His lips tightened. "He told me he was lucky. Diaz assured him that if he hadn't wanted to send you a message he would have killed him."

"And the message is that Diaz has Joe?"

He nodded. "He saw him at the castle. Diaz's men captured him in the woods near the village."

"What about Galen?"

"Galen wasn't with him."

"What?"

"They may have separated and only Quinn was captured. Galen definitely wasn't being held at the castle."

Eve frowned. "Galen wouldn't have left Joe."

Montalvo shrugged. "I can only tell you what Miguel told me."

And what he had said meant her last hope was gone that Diaz was lying about holding Joe prisoner.

"What happened? Why was Miguel captured?"

"Miguel thinks it was an informant. Diaz's men were searching the village."

"This Destando you told me about?"

"You can bet I'm going to be paying him a visit."

"May I see Miguel?"

He nodded. "Not for long. And he may not make much sense. He's under sedation."

"I'm not going to harass him. I want to tell him I'm here for him if he needs me. I guess I'm feeling guilty for my part in sending him into Diaz's territory."

"*You're* feeling guilty?" he asked bitterly. "None of it was your fault. It was Miguel's fault for disobeying orders and my responsibility for giving him a mission where anything could happen." He added grimly, "And did."

"I was angry. It might have influenced you."

"It didn't influence me. I did what I'd do if any of

my men disobeyed an order. If you make a mistake, you correct it."

Hard words. Hard man. And yet that last sentence echoed one of the philosophies that guided her own life. The mirror again. "I don't believe it's that black-and-white for you."

"Hell, no," he said roughly. "And right now, I'd do anything if I'd gone with him to that village."

"Didn't you think he had a better chance alone?"

"That doesn't stop me from remembering him propped against that wall, gagged to keep from screaming." He turned away. "I've got to call a specialist at your Emory University in Atlanta and arrange surgery for Miguel."

"And then?"

"Then I start moving on finding a way to get hold of Diaz and nail him to a cross." He strode down the hall.

The brutality of the words didn't shock her. The vision she'd seen earlier that evening was too vivid in her mind. Montalvo believed in revenge and it was natural that he'd want to punish the man who'd perpetrated that horror on the boy he cared about. She couldn't blame him. She was feeling angry and terrified that Diaz thought he could go through life hacking and maiming as if it were his right. The message he'd sent was very clear. Do as he commanded or risk Joe being the next victim. What the devil could she do?

She opened the door and went into Miguel's

bedroom. He was lying in the bed Joe had occupied. Both of his hands were bandaged and his usually olive complexion was pale, his mouth strained.

He opened his eyes as the door closed behind her. "I...should have...stopped Quinn," he whispered. "I didn't think they'd...catch him."

"Yes, you did wrong. I'm not going to tell you that it was all right just because you've been hurt." She came to him and stood beside the bed. "I will tell you that I'm sorry that you've suffered so much. Is there anything that I can do for you?"

He tried to smile. "Kill...the bastard?"

"Not a bad idea. I can't think of anyone who'd deserve it more."

"Just...joking. Not your job. The Colonel will... do it. He promised...me."

"Then I'm sure it's as good as done. Anything else?"

"Don't give in to Diaz. Never...give in. I thought my father was a bad man. Diaz is—" He shuddered. "Don't give in. No one should give in to him. He won't let Quinn live no matter what...you do."

"Did he say that?"

"He's...angry with you. He wants you dead. He wants to hurt you. Killing Quinn will hurt you." He looked down at his bandaged hands. "He likes to hurt. He laughed when they were pounding the stakes into...my hands."

Tears stung her eyes as she reached out to touch his arm. "Don't think about it. It's over."

"I think in time I can forget the pain. It's the sound I keep hearing over and over. The sound of the stake going into—" He stopped. "You're crying. I didn't mean to make you cry." His lips lifted in the faintest smile. "It's not so bad. Though I won't be able to play the piano again."

"And the next line is that you never played before. That's a very old joke." She said unsteadily, "And if you want to play the piano, I'm sure Montalvo will make sure you're able to do it."

"Me too." His eyes closed. "He...feels sorry this happened. He won't admit it but he...likes me."

"I believe that's an open secret."

"And he doesn't want to let me...help get Diaz." His words were becoming slurred. "Wrong. I have to do it."

"For pity's sake, you're wounded. You're not in shape to do anything."

"Didn't stop...Quinn."

"And Joe is being held by Diaz."

"Have...to...help. Maybe it will stop the sound..."

"Miguel, your job is just to concentrate on getting well. There's nothing else that—"

He was asleep. His chest was moving steadily in and out, his breathing deep and regular. Montalvo had warned her that Miguel was sedated and her visit couldn't be for long and she'd probably exceeded that limit. She was torn by pity and anger and a kind of maternal protectiveness as she gazed down at Miguel. He was only a boy, dammit.

She gently tucked the sheet higher around him and moved toward the door.

Don't give in to Diaz.

Easy to say. The last thing she wanted to do was to follow any order from that beast.

Joe. What about Joe?

Yet Miguel had said Joe was dead whether or not she disobeyed Diaz.

He would *not* die. She would not allow that to happen.

Think about it. There had to be an out. Diaz was a dragon who was scourging all of their lives. They couldn't let him win. Although right now it seemed as if that was what was happening, she thought bitterly.

She closed the door and went down the hall toward her own room. Grab a shower. Change her clothes and then sit down and try to puzzle a way out for all of them.

Her cell phone rang before she reached her door.

"How did you like my messenger?" Diaz asked. "I thought it was quite a dramatic way to convey my wishes."

"It was hideous. You're hideous."

"Sticks and stones may break my bones but words may never harm me. Isn't that the way the English saying goes? I didn't use words to break Miguel Vicente's bones. I gave my men a baseball bat."

"And then you crucified him."

"I thought it fitting. Rather biblical in flavor."

"Satanic in flavor."

"It's nothing to what I'll do to Quinn if you don't follow my orders to the letter. Did you know I boiled a man in oil once? It took him a long time to die. I was pleasantly surprised. I thought it would be over in the blink of an eye." His tone hardened. "I want the skull in my hands by tomorrow night. I want assurance by tomorrow afternoon that Armandariz believes you to be a lying bitch."

"I'd be a fool to do all that without some proof that you'd release Joe. I could never trust your word."

"That's true. But I'm in control here. You'll do as I say or Quinn dies."

She hesitated, a hundred frantic thoughts cascading through her mind. What did she know about Diaz? Dammit, she wasn't prepared for this. Okay, go with instinct. "And I may die too. Why should I risk my life when you're not offering me any chance of a way out?"

"Because you're a soft woman and he's your lover."

That was the strongest wild card Diaz was holding. She had to take it away from him. "I'd hate to have anything happen to Joe for old times' sake but he's no longer my lover."

Silence. "You lie. He followed you here. He took a bullet for you."

"But why did he have to follow me here? Why did I take this job? Money? If you investigated me, you have to know money doesn't mean that much to me."

"Money is important to everyone." He paused. "Why else?"

"Montalvo. I was bored with my relationship with Joe. Montalvo is new and exciting."

"You're fucking him?"

"Every chance I get."

"I don't believe you."

"Believe what you like. I've tried to keep our relationship under wraps because I didn't want to hurt Joe before I could make a final break. But life is looking very good to me right now and I'm not going to toss it away for a man I'm going to leave anyway. If I decide to do what you wish, I'm going to walk away safe and sound."

"Back to Montalvo?"

"Back to Montalvo. I'll put Joe on a plane to Atlanta and wave him good-bye."

"You're making a bad exchange. Montalvo's not going to live longer than the next few weeks."

"You haven't managed to kill him yet. He's a survivor. That's one of the things that excites me about him."

"Whore."

"Beast. Find me a safe way out and I'll find a way to get that skull."

Another silence. "I'll think about it." He hung up.

But he'd call back if she'd managed to convince him. Toward the end of the conversation she'd thought he'd accepted the lie as truth. Jesus, she'd taken a giant leap and wasn't sure if she'd plunged Joe off that precipice. She hadn't had any option. Diaz was using her love for Joe as a weapon that could kill both of them. The only way to keep him from dominating the situation was to take that weapon away from Diaz.

And what would she do when he called her back? Listen to his deal and then try to find a way to save Joe. At best, it would be a stopgap measure. She had to do better than that. She had to take the control away from Diaz. Initiate instead of defend. And she had no idea in hell how to do that.

It had better not remain a mystery for long, she thought desperately as she went into her room. She had to have a counterplan ready to meet any trap Diaz was going to set for her.

Go on. Do what she'd been starting to do when that call had shaken her to the core. Shower. Change. Get something to eat. And during every minute she was doing those mundane tasks keep thinking, keep searching for a way out. . . .

Diaz hadn't called back by the time she was ready to go downstairs. She hadn't really expected him to move fast. He probably had to consider whether there was truth in her words and then make a decision if he wanted to offer her what she'd told him she wanted.

She passed a mirror on the way to the door and grimaced. She had a right to look tired, since she hadn't slept in almost two days, but she was positively haggard. How pleased Diaz would be if he could see her now. Actually, she didn't feel nearly as exhausted as she looked. She was wired.

Montalvo glanced up as she entered the library. "Feel better? Miguel doesn't blame you for anything."

"Nor you?" She dropped down in the visitor's chair. "Though he may try to use his injury to manipulate you. He's capable of it."

"Yes, he is. And I fully expect to have to slap him down." He added, "After the bastard gets well."

"He wants to go after Diaz. He said you won't let him. That's good."

"Maybe. It might be better to give him a role. After what he went through he deserves to get some of his own back."

"I agree. But I'm more interested in getting Joe out of that castle than letting the two of you go after your revenge."

"Even if the one begets the other?" He didn't wait for an answer. "Has Diaz called you back yet?"

"Yes."

He stiffened. "And?"

"The same as before. A little added gloating about what he did to Miguel." She shuddered. "He enjoyed it."

"I don't doubt that."

"Neither do I." She straightened in the chair. "And I'm not letting him do that to Joe. So I've got to move quickly. He wants the skull. I'm going to give it to him. With all the embroidery that he asked me to tack on to the deal. Diaz wants me to convince Armandariz that I didn't tell the truth about the validity of the reconstruction. I'll need your help to intercede with Armandariz for me in both cases."

"You're going to tell Armandariz that you lied?" he asked harshly. "No way."

"Don't tell me that. I'll do whatever is necessary to get Joe away from him."

"I won't let you give him the skull."

"If you can think of any other way I'm open to suggestion."

"You're not going to give him the skull."

She sat there looking at him.

He muttered a curse. "He'll scoop you up and cut your throat if you go near him."

"I'm working on that. He's not totally in control any longer."

"The hell he's not."

"I told him that I wouldn't meet his terms unless I had an escape hole. That I wasn't going to risk my life for Joe's."

"And he believed you?"

"Perhaps. We'll have to see. I tried to make my holdout as reasonable as possible." She stared him in the eye. "I told him I was fucking you and that I was going to leave Joe anyway."

"Indeed?" he murmured. "Why?"

"I needed an excuse for being less than eager to get Joe out of his hands. It gave me more negotiating power."

"If Diaz believed you."

"I think he did. We'll see when he calls me back." She added, "And if he agrees, I'll set up the meeting place."

"No," Montalvo said flatly. "Forget it. It's not going to happen."

Despair tore through her. His refusal wasn't unexpected but she'd been hoping against hope. She stood up. "Is that your last word?"

He nodded and repeated, "It's not going to happen. I'm not going to cut you down from a crucifix, Eve."

She turned on her heel and walked out of the room.

Christ, she felt alone. She had desperately wanted Montalvo's help and it was clear she wasn't going to get it. She could see his viewpoint. He'd spent years bringing Armandariz to this point and he wasn't willing to give up the advantage. Okay, then she'd have to work through this by herself. She'd go back to her room and sleep for a few hours. She had an idea she wasn't going to get much in the foreseeable future. Then she'd sit down and try to puzzle a way out of this predicament.

·   ·   ·

She thought it would take time for her to go to sleep but she dropped off almost immediately.

She woke to the sound of the ringing of the phone four hours later.

Diaz?

She scrambled to reach the phone on the night-stand. "Hello."

"You sound sleepy. Wake up, Eve. We have things to talk about."

"Galen?" She sat up straight in bed. "Where are you?"

"At the moment? I'm in a blind in an oak tree about a mile from Diaz's fancy castle and damned uncomfortable. I'm not accustomed to the rough life anymore."

"I imagine Joe's a little uncomfortable himself."

"Not my fault." Galen's voice was suddenly sober. "I couldn't do anything with him. I tried to stop him. I wanted to be the one to rush into the dragon's lair but he wasn't having any of it. He said it was more logical that he do it. Actually, he was right. Diaz wouldn't have much use for me except to use my handsome head to decorate his fireplace. Quinn was much more likely to stay alive until he could finish the job."

"Killing Diaz? For God's sake, Miguel said Joe was still unconscious while he was there. He'll be lucky not to bleed to death."

"He may be waking up about now. I've been using the audio spy equipment to monitor the castle and it's weird he's not come around yet. I'd bet he's playing possum. And he won't bleed to death unless Diaz opens his wounds. It's not likely. Diaz enjoys live entertainment. He'll ignore Quinn while he's out cold."

"What?"

"Quinn's not stupid. Stubborn. Not stupid. He knew he was too weak to function as he usually did. So he decided he had to avoid confrontation until he could slit the toad's throat. He wasn't in top form so he couldn't chance getting close to Diaz in the castle. So we decided to blow the bastard up. We planted a nice hefty stash of dynamite around the castle. We were going to set it off once we were in the woods but it turned out the whole area was crawling with Diaz's men."

"That's what Miguel said."

"Anyway we were cornered and Quinn tossed me the detonator and told me to do the job. Then he ran out of the shrubbery and drew them away from me. He knew we weren't both going to be able to get away and he was too weak to make it." He paused. "He's got guts, your Joe, luv."

"You don't have to tell me that."

"I couldn't blow the castle. That's where they took Quinn. Like I said, I've been hanging out listening in on what was happening inside the castle with some of this handy-dandy surveillance equipment and looking for an opportunity. I figured my best bet would be to know what was going on so that I could bring in some reinforcements."

"Tell me where you are. Tell me how I can help."

"I'll fill you in on the important agendas first. I don't know how long I can stay in this blind. They've been searching for me since they got their hands on Quinn. I may have to go on the run again."

"Then talk, dammit."

He laughed. "Okay, then it's time that I started shorthand. One, I'm going strictly against Quinn's orders. He didn't want you involved. But I saw them carry that boy Miguel out of the castle on that cross. I think we need a little outside involvement." His voice sobered and the next words came hard and quick. "The first thing you have to know is that Montalvo is being..."

Excitement was surging through Eve as she hung up the phone fifteen minutes later. Excitement? Or hope? For the first time since she'd found out Joe was gone she felt as if she might see a way through this fog of ugliness generated by Diaz.

She threw back the covers and jumped out of bed. Get dressed. Galen was on-site and ready to help. She had to make plans of her own.

She glanced at the phone. It had been hours since Diaz had called. Was he trying to make her apprehensive? A psychological ploy? Perhaps. How the hell did she know?

Go on. Call, Diaz. I'm ready for you.

.   .   .

"I'm not going," Miguel said. "If you put me on that helicopter to Bogotá, I'll hijack it and come back."

"You won't try that kind of stupidity," Montalvo said. "I've taught you better."

"You've taught me loyalty and teamwork. I was stupid enough to get caught. I'm definitely stupid enough to force myself on you at a time like this."

"With two broken ribs and those hands?"

"Only the hands would bother me. I can get around the rest." He frowned. "And my fingers work. You could rig up something."

"Miguel…" Montalvo shrugged. "Let me think about it."

"She's not going to give you much time to think about anything," Miguel said. "When she was here, I could feel the impatience in her. She was hurting for me but she wants her man back."

He frowned. "He's not her man. Neither of them is that dependent on the other. It's not in their characters."

Miguel smiled. "You don't want it to be true. Interesting."

"Why should I care what—" Montalvo stopped. "No, I don't want it to be true, you perceptive rascal. You'd do well to concentrate on recovery and forget about my concerns."

"But your concerns are my concerns. I can't help

being involved. It's your fault for saving me from having my head blown off."

Montalvo sighed. "I'm beginning to regret that moment."

Miguel shook his head. "It's no good you telling me that. I saw your face when you were taking me off that cross. You were as tender as Mary with Christ at Calvary."

"I believe I'm going to be ill. You're not Christ. I'm not Mary. You can't even get the sex right."

"Well, something like that."

"I can see you're going to hold that Jesus image up to me for the rest of your life."

"Possibly." His smile faded. "I told you what I had to do. Now set it up so that my mission paves the way for your mission."

"You've had your answer."

Miguel stared him in the eye. "And you've had your answer. I won't back down. I don't care if it complicates everything. Work it out."

Montalvo got to his feet. "Maybe. It all depends on Eve. I don't know what the hell is happening right now." He moved toward the door. "In the meantime go to sleep and stop thinking up things to torment me."

"It's my duty." Miguel closed his eyes. "I must keep you humble, Colonel. I embrace the task gladly."

"I'm sure you do," he said as he left the bedroom.

Blast the boy, he thought with exasperation. He was relieved that Miguel was progressing so rapidly but not that his will was gaining determination on a pace with his physical strength. He'd always had a power and mental ability far beyond his years but that episode at the castle had changed him. No, not changed, just made his character deepen, harden.

And why the hell shouldn't it have done that? An experience of that nature was enough to drive some men mad. He was lucky that it had only caused Miguel to toughen. The boy was totally remarkable.

And it was time Montalvo started to move against that slimeball of an informer who had betrayed Miguel, he thought grimly.

He headed downstairs to go pay a visit to Destando.

The call from Diaz to Eve came four hours later.

"Very well," he said. "I'll arrange a meeting in a place other than the castle to receive the skull if my informants tell me that Armandariz is not going to be a problem."

Eve felt a surge of relief. "He won't be a problem. Where?"

"The woods on the other side of the village."

"Where you could have thirty sharpshooters ready to pick us off after you have the skull? I don't think so."

"Take it or leave it."

"I'll leave it. I won't die for an affair that's run its

course. I told you I wanted to live. You've given me no chance at all."

"Then I kill Quinn."

"If that's what you have to do. Call me back if you change your mind."

"Wait." Diaz hesitated before saying sourly, "Perhaps we can come to an agreement. What do you consider a safe exchange?"

"A helicopter pickup for Joe and me immediately after the exchange to whisk us both back to Bogotá. I'm going to ask Venable with the CIA to send a copter to get us out. Where's your helicopter pad?"

"On the grounds in back of the castle."

"Too dangerous for me. Where else can he land?"

"There's a pad on the outskirts of the village near the cemetery."

She was silent. "The cemetery is too out in the open. I'd be a target. Anywhere else?"

"Maybe the church on the cemetery grounds."

Yes. She tried to sound uncertain. "I don't know..."

"I'm tired of fooling with you. It's the church or the deal is a wash."

She waited a few seconds and then said reluctantly, "I suppose the church would be safe enough. I won't have the skull with me but it will be close by. When I see that you're the only one in the church, I'll go and fetch it. And I'm going to ask the helicopter pilot to skim over those woods across from the cemetery and use infrared to make sure there's no one waiting to put a bullet in the copter's gas tank when we take off."

"My, how suspicious you are."

"I won't even deign to answer that one. I saw what you did to Miguel. You're a butcher."

"Montalvo likes the boy. I had an idea it would bother him."

"Then you'll be glad to know it did. He won't leave his side."

"And that should make it easier for you to deliver the skull," he said mockingly. "He won't miss you in his bed."

"Nothing about this is going to be easy. I'm dealing with a man who's plotting and planning how to get what he wants and still manage to kill me. Even when I get Joe safely to Bogotá, I'm going to have to come back and face Montalvo, who is going to be mad as hell I spoiled his plans."

"That's true. He may kill you."

"He won't kill me. We're too good together. But I'm going to have to handle him carefully."

"Only for a little while. I told you I intended to arrange his death within the next few weeks. You'd do better to stay in Bogotá."

"I'm touched by your concern," she said sarcastically. "But I'll manage my own business, thank you."

"I don't care about your shoddy little affairs. You and Quinn are nothing to me." His voice became cold. "I want the skull delivered by midnight tomorrow night. If it's not, I'll send Quinn back to you in a dozen separate baskets."

Don't let her voice show the terror that thought brought. "You're beginning to lack imagination. The crucifix was much more effective."

"Are you mocking me? You believe you're so strong and intelligent. I detest women who think they're as good as men. In the end they find out how weak they are."

"Like your mother, Diaz? It takes a real man to kill the woman who bore and raised him." Shut up. She had what she wanted. She didn't want to ruin everything because he infuriated her. "I'll be at the church tomorrow at midnight. If I have any trouble getting the skull, I'll—"

"No ifs," he said harshly. "You *will* do it." He paused. "You may be through with Quinn but you have a fondness for Jane MacGuire. Did you think you could hide her away from me forever?" He hung up.

He was bluffing.

Jane was safe.

Jesus, but she had to be sure.

She phoned Venable. "Diaz just mentioned Jane and he sounded very confident."

"She's safe." He added, "Okay, we think her safe house was compromised. One of the agents was followed back to the house but he noticed the surveillance. They pulled out of the area a few hours later and she's been relocated in Flagstaff."

Close. Damn close. "And they weren't followed to Flagstaff?"

"My guys are careful, Eve. Stop worrying about your daughter and start worrying about yourself. What you're doing at Diaz's place is very risky."

"Not if you get that helicopter on the ground at the right time." No, he was right, it didn't matter if everything went like clockwork. It was still going to be dangerous. "I have to do this, Venable."

"I know," he said wearily. "I wish we could help more."

"Soldono explained the delicacy of CIA negotiations," she said sarcastically. "You wouldn't want to offend any slimeballs like Diaz."

"It's a dirty, fixed game. We do what we can to make the stakes as low as possible for the winners. Call me when you leave the compound and I'll make sure the helicopter is in the area." He hung up.

Jane was safe. Venable was doing what he could to help her. She had managed to back Diaz into the corner she needed him to be in. Everything was as good as it could be, considering that nothing could possibly be good as long as Diaz had Joe.

15

It's the church," Diaz said to Nekmon as he hung up the phone. "Tomorrow at midnight."

"Where do you want men positioned in the village?"

"Nowhere. She's pulling in the CIA to get them out. We don't want an incident in my territory." He smiled maliciously. "Much better to have it closer to Montalvo's compound. Then we can claim he ordered it shot down because he was angry with the bitch. He has ground-to-air missiles and the CIA knows it. Station a man in the ruins of that tower thirty miles from here. She'll think she's free and clear and then we'll incinerate the whore."

"You're going to let her get on the helicopter?"

"Why not? It's the best way to get rid of the bitch. The CIA won't be a problem as long as we don't directly interfere with their agents. Kill a CIA agent and the Agency will be very difficult to deal with." He got to his feet. "Have you found Galen yet?"

"We picked up a phone signal in the woods about ten miles from here."

"And you didn't catch him?"

"He was gone by the time we got to the source," Nekmon said. "He seems to be moving constantly. But he's not leaving the area."

"Perhaps he's looking for a way to rescue his friend Quinn," Diaz said. "I'm going to be most displeased if he manages to get in my way tomorrow night. You don't want to know how displeased, Nekmon."

"He won't be an obstacle," Nekmon said. "I give you my word. By the way, Quinn has regained consciousness."

"Good. I was afraid I was going to have to bargain with a corpse. Is he going to live?"

Nekmon nodded. "As you know, he was somewhat damaged in the struggle to take him. Do you want to see him?"

Diaz thought about it. He was tempted to give Quinn a reason to remember him. The Duncan woman still had some feeling for the bastard or she wouldn't be going to these lengths to free him.

No, better not. Everything should be smooth on the surface when they met at the church.

"Later." He moved toward the door. Spilling blood was exciting, heady, and energizing. But sex was almost as good and he still had the young farm girl here at the castle. She was proving very amusing. She had started out as a frightened doe but recently he had noticed flashes of spirit when the pain had been too great.

Yes, she would be a suitable substitute for the satisfaction he would relinquish from toying with Quinn.

Soldono was on the veranda when Eve tracked him down that evening.

"I've been looking for you," Eve said. "I need your help. Where can we talk?"

"Problems?" He took her elbow and guided her across the veranda. "This is as good as anywhere." He shook his head. "Now that poor Miguel has been taken out of guard duty, surveillance isn't what it used to be."

"You told me that you could get me out of the compound and back to the village without Montalvo knowing about it."

He went still. "Is that what you want to do?"

"No, but if you can do that, I figured you could help me in another way. I want you to arrange a meeting with Armandariz for me. I can't go to him. It's too far and Montalvo would find out and track me down. Armandariz will have to come fairly close to the compound."

"Why do you want to see him?"

She grimaced. "I have to convince the neurotic bastard that I lied to him and erase everything that

Montalvo wanted to accomplish. To top it off I have to persuade him to give me back the reconstruction."

Soldono whistled softly. "I can see why he'd want to track you down. Montalvo might just put a bullet in you."

"I'll take the chance. It's the only way I can save Joe. Montalvo doesn't give a damn about him. Can you do it? You've dealt with the rebels, haven't you?"

"I've dealt with everyone in this stinking jungle at one time or another."

"Then will you help me?"

"I shouldn't do it. And you shouldn't trust any bargain you make with Diaz."

"I don't have a choice." She added unsteadily, "You saw what he did to Miguel. That's not going to happen to Joe."

He frowned thoughtfully. "I don't know if I can convince Armandariz."

"Try. He wants to believe his daughter's still alive. That should take him halfway. He doesn't like Montalvo and that may bring him the rest of the way. Will you do it?"

"How soon do you have to meet with him?"

"Tomorrow morning. And ask him to bring the reconstruction with him. He may not go along with it but we have to make the attempt."

"This isn't smart, Eve."

"It's the best I can do. I won't have Joe killed." She repeated, "Will you do it?"

He hesitated and then slowly nodded.

"Thank God." She squeezed his arm. "And thank you, Soldono."

"You can thank me by getting out of this in one piece. My job is keeping you safe, not Quinn." He turned away. "And I'd better get my ass in gear. I'll need to go some distance into the jungle if I'm going to phone Armandariz with no risk of being monitored. And it may take a long, long discussion to get him here." He glanced back over his shoulder. "Change your mind, Eve. This is too risky. If the rebels don't kill you, Montalvo will."

"Why not throw in Diaz?" she asked. "There's no win-win situation here. I just have to survive and keep Joe alive." She turned on her heel. "I'll be in my room waiting for you to tell me what's happening."

Soldono didn't show up at her room until almost 2:30 A.M.

"This morning before dawn," he said when she opened the door. "Sorry you're not going to get much sleep but it's safer for me to smuggle you out of the compound at that time."

"That doesn't matter. Where's the meeting?"

"At a clearing about five miles from here."

"Is he going to bring the reconstruction?"

He shrugged. "He wouldn't commit himself. You'll see when you get there. I did the best I could."

"You did very well. Thank you, Soldono."

"I'll meet you on the veranda at five-thirty A.M.

We've got to be over the wall and on our way fifteen minutes later."

"How can you be sure that we'll be able to get out?"

"I'm not sure. But the west wall was guarded by a man named Destando and Montalvo paid him a visit last night."

She stiffened. "Destando? He's the man Miguel said could be the informant."

He nodded. "I heard a shot about five minutes after Montalvo went into Destando's quarters. Evidently Montalvo took care of his leak. If the west wall is guarded, it won't be by anyone experienced. Quinn and Galen went over the west wall. I'm wondering if Destando was deliberately remiss in his duty that night."

She watched him walk away and drew a deep breath.

So far, so good.

"Armandariz should be in the glade just ahead," Soldono murmured. "I can't go any farther. He said for you to come alone. I'll stay here and guard your back."

"If Armandariz has as many guards milling around as he did in the camp, that's not going to be very effective." She moved down the path. "But thanks for the thought."

"Don't push him too hard," Soldono said. "He

wasn't eager for this meeting. If he gets too angry with you for lying to him, he might cut your throat."

"I'll push him as hard as I have to." She strained her eyes to see in the darkness that was only marginally lessened by the coming dawn. "I have no choice."

Soldono was leaning against a tree and straightened when she came down the path an hour later. "I was getting worried."

"So was I." She started down the trail. "He didn't want to believe me. I was too convincing before."

"But he finally did?"

"After telling me that if I didn't leave Colombia by the end of the week, I'd go home in a casket."

"But he didn't give you the reconstruction?"

"On the contrary, he threw it at me."

"You don't have it with you."

"I hid it on the way back. I couldn't chance Montalvo catching me and taking it away. I'll pick it up on the way to meet Diaz." She paused. "I'm going to need your help there too. Phone Venable and tell him to have one of his men pick me up here at ten tonight and drive me to the hill outside of Diaz's village. I'll make my own way from there."

"He's already consented to giving you the helicopter escort. He might not want to—"

"Just ask him."

"What about Montalvo? He's no dummy. Won't he know you're up to something?"

"I'll be visible during the early evening and he won't expect me to stick around later." She added grimly, "He knows I'm mad as hell with him and our relationship has been very cool." She looked up at the sky and started to trot. "It's beginning to turn light. We have to get back to the compound...."

11:55 P.M.

Nekmon phoned Diaz at the church a few minutes before midnight. "She's coming. She's down from the hill and just came out of the forest."

"Alone?"

"Yes, absolutely." Nekmon paused. "She's not carrying anything."

"She said she wouldn't bring it to the church. She'd just better have it close by." He turned to Joe Quinn. "She's coming to rescue you. Isn't that sweet? What devotion. I do love to see a woman protect her man. Too bad she believes she's trading you in for a new model."

"You're lying."

"I have a few doubts myself but since I have little faith in the human race, I think it likely she's as faithless as most women. Montalvo had the reputation for being very good with the ladies when he was in the rebel army. Sex is sex."

"Shut up, Diaz."

"Ugly." He backhanded him across the face. "Will

you never learn? I really should take you back to the castle instead of proceeding with the current plan. I didn't get my fill of you."

Joe's eyes were blazing in his bleeding face. "Do it. Let's go."

"So that I won't get my chance at Eve Duncan? She really doesn't deserve you. How can I convince you of that?"

"You can't."

"Nevertheless, I'll try. Disillusionment can be a torture in itself, I've discovered. Women are instinctively self-serving, Quinn. They try to mask it by preaching fairness and goodness but it's always to make their own position in life more secure. Christian behavior dictates that they be treated with kindness and tolerance. It doesn't matter how they interfere with a man's drive to better himself. It's always best to use them and then walk away. You'll know better next time."

Joe didn't answer.

"Providing you go on living after tonight." Diaz moved over to the window. He could see the woman walking swiftly through the cemetery. She should be here in a few minutes.

She was passing his mother's tomb now. Do you see her, Mother? She's another one like you. So sure she's right. Despising me for being evil and yet she excuses her own sins. It's going to be a pleasure killing her. Just as it was a pleasure killing you.

·   ·   ·

Eve stood before the church door, hesitating.

"Diaz."

"Come in," he called. "We're waiting for you."

"That's what I'm afraid of," she said. "Come out into the open and bring Joe with you."

"You don't trust me?" he asked mockingly. "I don't know why. Haven't I done everything you've asked?"

"You're entirely too fond of torture. What's to stop you from grabbing me as soon as I walk through those doors and trying to make me tell you where I placed the skull?"

"An excellent idea."

"Come out here."

"Did it occur to you that I could have had a sniper behind every tombstone in the cemetery to pick you off?"

"As you must know, Venable's helicopter pilot did a sweep before I left the forest." She held up a small radio receiver. "He said that there were possibly two men in the forest but none in the cemetery."

He chuckled. "There are three in the forest. And any one of them could have killed you before you reached here."

"But that wouldn't have served you. What about the skull?"

"Yes, what about the skull? Where is it?"

"Bring Joe out and we'll talk about it."

He turned and said over his shoulder, "Come along, Quinn. The lady has a desire to see your handsome face."

A moment later he appeared in the doorway. "Here we are. Now tell me where the skull is."

He looked no different from the newspaper photo she had seen of him. A little heavier, a little older, perhaps. "I'm not going to—" She inhaled sharply as she saw Joe with hands bound behind his back, behind Diaz. "My God. What did you do to him?"

"Nothing much. I had no time," Diaz said. "He was unconscious at first and then I had to be careful to make sure I had something to trade you."

The bruises on Joe's swollen face made him almost unrecognizable. "It must have been a real thrill beating up on an unarmed man."

"You shouldn't have interfered, Eve," Joe said. "Why the hell did you?"

"If you don't know the answer to that, then there's no use talking to you." She turned to Diaz. "The helicopter is going to land in four minutes. When Joe's on board, I'll tell you where to find the skull."

"Not good enough. I want it in my hands before I release you."

She had thought that was the way it was going to play out. "I'll stay behind."

"No!" Joe took a step forward. "Hell, no."

"Don't worry, I'm not sacrificing my life for you," she said. "He's not going to kill me. If he did,

Armandariz would hear about it and begin to suspect that what Montalvo said was really true."

"No!" Joe said.

"This is no longer up to you, Joe." She turned back to Diaz. "I mean it, no skull until you get Joe on that helicopter."

"You're willing to trade your life for his?"

"You heard what I told Joe. You're not stupid enough to kill me and risk what you've been bargaining for." She looked up at the sky. "I hear the helicopter. He should be landing soon." Her glance shifted to Diaz. "Well?"

He shrugged. "I'll let Quinn go as long as I have you. If you try to cheat me, I won't hesitate to cut your throat."

"I won't go." Joe's eyes were blazing. "What do you think I am, Eve? When did you decide I was namby-pamby enough to let you run over me? There's no way that—" He broke off as Diaz's fist crashed into his stomach with brutal force.

His knees buckled and he would have fallen to the ground if Eve hadn't sprung forward and caught him. She was brought down to the ground with him by the heavy weight of his body. She glared at Diaz. "You bastard."

"I was tired of arguments. I'd already made my decision."

Her arms tightened protectively around him. The blow had knocked the breath from his body and he was struggling for air. "He's wounded and helpless. Cut him loose."

"When he's tucked into the helicopter. He's not that helpless. Some men never give up. He killed three of my men before they took him." Diaz raised his eyes to the sky to watch the blue-white light of the helicopter spear the ground. "Ah, here it comes."

The wind from the rotors was blowing her hair across her face as the helicopter descended. Just a few minutes more and it would be down and Joe would be safe.

Hurry. Please, hurry.

Joe was struggling, trying to sit up and get away from her. She could feel the anger and outrage in every muscle of his body. Who could blame him? She had damaged his independence and his pride and that was unbearable for him. "I had to do it," she whispered. "I'm sorry, Joe."

"So am I." He pronounced every word with precision. "Let me go."

She slowly released him. "It's going to be okay, Joe." She wasn't sure if she was lying. Even if they got out of this alive, she couldn't be sure that anything would be okay for them again. She got to her feet. "Try to believe me." The helicopter had landed and the cockpit door was opening. Two men got out of the aircraft and came toward them.

Diaz pointed his gun at the men.

She stepped between them and jerked her head at Joe. "Untie him and then get him out of here."

"Wait until he's in the helicopter to cut him loose," Diaz told them. "She's trying to save his dignity but it will be much easier for you."

The pilot looked at her. "Ma'am?"

She turned away. "Just get him out." She didn't want to see him struggle. "Don't hurt him."

She heard Joe's muttered curse and then the closing of the door of the helicopter. A moment later she heard the whine of the rotors and glanced back to see the aircraft take off.

He was gone. He'd be safe. Her relief was mixed with sadness. Jesus, she'd *hated* to do it this way.

"The skull," Diaz prompted.

She tore her eyes from the helicopter. Get down to business. "Very well." She turned on her heel and strode back through the cemetery in the direction from which she'd come. "Follow me."

"I wouldn't think of doing anything else. But tell me where we're going."

"Not far."

"Where?"

"We're almost there." She glanced at the tomb they were passing, where Diaz's mother was interred. "It's really amazing that you were born to a woman, Diaz. I'd think that you'd be hatched by some vermin under a rock. It didn't surprise me that you tried to use a snake to kill me since you're so alike."

"Are you trying to make me angry? Why?"

"Because I'm angry. I don't like what you did to Joe. What you made me do to him."

"Too bad. Where's the skull?"

"Here." She stopped just beyond the tomb. "But you'll have to dig for it."

"Dig?" His eyes narrowed on her face and then went to the grave beside which she was standing. "The Armandariz woman's grave?"

"I thought it fitting that I return her skull to her resting place."

"You're lying. How would you do that? I've had you watched since you reached the hill. You had no time to come here and plant the skull."

"And you probably had the church watched. If I'd done it myself, it would have been suicidal and I've already told you I've no desire to do that."

"If you didn't do it, who did?"

"Sean Galen. I told him where I'd hidden the skull in the jungle outside the compound and he went to get it. He slipped in under your nose and buried the skull."

"Galen." He frowned. "He's been causing me a good deal of disturbance. I believe I'll have to deal very harshly with him." He looked around the cemetery warily. "And where did Galen go?"

"Are you afraid he's going to pop out from behind one of those tombstones? You know he's not here. Your men must have surveillance on the entire area."

"Yes." He looked back at her. "But I never trust the predictability of a woman. They don't think rationally."

"Do you want the skull?" She picked up a shovel leaning against the tomb. "Dig."

He stared at her for a moment and then leveled the gun at her head. "I think not. I don't do hard labor. Suppose you do it for me?"

Disappointment and fear surged through her. She'd hoped to distract him. There was no help for it.

She started to dig.

"The helicopter should be approaching the tower within the next ten minutes, Perez," Nekmon said into the phone. "Bring it down. Blow it out of the sky."

He hung up the phone and brought the binoculars up to his eyes again. What the hell was happening down there? The woman was digging. Was Diaz making her dig her own grave? It was possible. He'd seen him do it before to those missionaries who'd made him so angry preaching against him to the farmers.

Yes, that must be it. He remembered him threatening to bury her in the same grave with Montalvo's wife and he was much angrier with her than he had been with the missionaries. There had been no doubt in Nekmon's mind that Diaz would kill Eve Duncan and he had been bewildered when she had not been put on the helicopter with Quinn.

Oh, well, it was only a delay and none of his business. Nekmon had done his part and couldn't be blamed. Let Diaz toy with the woman to his heart's content.

In a few minutes Quinn and the CIA agents would be incinerated by the missile. The woman would be shot and disposed of and life could get back to normal. All this uproar since she'd arrived on the scene had been very annoying.

She'd stopped digging and was glaring at Diaz. She was saying something to him.

If her words were as provocative as her demeanor, she might not live to finish digging that grave.

16

Perez could hear the faint sound of the helicopter in the distance. It was still too far away but it would be on him before he knew it.

He steadied the missile launcher on the stone sill of the window. He would probably only get one shot and it had better be a good one. Diaz did not excuse failure.

He would not fail. He was the very best, Perez thought. Diaz would not have chosen him to take down the helicopter if he hadn't known how good he was.

The helicopter was closer. He could see it now, gleaming in the moonlight.

Come a little nearer, little bird. I'm going to pluck your feathers. . . .

12:40 A.M.

"If you want me to keep on digging keep your mouth shut," Eve said. "I'm tired of that poisonous slime you're spitting out."

Diaz's lips tightened. "Have you noticed I have a gun pointed at your head? I'll say anything I like to you."

"You don't want me dead. Armandariz would know that—"

"You think you're safe because of that bullshit? I can get around it. Though it would have been better if you'd boarded that helicopter with Quinn. Keep digging."

She tensed and then sank her shovel into the earth again. "What do you mean?"

"Presently. When you hand me the skull. If it's truly buried here, as you told me. I'm beginning to doubt it."

"It's here." She shoveled more quickly. "A few more inches... There!"

The dull gleam of the brown leather of the case was revealed as she scraped the dirt from around it. She picked up the case and held it out to him. "Now tell me what you meant when you said it would have been better if I'd gotten on the helicopter."

"Open it."

She unsnapped the case and lifted the lid.

He shone the flashlight down at the reconstruction. He gave a low whistle. "Yes, that's the bitch. You did a good job."

"What did you mean?" she repeated.

"It's true I don't want to disrupt my very tentative relationship with the CIA. To kill an agent would bring pressure to bear to wipe me out." He reached out and took the case. "But if Montalvo does it, then everyone goes after him. The helicopter should be blown out of the air in his territory in about three minutes."

"No!"

"Yes. I don't think we can hear it but we may be able to see the sky light up to the west. I believe we'll wait and let you see it before I kill you."

She climbed out of the grave. "You son of a bitch."

"Of course, we'll have to transport your body to the wreckage immediately so that you'll be found with Quinn's remains. A little gasoline bonfire and your body should be similar to the other corpses."

"They'll find the bullet wound when they do the autopsy. The burns wouldn't mask it."

He snapped his fingers. "That's right. What a fine scientific mind you have. I might have made a mistake. Let's see, then I'll have to break your neck, won't I?"

"If you can catch me, bastard." She wheeled and tore down the path in the direction of the church.

She heard him laugh behind her. "Run. You can't get away. Nekmon has been watching us from the hill. He knows that I have what I need and he'll be calling the castle to have my men come down to scoop you up. I may have them break a few more bodily parts other than your neck."

She glanced at her watch as she threw open the church door. Three minutes. God, she'd cut it close. "Sure, have them come after me," she called back to him. "You're too much of a coward to do it yourself. You beat up men who can't defend themselves. You crucify boys who are better men than you'll ever be. You think of yourself as a king of all you survey, but you'd be nothing without those goons." She glanced over her shoulder. That had gotten him. He was stalking after her.

Her gaze shifted to the castle. Activity. The gates were opening to let Diaz's men stream out.

And Diaz had almost reached the church.

The sky to the west lit up.

The helicopter!

"No!"

The Compound
12:44 A.M.

It was time. It was going to happen.

Miguel tensed beneath the sheet. Sweet Mary, he had waited too long for this. He was actually trembling like a baby.

Soldono stuck his head in the door. "How are you doing, Miguel? Dr. Diego said you couldn't sleep and wanted some company. You're lucky I'm a night owl."

Miguel nodded. "So is the Colonel. But I'm still being terribly neglected. He's in the library, busy trying to arrange to send me away from here. And Eve didn't even pay me a courtesy visit today."

"I believe she's busy too." Soldono sat down in the bedside chair. "We seem to be the only ones with a little leisure time." He smiled. "Would you like a midnight snack? I'll send for a tray."

"Are you sure you haven't been told to keep an ailing man from being bored?"

"Who would tell me? I take orders from Venable. I'm afraid he doesn't think you of enough importance to waste my time."

"Ah, what a blow to my ego," Miguel said. "And I was considering leaving the Colonel and going to Venable and asking for a job. Don't you think I'd make a fine CIA agent?"

"I think you're pulling my leg. What do you want to eat?"

"The Colonel is feeding me steaks to replenish my blood supply." His smile faded. "I hear I must thank you for donating blood to me."

"It was nothing. I would have done it for anyone."

"But I was the one in need," Miguel said. "I don't like to be in need. It hurts my pride. I've never felt more helpless in my life than when I was being nailed to that cross."

"You don't want to think about that, Miguel."

"But I do think about it. I can't get it out of my head. The spikes being driven into my hands and all the time Diaz standing above me and gazing down at me and smiling. It was nothing to him. He acted as if he did this every day of his life. So casual. He even took a phone call while he watched them do that to me."

Soldono leaned back in the chair. "Oh?"

"He probably thought I was in too much pain to pay any attention to what he was doing. He didn't realize how every sound, every sight, was magnified, and recorded in my mind. With every pound of that hammer..."

"I'm with Diaz. You must be remarkable, Miguel. I wouldn't think you'd be able to concentrate on anything but what was happening to you."

"What a curious coincidence that you'd use that phrase."

"What phrase?"

"You said, 'I'm with Diaz.'" He smiled. "And you are with Diaz, Soldono. You were the one on the phone with the bastard that night."

Soldono stiffened warily. "You're crazy."

"No, he used your name. Just once. He said, 'Are you sure, Soldono?' You must have been telling him about Eve going to Armandariz's camp."

"Nonsense. You were delirious with pain."

"No. You're his mole in this camp. How long have you been in his pay?"

"You're nuts. It was Destando who was in Diaz's pay. For God's sake, Montalvo shot the bastard."

'No, he wanted you to think he had shot him so that you wouldn't realize we suspected you. Destando has been lying low all day on the Colonel's orders. How long has Diaz had you in his pocket?"

Soldono didn't answer.

"How long, Soldono?" Miguel asked softly.

He was silent a moment and then shrugged. "Not long. He wouldn't meet my price. It wasn't until lately that he was desperate enough to make it worth my while." Soldono's gaze was cold. "And you're a fool to confront me like this when you're helpless in bed. You must know I have to kill you."

"To protect your interests with Diaz?"

"Diaz will need me as long as I have contacts with the Agency. I have to maintain those contacts. When I leave the Agency, I'm going to go home and fake a terrific windfall on the stock market. None of this living in the jungle like an animal for me. I'll have a grand horse farm in Kentucky and be respected." His eyes narrowed. "So Montalvo knows?"

"Definitely."

"Then I think after I leave here, I'll have to go and take care of him. The library, you said?"

"That's what I said." Miguel watched him reach in his pocket and draw out a gun and point it at him. "You'd really shoot an unarmed man?"

Soldono's lips twisted. "I really would."

"That's what I thought." Miguel's forefinger pressed the trigger of the sawed-off shotgun he was cradling beneath the sheet. The sheet was blown off Miguel by the force of the blast.

And Soldono's head was blown off his body.

12:48 A.M.

"Are you hiding from me?" Diaz asked mockingly as he peered at the dark pews. "You were very brave a few minutes ago, whore. Where is that courage now?"

He began to go slowly down the aisle, shining the flashlight on either side. "Are you praying in my fine church? It won't do you any good. You'll be dead in a few minutes. Did you see the sky when the helicopter blew? Do you think when you join Quinn in the afterlife that he'll forgive you for betraying him with another man? He tried to tell me that he didn't believe me, but a man always believes a woman will fuck another man given the chance." He stopped, frowning. "Come out, bitch. I'm getting impatient and you don't want to—"

"You're not the only one who's impatient."

Diaz froze. He whirled to stare at the man standing in the doorway. "Montalvo?"

"Who else?" He melted to the side so he wasn't silhouetted against the door. "Are you ready to die? You asked Eve if she was praying. It wouldn't do you any good to pray. You're so steeped in foulness that even Satan wouldn't take you."

Diaz got off a shot as he dropped behind one of the pews.

"Missed."

He could hear Montalvo moving to the left.

He fired again.

"Missed again. You've spent too much time in that castle counting drug money," Montalvo said. "There's an art to cat and mouse. I learned it in the army." He paused. "So did Nalia."

Montalvo's voice seemed lower and to the right, Diaz judged. Make him keep talking until he could zero in on him. "That whore was no challenge to me. I gathered her up and crushed her. Alive or dead she's nothing. I have her head right here."

"You're wrong." It was Eve's voice from far across the room. "Nalia may be dead, but she's the one who trapped you tonight."

"I told you not to be in the church when I got here, Eve," Montalvo said roughly. "Now get the hell out of here."

"I had to be sure," Eve said. "I didn't see you at the tomb. I wasn't sure you'd made it."

"Tomb," Diaz repeated.

"Your mother's tomb," Montalvo said. "I made it here earlier this evening and jimmied the lock. I thought she wouldn't mind if it meant you were disposed of like the garbage you are."

Diaz began cursing. That bitch mother was trying to destroy him even from beyond the grave. No, he mustn't lose control. He was still master here. Soon his men would be pouring into the church and killing these vermin. He started crawling toward the door.

The floor shook as an explosion rocked the earth!

"What the hell?"

"It's your splendid castle, the center of your universe," Montalvo said. "Or at least it was. That blast should have turned it into rubble. By the sound of the explosion, Galen and Quinn did a good job of planting that dynamite."

"I'll build another one," Diaz snarled. "I have money. I have men. You can't—"

"You have no men," Eve said. "Armandariz was waiting to gather them up when they poured out of the castle. Another of his troops is setting the coca fields on fire now. You have nothing. They'll bury you in a pauper's grave."

"No!" he screamed. He began shooting at the corner where he'd heard her voice. "You're lying. You're lying."

"It's time to end it," Montalvo said. "Past time."

He was near the altar! Diaz turned and got off another shot. He didn't wait to see if he'd gotten the bastard. He had to get out. He had to see if it was true. He had to see—

His body collapsed on the floor as Montalvo jumped on top of him. He struggled to turn and lifted the gun. Montalvo knocked it aside. "No guns. I'm not going to shoot you. I've waited too long for this." His hands closed around Diaz's throat. "Is this how you were going to kill Eve, Diaz? You would have taken your time, wouldn't you? You like the pain to be slow and deep."

"Yes." Diaz glared up at him and began to curse. "I'll get out of this." He tore at his hands. "I'm stronger and smarter than you, than anyone. I won't let—"

"The hell you are." Montalvo's hands tightened, slowly choking him. "You're scum. Die, scum."

He was dead.

Eve could see the limpness of Diaz's body as she came across the church toward where Montalvo was still astride him.

She picked up Diaz's fallen flashlight and shone it down on his face. His eyes were wide open and staring up at her. Yes, dead. But Montalvo still wasn't moving to get off him.

She shone the light on Montalvo's face and inhaled sharply. Bloodlust. She had seen that expression on Joe's face in the heat of battle and it still shocked and terrified her. "I believe you can get off him now," she said quietly.

He stared blindly at her and then shook his head as if to clear it. "Yes." He slowly released Diaz's throat. "It's ... done." He got to his feet. "You should have gone out the back door as we agreed."

"I didn't agree. You told me to do it. I decided that

wasn't what I wanted. I had to know for sure that Diaz didn't get away. He's hurt too many people."

"Yes, he has." He was still staring down at Diaz. "He believed until the very end that he'd be the one to survive."

Her lips twisted. "Survive and prosper."

"I wanted him to know he was defeated and going to die. I'm not sure he did."

"Unless it's a sudden death, I think everyone knows before the last breath." She paused. "There was an explosion. I saw the light in the sky. That wasn't supposed to happen. It scared the hell out of me. You promised me that Joe would be safe on that helicopter."

"He is safe. I set it up so that—"

"You can't be sure of that," she said fiercely. "What was that explosion?"

"I'll find out." He dialed the phone as he walked toward one of the arched windows. "It looks like something from that American movie *Independence Day* out there. Come and look."

She followed him to the window. The castle was engulfed in flames, and smoke wreathed the ruins and cast a dark haze over the village.

Men running toward the castle.

Screams.

Shots.

A machine gun mounted on a truck was driving down the street and spewing out bullets and death as Diaz's men returned the fire.

Montalvo had finally made a connection and was talking into the phone.

She tensed, her gaze on his face. No expression, dammit.

He listened for a moment and then said, "No, go back to the compound. We'll meet you there."

"What's happening?" she asked as he hung up the phone.

"Quinn is alive and free and angry as hell. That's what you wanted to know, isn't it?"

Relief poured through her. "That's what I wanted to know. It's not that I didn't trust you but—"

"But you didn't trust me." He smiled faintly. "Not entirely. But at least there was some trust there or you would have been hysterical instead of mildly suspicious."

"Sometimes the best-laid plans go awry."

"Not usually. I've never believed in that saying."

"What about the explosion?"

"The tower was too inaccessible to send a force in to bring down the sniper."

"You sent twenty men to meet Galen and take care of it. That wasn't enough?"

"There would have been casualties. It turns out that Galen has a horror of casualties. He camped out in the jungle outside the tower and checked out the missile launcher last night. He thought he could disable it. So he waited until the sniper left the battlements and went downstairs, presumably to piss and eat. Galen went into the tower, disabled the missile, and got out by the skin of his teeth."

"The explosion," she repeated.

"When the sniper fired the missile, it exploded as Galen intended. That was the tower blowing up."

"Thank God." She turned to once again gaze out at the turmoil in the streets.

"Independence Day?" Montalvo asked softly.

She nodded. She and Montalvo had caused this to happen. They had planned and worked and executed the plan and now it was happening. The knowledge gave her a sense of bonding and closeness to him that she had never felt before toward anyone.

She drew a deep breath and took a step away from him. "When can I get back to the compound?"

"Don't be impatient. We have a major conflict going on outside." He handed her a gun and headed for the door. "And I should be out there with my men. Stay here. I'll come back for you when it's safe."

"What about Nekmon and the other men staked out in the forest?"

"They should have been disposed of by now. I ordered them to be taken out as soon as the castle was blown." He stopped at the door. "I mean it. Don't leave here. There are bullets flying everywhere. I'm not going to lose you at this stage of the game."

"You can't lose what you don't—"

He had already run out of the church. She watched him duck down and keep low as he ran through the streets toward the castle. It was true;

there were shots and grenades going off constantly. He'd be lucky if he reached his men before he
took a bullet. The thought sent a thrill of panic
through her.

"Keep safe," she whispered. "For Christ's sake,
don't die now, Montalvo."

Galen met Eve in the courtyard when she arrived
back at the compound. "Okay?"

"Of course I'm okay." She jumped out of the jeep.
"How is Joe?"

"He had to have some stitches replaced and Diaz
broke another rib but he's as good as can be expected. Where's Montalvo?"

"Still at the village. He and Armandariz are doing
a cleanup. He sent me here as soon as he thought it
was safe." She smiled grimly. "Some of Diaz's men
are holed up and shooting everyone they spot. The
idiot will be lucky to get out with his skin intact."

He raised an eyebrow. "You're very concerned
about Montalvo."

"What do you expect? He's not a stranger, after all.
We've been practically living in each other's pockets
ever since I got here."

"Yes, I can see how that would promote a certain
intimacy. A relationship born under the sword, so to
speak."

"We're not intimate." Yet those moments in the
church had possessed a strong sense of intimacy she

couldn't deny. "It's over. May I see Joe? He's not under sedation?"

"Are you kidding? After what he's been through with these wounds, he'd have shot anyone who tried to drug him now. He's on the veranda."

"But you're the one who came to meet me."

"He was concerned about you. He wanted to go back to the cemetery and rescue you. He was relieved when I told you were on the way back here."

She smiled bitterly. "Not relieved enough for him to want to see my face." She wearily shook her head. "I didn't expect anything else. I know how Joe thinks. I hurt his pride. It will take a while for him to forgive me." She paused. "If he ever does."

Galen shrugged. "I can sympathize with him. I'd have problems with being a pawn instead of a player. It would chafe like hell."

"Then he'll have to deal with it." She started up the steps. But Joe wouldn't have to deal with it unless that was his choice. He could turn his back and walk away. The thought sent a jolt of pain through her. Face it. She had done what she had decided had to be done and there might be terrible consequences. Confront them and try to work through them.

Joe was standing by the balustrade on the veranda looking out at the jungle when Eve opened the French doors.

"Shouldn't you be sitting down?" she asked

quietly. "Galen said you had to have your stitches redone."

"I don't feel like sitting down." He turned to face her. "It makes me feel weak and ineffectual. I've had enough of that to last a lifetime."

"You weren't ineffectual. You're the one who laid those explosives. You took the beatings that bastard handed out and never flinched." She paused. "You were a hero, Joe."

"Bullshit. I didn't finish the job." He stared her in the eye. "You did. You and Montalvo. I was useless after I was captured. Just a glorified punching bag."

"You *weren't* useless. If you hadn't set those explosions, Montalvo might not have been able to persuade Armandariz to stage the attack. Everything fell into place."

"What fell into place?"

She frowned. "Didn't Galen tell you?"

"I want to hear it from you. I want to watch your face."

"Do you think I'd lie to you?"

"No, that's not why I want to do it. Tell me."

"When Diaz told me that you'd been captured, I knew I had to make a deal with him. But I couldn't be sure he'd keep it, so I had to involve Montalvo. At first, he refused me and I thought I'd have to go it alone. But I went back and wore him down after I got the call from Galen. He knew there was a chance then. He already knew that Soldono was Diaz's information source and was monitoring his calls. We needed to make sure that Soldono gave Diaz the right information. That was my job."

"Was it your job to meet him in that cemetery and risk your neck?"

"Yes. It was the only way I could be sure of saving you. And it all had to go like clockwork if we were going to wipe Diaz out in one night. Armandariz setting off the explosion and the attack on the castle. Montalvo sending Galen to take care of the sniper in the tower after Galen told us what Diaz was planning. Galen had been monitoring what was going on at the castle with that fancy surveillance equipment you brought with you. Montalvo's part was to take out Diaz so that he couldn't call for more reinforcements. We couldn't tip any part of the plan or the rest might not work."

His lip curled. "I can see the two of you huddled together conspiring."

"We did a lot of that," she said. "We had to make sure Soldono didn't tumble to what we were doing until the right moment."

"Cozy."

"Not at all." Her lips tightened. "What the devil are you trying to say?"

"Did you fuck him?"

She absorbed the shock and then said, "No, I didn't. Did you think I did?"

"Diaz said you told him you did."

"To give me a better position to bargain. I'd think you'd figure that out."

"It was hard to figure anything out when every word was punctuated with a fist in my stomach. It sort of drove his point home."

She flinched. "I can see that it would. Do you believe him?"

He met her eyes and then shook his head. "Not when I'm sane."

"Diaz said in their hearts all men believe women are whores."

"Diaz is wrong. But there's a streak of the primitive that makes us think women will always go to the strong. It's something I can't fight."

"The hell you can't," she said unsteadily. "And you are strong, Joe. Even if you were in a wheelchair, you'd still be stronger than any other man I've met."

"I won't ask if that includes Montalvo."

"I did *not* fuck him."

"But did you want to?" He moved toward the door. "I think the answer is yes. I don't even want you to deny it. I don't think I'd believe you. Hell, you may not even realize that you do."

"But of course you can see right into my psyche as if it were a blueprint."

"Yes, I know you. Maybe better than you know yourself."

He had reached the door and panic seared through her. "Don't you dare leave. We have to talk."

"Not now. I'm a little raw at the moment. Okay, I have an ego and you stung me by closing me out of the action. That could be part of it. And after all these years of dealing with your obsession about finding Bonnie maybe I'm just tired. I don't know. I have to do some thinking."

"Joe..."

He gazed back at her. "I know you care about me. I know you're upset and hurt. I can't help you this time, Eve." The French doors closed behind him.

Jesus.

She sank into the rattan chair and huddled there. She had hurt him and that was the last thing she wanted to do. She had to find a way to help him, heal him. Yes, she was hurting, too, but she was afraid no one could help her.

Those last words had sounded too much like good-bye.

17

Eve was still on the veranda when Montalvo came back to the compound four hours later.

"Eve?"

She stirred and sat up straight in the chair. "Is everything secured at the village?"

"A few pockets of resistance. Armandariz can take care of the rest." He squatted in front of her chair. "I came to take care of you."

"I'm fine."

"Liar." His fingers moved delicately over her jawline. "You're tense as a violin string. Galen said you'd gone out here to talk to Quinn."

She nodded jerkily.

"And it didn't go well."

"You could say that."

"Why?"

"He thinks I want to go to bed with you."

His fingers continued to stroke her cheek. "Do you?"

"Sometimes." She hadn't realized she'd blurt out the truth that she hadn't fully admitted to herself. "But it's only sex. And I won't do it."

He sighed. "I'm afraid that's true. But what a splendid match we'd make. It would be beyond belief." He touched her lips with his forefinger. "Just once, Eve?"

She shook her head. "Even if there weren't Joe I couldn't risk it. You're . . . I think you'd be too much."

"Too much what?"

"Too much darkness, too much intensity, too much passion." She shrugged helplessly. "Too much."

"I'm working on the darkness. I believe I have a chance to come into the light now that I've brought Nalia home and killed Diaz. The intensity and the passion?" He smiled. "No way. I told you that we mirrored each other. It may be those qualities that are my most potent ammunition."

Her lip was tingling beneath his touch and she turned her head. "I like my life. I love Joe. You'd . . . devour me."

"I might try." He rose to his feet. "You're feeling insecure at the moment or you wouldn't be so lacking in confidence. I think I'll leave you alone to pull yourself together. You don't know how difficult it is to be this restrained." He gazed down at her with a smile. "What a team we'd be, Eve. We'd have it all."

She shook her head.

He studied her face. "You don't want to take that first step. I'd help you, Eve. There's so much more between us than sex."

"I love Joe," she repeated.

"Of course you do. But there's a place for me too. I can't promise I won't try to squeeze Quinn out. We're both alpha males. But I can be patient. I know what we have in store for us. I see it. I can *feel* it."

And he was making her feel it too, she realized. He was blurring the images and drawing her into the circle of intensity as he always did. Fight it.

But dear God, she was weary of fighting.

"I could push it," he said softly. "You're hurting and I may never get another chance when you're this vulnerable." He shook his head. "But that's not good enough for me. I want you to walk toward me and take my hand. I want you to stand beside me as you did in that church, strong and independent and joined in purpose." He turned and headed for the door. "So I'll wait. My time will come."

He was gone.

Relief cascaded through her.

Relief . . . and disappointment.

Jesus, what the hell was happening to her? She had always known where she was going and this bewilderment was tearing her to pieces.

Forget it. Go to bed. It wasn't as if she were the one to make a decision, she thought bitterly. She wasn't sure Joe still wanted her. Montalvo had already said she wasn't enough for him right now. She might very well end up alone.

And it would probably serve her right. Perhaps a person as obsessed as she should be alone. That way she wouldn't hurt anyone but herself.

She got to her feet. No use sitting here brooding. She would shower, start to pack, and then go to sleep. Tomorrow she'd talk to Montalvo about arranging for her to go back to Atlanta.

It was time to put her life back on track.

"Eve? Are you asleep?"

She turned over in bed to see Joe silhouetted in the open doorway. "No. Come in."

He closed the door and crossed the room to the bed. "I was going to wait until morning. But I couldn't do it."

"It's close enough." She glanced at the clock on the nightstand. "It's almost four A.M. That's morning." She sat up in bed. "And I couldn't sleep anyway." She tried to smile. "You pretty well blew me away."

"I know. I had...issues."

"Obviously. Will it help if I tell you I understand every single one?"

He sat down on the bed beside her. "It helps."

"Should I turn on the light?"

"Not now. There's enough moonlight coming in that window." He was silent a moment. "I can work my way through most of those issues. Once I'm healthy I don't believe you're going to treat me like a second-class citizen. You never have before."

"You were never hurt and in danger before. I don't promise I wouldn't do the same thing again. I love you, Joe. Protection goes with the territory. It's self-preservation for me as well as you."

"Then I'll have to be damn sure I don't get wounded again. I can't take it." He paused. "And I'm not afraid of Montalvo. I can find ways to make you forget him. He's the new kid on the block. I know you better than he ever could."

I looked at you and saw myself.

"Yes."

"That wasn't very convincing."

"I'm convinced you can do anything you want to do."

He reached out and took her hand. "Except one thing."

She knew what was coming and instinctively tensed.

"Bonnie. I can't make you forget Bonnie."

"No, you can't," she said unevenly. "Not ever. And if that's becoming a problem, it's the one thing I can't solve."

"It's a problem. I used to think if I could just find her that it would be over. But it's not happening and you almost died this time trying to find her."

"And so did you."

"Yet when we get back to the U.S., you're going to go after that lead Montalvo got for you."

"Yes." Her hand tightened. "So if you're smart, you'll leave me. You don't deserve this."

He looked down at their joined hands. "Do you want me to leave you? Will it make it easier for you?"

"God, no."

He was silent a moment. "Then I think I'll stick around." He kicked off his shoes. "Scoot over. The last time I held you, I was so drugged I couldn't appreciate it."

She shifted over in bed and he enfolded her in his arms. Lord, he felt good. "I love you, Joe," she whispered. "This is all I want. You're all I want."

"That's good to know." He kissed her temple. "And I'll work very hard on keeping the status quo intact."

"So will I," she whispered. "Forever..."

Montalvo was in the library when she came downstairs later that morning. "Good morning." His gaze searched her expression. "You're...serene. I'm not sure that's good for me."

"I want you to arrange transportation to send Joe and me home."

He nodded. "Ah, a reconciliation. Definitely not good for me."

"Will you do it?"

"Of course. I'll have you out of here by late this afternoon." He stood up. "Do I get a fond kiss good-bye?"

"No."

"Coward." He smiled. "I've never kissed you and I thought it would be interesting. But I agree it's better not to run the risk. It would get in the way."

"No risk," she said. "How is Miguel?"

"Much better now that I let him shoot Soldono." He grimaced. "But Venable isn't as pleased. He wanted to bring Soldono back to your justice. I don't trust courts." His expression darkened. "And Miguel deserved his revenge."

She shivered as she remembered the boy hanging from that cross. "When are you taking him to the hospital in the U.S.?"

"As soon as I wind up my affairs here. I'm closing the compound."

"What?"

"I'm retiring. I have all the money I could possibly need. I've accomplished what I set out to do." He inclined his head at her. "*We've* accomplished what I set out to do. Armandariz and I are burying Nalia's remains in the cemetery in the village where she was born."

"Then she's truly home," she said softly.

He nodded.

"Good. That makes me very happy." She turned to go back upstairs.

"And as soon as I get Miguel on his feet, I'll be keeping my promise about Bonnie's killer."

"I have the names. Joe and I can follow through on it."

"But that wouldn't be keeping my promise."

"We can do it," she repeated.

He studied her expression. "We'll discuss it another time."

"No, I don't want you near me, Montalvo."

He nodded slowly. "Quinn is feeling threatened?"

She didn't answer.

He tilted his head appraisingly. "Or are you the one feeling threatened?"

"We can handle it ourselves." She started up the stairs. "Just as we've always done."

The sun was setting as Eve, Joe, and Galen got into the jeep.

"Why don't you go down and tell her good-bye?" Miguel asked from his bed across the room from the window where Montalvo stood looking down at the courtyard below. "It's what you want to do."

Turn around, Eve. You know I'm watching you.

"How do you know what I want to do?" Montalvo asked.

"I have nothing to do but lie here and think," Miguel said. "And since I have a very boring selection of subjects I chose you." He paused. "You let her go. I didn't think you'd do it."

"She's not ready for me yet. It would have been a disaster if I'd not walked carefully."

"But you could say good-bye."

"It wouldn't have been satisfactory for either one of us. She's very defensive about Quinn." He smiled. "And not saying good-bye is not a bad thing."

Turn around and look up, Eve.

She gazed straight ahead as the driver started the car.

I'm here, Eve. Just a glance . . .

Her shoulders tensed and for a moment he thought she'd look back.

She didn't do it. Her shoulders were straight, her eyes still straight ahead as the driver drove through the gates.

Of course she hadn't looked back. It would have been foreign to her character to give in to that impulse.

But for an instant she had thought about it and that was a triumph too.

"They're gone." He turned away from the window and strolled back to the bed. "By tomorrow they'll be safely tucked away in their cozy cottage by the lake."

"You don't seem upset."

"There's no use being upset." He poured a cup of coffee for Miguel and lifted it to his lips. After the boy had taken a few swallows he set the cup on the saucer. "It's counterproductive. And you know that's not my way."

"So what will you do?"

"I'll go and put my Nalia in her final resting-place. Then I'll take you to that Emory Hospital and get you well. I'm very tired of waiting on you like this. I think you're beginning to enjoy it too much."

Miguel smiled slyly. "Maybe."

"And then I'll put you into a school and make you slave at the books."

Miguel's smile faded. "I'm staying with you."

"Who said I wouldn't be there?"

"All the time?" Miguel asked suspiciously.

Montalvo's glance returned to the window. "I might take a few excursions while you're otherwise occupied."

Miguel's jaw set. "I won't be 'otherwise occupied.' Not if it means you're dumping me somewhere. I don't give a damn about your books."

Montalvo looked back at him and he slowly shook his head. "What am I going to do with you, boy?"

"Keep me around. We've got to be together, Colonel."

Montalvo nodded, and carefully avoiding Miguel's bandaged hands, he grasped his forearm with affection. "I believe you're right," he said softly. A warm smile lit his face. "We've got to stay together."

18

Lake Cottage

The sun was going down and casting a glory of pink-and-purple mirror images on the lake.

Mirror . . .

Would she ever be able to think of that word without remembering Montalvo, Eve wondered as she leaned back against a pine and linked her arms about her knees.

Of course she would. It would only take time. Good heavens, she hadn't thought of him more than a few times during the entire two months that had passed since they had left the compound. In a year she wouldn't remember Montalvo existed.

"Yes, you will."

She glanced sideways to see Bonnie leaning against the tree a few yards away. A surge of love swept through her.

"You know nothing about it," she said. "You're a kid."

Bonnie sighed. "I told you that doesn't make any difference now."

"You always tell me what I want to hear. That's very suspicious, you know."

"I want to make you happy. It doesn't mean I don't tell you the truth."

"As you see it."

A luminous smile lit Bonnie's face. "As I see it."

"I am happy," Eve said softly. "Whenever I see you, I'm happy. Of course, that makes me pretty wacko."

"And are you happy with Joe now, Mama?"

"Of course I am." It was the truth. Why shouldn't she be happy? They had each other and the peaceful life they had almost lost. "Why do you ask?"

Bonnie just looked at her.

"Okay, there are things to work out. It's not as... smooth."

"Smooth isn't always good. Perhaps you needed shaking up, Mama."

"Not like that," she said dryly. "I'll pass."

"He was good for you."

"Montalvo? You don't know what you're talking about."

"It was like being caught in a storm. You had to fight to survive, but it excited you. It made you come alive. I like to see you all glowing and intent."

"I'm glad I made you happy. It wasn't so much fun for me." She gazed out at the lake. "And it's over. I'm only waiting for Joe's wounds to finish healing and we'll be going after a man who may have killed you. Did he do it, baby?"

"I told you that I don't think about things that happened that night. It makes me—I don't think about it."

Eve closed her eyes as she thought about the horror of that night. "I forgot," she whispered. "I'm sorry, baby. I could just use a little help."

"You'll have help. You have Joe." She smiled. "And you'll have Montalvo."

"I don't have Montalvo. I'll probably never hear from him again."

"You'll hear from him. He's there, waiting."

"Then I'll send him on his way. I don't need him."

"Whatever you say," Bonnie said gently. "It's getting dark. Joe's going to make steaks on the barbecue tonight. He's wondering where you are."

"Then I'd better go back to the cottage." She opened her eyes. "I don't like to—"

Bonnie was no longer there. She felt the familiar pang of sadness and loss.

"Good-bye, baby," she whispered.

She got to her feet and strolled down the path toward the lake cottage.

Joe had come out on the porch and waved to her.

She waved back at him.

Contentment and love flowed through her as she saw Joe leaning on the porch rail and smiling at her. Her pace quickened with eagerness as she moved toward him.

If you loved
STALEMATE,
read on for a sneak peek at

QUICKSAND

The next heart-stopping thriller

featuring Eve Duncan

by Iris Johansen

Coming Spring 2008
from St. Martin's Press

QUICKSAND

On sale March 2008 from St. Martin's Press

The phone was ringing again, Eve realized impatiently. It was the third time in fifteen minutes and she supposed she'd have to answer it. It couldn't be that important. Joe or Jane would have called her on her cell phone when she hadn't answered. They knew how absorbed she became when she was working.

She glanced down at the ID. Bloomburg, Illinois. Sheriff James Jedroth. It had to be another police department asking her to do a reconstruction. Since she'd become so blasted famous those requests never stopped. But it was nearly ten at night and evidently Sheriff Jedroth didn't understand the concept of business hours. Well, Eve didn't either, so she might as well answer.

"Eve Duncan."

"Do you still miss your little Bonnie?"

Shock rippled through her. "I beg your pardon."

"She had curly red hair and on the last day you saw her, she was wearing a Bugs Bunny T-shirt."

"Is this some kind of sick joke, Sheriff Jedroth? I'm not amused."

"I'm amused. Amused and excited and full of anticipation. I haven't felt like this for years. I didn't realize I was getting stale and that the kill was losing its luster. Then I heard your name on your voice mail and suddenly felt reborn."

"Kill." Her hand tightened on the phone. "Who is this? You're not a sheriff, are you?"

"I impersonated a sheriff once. It was in Fort Collins, Colorado. Children are taught to trust policemen."

"Who are you?" she repeated. "I don't know you. Why are you calling me?"

"Bonnie knew me. She knew me very well before the end."

Pain surged through Eve. "You son of a bitch. What are you trying to tell me?"

"You shouldn't have tried to track me down. Now I'll have to punish you. I never let myself be victimized without making sure that my pain is reciprocated." He chuckled.

"I didn't try to track you down. I don't even know your name."

"Henry Kistle."

Kistle. The name of the man Montalvo had given her as one of the possible murderers of her daughter.

"Yes, you know me. You set that asshole Jedroth to watch me."

"Where are you?"

"It would be no use to tell you. I've just left town. I'll be hundreds of miles away from here before you can call and get someone to find me. I know about red tape."

"What . . . do you know about Bonnie?"

"That she was seven years old and a beautiful child. Do you know how many pretty little girls I've killed since your Bonnie died? Though I always regard her as my inspiration. She was like a burning arrow lighting the darkness. I remember how—"

"Shut up." She couldn't take anymore. "Don't talk about her."

"I'm done for the time being. I just wanted to touch base with you. I needed something to keep me up and zinging."

"Zinging?"

"That's what life's about. You have to keep on top of it, keep excited and moving. I got a little buzz earlier tonight but nothing like the one I'm feeling now. It's not as good as a kill but maybe you could make the next kill extraordinary."

"What kill?"

But he had hung up the phone.

TEN YEARS OF EVE DUNCAN FORENSIC THRILLERS

Iris Johansen's heroine Eve Duncan first won the hearts of readers over a decade ago in *The Face of Deception*. Fans have watched Eve grow from a young forensic sculptor shattered by the murder of her child into a wise and capable woman, assisting her adopted daughter, Jane, who now has missions all her own. Here's a look back at the Eve Duncan books that have chilled spines while thrilling imaginations. . . .

●

THE FACE OF DECEPTION (October 1998)

An unidentified skull . . . a trail of terrifying secrets . . . and a woman whose talented hands could reveal the shocking truth . . .

As a forensic sculptor, Eve Duncan helps identify the dead from their skulls. Her own daughter murdered and her body never found, the job is Eve's way of coming to terms with her personal nightmare. But more terror lies ahead when she accepts work from billionaire John Logan. Beneath her gifted hands a face emerges from the skull he has given her to reconstruct—a face no one was ever meant to see. Now Eve is trapped in a frightening web of murder and deceit. Powerful enemies are determined to cover up the truth, and they will make certain that truth goes to the grave . . . even if Eve gets buried with it.

Praise for *The Face of Deception*

"One of her best . . . a fast-paced, nonstop, clever plot in which Johansen mixes political intrigue, murder and suspense." —*USA Today*

"The book's twists and turns manage to hold the reader hostage until the denouement, a sure crowd pleaser." —*Publishers Weekly*

"Johansen keeps her story moving at breakneck speed."
—*Chicago Daily Sun*

A Look Inside THE FACE OF DECEPTION:

"Ms. Duncan."

She stiffened, then whirled around.

"I'm sorry, I didn't mean to frighten you. I'm John Logan. I wonder if I could speak to you?"

John Logan. If he hadn't introduced himself she would have recognized him from the photo. How could she miss that California tan? she thought sardonically. And in that gray Armani suit and Gucci loafers, he looked as out of place in her small backyard as a peacock. "You didn't frighten me. You startled me."

"I rang the doorbell." He smiled as he walked toward her. There was not an ounce of fat on his body and he exuded confidence and charm. She had never liked charming men. Charm could hide too much. "I guess you didn't hear me."

"No." She had the sudden desire to shake his confidence. "Do you always trespass, Mr. Logan?"

The sarcasm didn't faze him. "Only when I really want to see someone. Could we go somewhere and talk?" His gaze went to the door of her lab. "That's where you work, isn't it? I'd like to see it."

"How did you know where I work?"

"Not from your friends at the Atlanta P.D. I understand they were very protective of your privacy." He strolled forward and stood beside the door. He smiled. "Please?"

He was obviously accustomed to instant acquiescence, and annoyance surged through her again. "No."

His smile faded a little. "I may have a proposition for you."

"I know. Why else would you be here? But I'm too busy to take on any more work. You should have phoned first."

"I wanted to see you in person."

●

THE KILLING GAME (September 1999)

A merciless killer on the hunt . . . an innocent child in his sights . . . a woman driven to the edge to stop him . . .

The killer knows Eve Duncan all too well. He knows the pain she feels for her murdered daughter, Bonnie, whose body has never been found. He knows that as one of the nation's top forensic sculptors she'll insist on identifying the nine skeletons unearthed on a bluff near Georgia's Talladega Falls. He knows she won't be able to resist the temptation of believing that one of those skeletons might be her daughter's. But that is only the beginning of the killer's sadistic game. He wants Eve one-on-one, and he'll use his ace in the hole to make sure she complies. And he won't stop playing until he claims the prize he wants most: Eve's life.

Praise for *The Killing Game*

"Johansen is at the top of her game. . . . An enthralling cat-and-mouse game . . . perfect pacing . . . The suspense holds until the very end." —*Publishers Weekly*

"Most satisfying." —*New York Daily News*

"An intense whodunit that will have you gasping for breath." —*Tennessean*

"For a well-plotted thrill-a-minute read, you can't go wrong with this one." —*Southern Pines (NC) Pilot*

A Look Inside THE KILLING GAME:

She kicked off her shoes as soon as they reached the terrace and watched Joe take off his shoes and socks and roll up his pant legs. It reminded her of the last time she'd seen him on his speedboat, bare-chested, khakis rolled up to his calves, laughing over his shoulder at Eve and Diane as he weaved the boat across the lake. "Do you still have the lake cottage?"

He nodded. "But I gave the Buckhead house to Diane as part of the settlement."

"Where do you live now?"

"An apartment near the precinct." He followed her down the path toward the beach. "It's fine. I'm not there much anyway."

"I can tell." Her feet sank into the cool, soft sand. This was better. The sound of the surf was calming, and being alone with Joe was soothing too. They knew each other so well, it was almost like being by herself. Well, not really. Joe never let her forget who and what he was. It was just that they . . . meshed. "You're not taking care of yourself. You look tired."

"It's been a rough week." He fell into step with her and walked in silence for a few moments "Did your mother tell you about Talladega?"

"What?"

"I didn't think she would. It's all over the newspapers but she wouldn't want to tell you anything that might jar you away from here."

She stiffened. "What's happened?"

"Nine skeletons were found on the bluff near the falls. One of them is a little girl. Caucasian."

"How . . . little?"

"Seven or eight."

She drew a deep breath. "How long has she been buried?"

•

THE SEARCH (June 2000)

He strikes without warning. He kills without mercy. He's only just begun.

As part of an elite K-9 search-and-rescue team, Sarah Patrick and her golden retriever, Monty, have a gift for finding what no one else can. But their latest assignment is not like the others. This time Sarah is being forced to take part in a deadly mission . . . by a man who knows enough about her past to ensure her cooperation.

Billionaire John Logan's top secret venture has been sabotaged, its facilities destroyed, and its handpicked staff massacred. The sole survivor is being held for ransom. Logan knows that the only way to save the man—and the secrets he holds—is to find him as soon as possible.

Sarah is furious when she is strong-armed into joining Logan on his search. And once she takes the perilous assignment, not even Logan's promises that she and Monty will be safe may be enough to protect them. Because a killer is devising a sadistic vengeance . . . and he may soon find use for Sarah.

Praise for *The Search*

A Look Inside THE SEARCH:

The DNA report that had just come through had confirmed these bones were her daughter's.

Tears were running down Eve's mother's face, but Eve was not weeping. Her expression reflected peace, sadness, and completion. She had wept her tears for Bonnie long ago. Her daughter was home now.

But Sarah felt tears sting her own eyes as she tossed the rose in her hand on top of the casket.

Good-bye, Bonnie Duncan.

"I think we should leave the family alone to say their good-byes," John Logan said in a low voice. "Let's go back to the cottage and wait for them."

Sarah hadn't been aware that he had moved to stand beside her. She instinctively shifted away from him.

Logan shook his head. "I know how you feel about me, but this isn't the time to burden Eve with it. We've got to help her get through this."

He was right. She hadn't been pleased when she had seen him drive up to the cottage a few hours before it was time to go to the burial site, but she couldn't fault his behavior toward Eve and Joe. He had been both sympathetic and supportive. And he was also right about leaving the family alone now. She turned away from the grave and started the short walk around the lake toward the cottage. It was pretty here, she thought. Eve had chosen a lovely spot on a small hill overlooking the lake to bury her daughter.

"Where's Monty?" Logan asked as he caught up with her.

"I left him in the cottage. Being at a grave site would have upset him"

"Ah, yes. I'd forgotten what a sensitive canine your Monty is."

"More sensitive than some people."

•

BODY OF LIES (March 2002)

A past she thought buried . . . a murder she was driven to solve . . .

Forensic sculptor Eve Duncan has been summoned to Baton Rouge by a high-ranking government official to identify the remains of an unknown murder victim. Eve wants nothing to do with the project. She has finally found peace from her own tragic past, living a quiet life with Atlanta detective Joe Quinn and her adopted daughter, Jane. Then a stunning series of seemingly unrelated events turns Eve's new world upside down.

A killer so deceptive, he leaves nothing behind but his victims . . .

Now, in a special government facility, she takes on the project of identifying the victim's skeleton. But she hasn't even begun when the first death occurs. Someone totally ruthless, someone who can strike anywhere at any time and with seeming immunity, is determined to put a halt to her work, her life, and the lives of those she loves. Eve has stumbled onto a chilling conspiracy. There is only one person who can give her the devastating truth . . . and he is already dead.

A Look Inside BODY OF LIES:

"Will you come with me?" Jane moved toward the door. "You have to see—"

"See what?"

"Bonnie . . ."

"What do you mean—"

Jane was gone, running down the porch steps and down the path.

"Jane!"

Eve ran after her but didn't catch up until she was almost up the hill. "Why are you—"

Then she saw it.

"I didn't know what to do." Jane's voice was uneven. "I tried to clean it up."

Blood smeared, dripping over the headstone.

Eve shuddered. "What did you— What happened here?"

"I don't know. I came up today to clean off the weeds

and it was like this. No, not like this. I made it worse. I'm sorry, Eve."

"Blood."

"No, I don't think so. At first, I thought— But it's paint or something." She edged closer to Eve. "I couldn't get it off."

"Paint?"

Jane nodded. "Someone drew a big X through Bonnie's name and everything else on the tombstone." She took Eve's hand. "Who would do this to you?"

Eve couldn't imagine who would commit a horror like this. She felt . . . bruised. "I don't know." It was hard to think. "Maybe some kid who thought it was funny to desecrate a grave." But not her Bonnie's grave. Not her Bonnie. "I can't think of anyone else."

●

BLIND ALLEY (SEPTEMBER 2004)

Eve Duncan's job is to put a face on the faceless victims of violent crimes. Her work not only comforts their survivors—but helps catch their killers. But there is another more personal reason that Eve Duncan is driven to do the kind of work she does—a dark nightmare from a past she can never bury. And as she works on the skull of a newly discovered victim, that past is about to return all over again.

The victim is a Jane Doe found murdered, her face erased beyond recognition. But whoever killed her wasn't just trying to hide her identity. The plan was far more horrifying. For as the face forms under Eve's skilled hands, she is about to get the shock of her life. The victim is someone she knows all too well. Someone who isn't dead. Yet.

Instantly Eve's peaceful life is shattered. The sanctuary of the lakeside cottage she shares with Atlanta detective Joe Quinn and their adopted daughter, Jane, has been invaded by a killer who's sent the grimmest of threats: the face of his next victim. To stop him, Eve must put her own life in the balance and question everything and everyone she trusts. Not even Quinn can go where Eve must go this time.

As the trail of faceless bodies leads to a chilling revelation, Eve finds herself trying to catch a master murderer whose grisly work is a testament to a mind warped by perversion and revenge. Now she must pit her skills against his in a showdown where the stakes are life itself—and where the unbearable cost of failure will make Eve's own murder seem like a mercy killing.

Praise for *Blind Alley*

"[Johansen's] new tale will please both fans and new converts with its unpredictable journey from Atlanta to the archaeological digs of Herculaneum in Italy."
—*Booklist*

"Johansen's back . . . solid thriller, intriguing suspense." —*Kirkus Reviews*

A Look Inside BLIND ALLEY:

"Okay," Eve murmured as she turned the pedestal to the light. "Here we go, Ruth. Measurements only take us so far. Help me out. I can't do this alone."

Smooth.

Start on the cheeks.

Work fast.

Don't think.

Or think about Ruth.

Think about brining her home.

Do the upper lip.

Smooth.

A little less?

No, leave it alone.

Smooth.

Her hands moved swiftly, mindlessly.

Who are you, Ruth?

Tell me. Help me.

The middle area between nose and lip. Shorter?

Yes.

Smooth.

Smooth.

Smooth.

It was three hours later when her hands fell away from the skull and she closed her eyes. "It's the best I can do," she whispered. "I hope it's enough, Ruth. Sometimes it is." She opened her eyes and stepped away from the pedestal. "We'll just have to— My God!"

"You haven't finished her," Joe said from the doorway. He came over to the workbench and took out her eye cast. "You know which ones to give her."

"Damn you, Joe."

•

COUNTDOWN (MAY 2005)

"Don't kill her. She's no good to us dead." These words haunt Jane MacGuire after a shocking attack shatters her world in an instant. Was it a random kidnapping attempt—or the countdown to something far more sinister?

Who is after her—and what do they want so badly they'll kill anyone in their way? That's what Jane is determined to find out, without the help of the police, the FBI, or her adoptive parents, forensic sculptor Eve Duncan and her husband, Joe Quinn, of the Atlanta PD—because whoever is after her won't hesitate to hurt those she loves the most. Now Jane will go on the run with the only man who may be more dangerous than those who are pursuing her. A smuggler, a con man, and who knew what else, Mark Trevor had his own mysterious reasons for wanting to keep Jane safe and out of the hands of a killer obsessed with a two-thousand-year-old mystery that could rock the modern-day world.

Orphaned at an early age, Jane grew up the hard way, but she was given a new life, a loving family, and a chance to pursue her interest in one of the greatest archaeological finds ever unearthed. Now someone was trying to destroy that new life before it could even get started. The past is returning with the kind of vengeance that knows no mercy. The countdown has already begun, and it's approaching zero faster than anyone thinks.

Praise for *Countdown*

"Johansen delivers a top-notch sequel filled with great chases, original characters, and intricate plot twists, creating a unique supernatural twist on the classic thriller." —*Booklist*

"Action, romance, castles, bomb plots and a booby-trapped hideaway in snowbound Idaho—what more could Johansen fans want?" —*Publishers Weekly*

A Look Inside COUNTDOWN:

"You don't know zilch right now. Listen, Mike, we both grew up on the streets, but we were lucky. We've been given a chance to climb out."

"Not smart enough. Paul's right. . . ."

"You're all muddled." The alley was yawning just ahead. Her hand tightened on the key as she pressed the unlock button and pushed him toward his Saturn. "You can't even remember what—"

Shadow. Leaping forward. Arm raised.

She instinctively pushed Mike aside and ducked.

Pain!

In her shoulder, not her head, where the blow was aimed.

She whirled and kicked him in the belly.

He grunted and bent double.

She kicked him in the groin and listened with fierce satisfaction as he howled in agony. "Bastard." She took a step toward him. "Can't you—"

A bullet whistled by her ear.

Mike cried out.

Dear God. She hadn't seen the gun.

No, her attacker was still doubled over, groaning in pain. Someone else was in the alley.

And Mike was falling to his knees.

Get him out of here.

She opened the door of the Saturn and pushed him into the passenger seat.

Another shadow running toward her from the end of the alley as she ran around to the driver's seat.

Another shot.

"Don't kill her, you fool. She's no good to us dead."